WHAT

GOES

UP

WHAT GOES UP

A MAX ROSEN MYSTERY

ALLEN WEINER

This is a work of fiction. Names, characters, businesses, places, events, locales, and incidents are either the products of the author's imagination or used in a fictitious manner. Any resemblance to actual persons, living or dead, or actual events is purely coincidental.

©Copyright 2020 Allen Weiner
All rights reserved

It is not legal to reproduce, duplicate, or transmit any part of this document in either electronic means or printed format. Recording of this publication is strictly prohibited.

Paperback ISBN: 978-1-7360947-1-6
Ebook ISBN: 978-1-7360947-0-9

Copyediting, Cover Art, and Layout by
Vicky Haygood Editorial and Book Design Services

This book is dedicated to:
Kathy
who taught me the meaning of true love ways.

Contents

Prologue	1
Chapter One	3
Chapter Two	10
Chapter Three	19
Chapter Four	27
Chapter Five	35
Chapter Six	43
Chapter Seven	51
Chapter Eight	61
Chapter Nine	72
Chapter Ten	81
Chapter Eleven	90
Chapter Twelve	100
Chapter Thirteen	109
Chapter Fourteen	121
Chapter Fifteen	131
Chapter Sixteen	143
Chapter Seventeen	152
Chapter Eighteen	168
Chapter Nineteen	178
Chapter Twenty	191
About Allen Weiner	208

Prologue

Sunday, November 12, 2017 was an unseasonably warm day in Austin, Texas. The town was quiet at 7 a.m. after celebrating UT's win the previous day over Kansas, 42–27. Traffic was light in the Shoal Creek area of the city, save for churchgoers and tourists searching for fantastic breakfast tacos.

Shortly after seven, Toby, an oversized rescued golden retriever, came along the bed's far side and nudged Max Rosen. Max was a light sleeper, so instantly looked over to see his sad-faced dog, standing with his leash gripped between his teeth.

"Okay, Toby, I know you need to go out," Max said, putting on his glasses and taking a sip of water from the glass on his night table. Max's wife, Marcia, was a sound sleeper and dozed away, unaware of Toby's request. Given the dog's age and medical issues, it was probably more than a simple request.

Max threw on his Phillies zippered sweatshirt and took the leash from Toby.

"When you gotta go, you gotta go," Max whispered to Toby. "Let's go out and see who's up so early."

The man and his dog were quite the scene for passersby. Toby never walked more than one step away from his human, and Max talked nonstop to his beloved pet. The two walked toward Anderson Lane, the main drag by the house.

"Toby, let's play a game. Between here and the main street, count the number of homes with the Sunday newspaper out front. I will give you the over/under at ten."

Toby looked over at Max as if he understood. The handsome golden wagged his tail, and the early morning duo set sail.

While the daily newspaper in Austin wasn't much, it was the paper of record for Texas's capital city. The *Globe* recently was sold from a major media conglomerate to a smaller chain whose focus was on cost-cutting and presenting the news in a far more conservative bent than its predecessor.

As Max and Toby walked, they counted only three driveways with Sunday newspapers. "Everyone gets their news online," Max told Toby. "And who blames them? Today's paper has yesterday's news and sports scores."

Toby came into Max and Marcia's life three years before, long after Max made his mark heading the project that launched the first daily newspaper on the web. Max missed unfolding the large Sunday paper and poring through the inserts, comics, and sports pages even with that accomplishment. He missed it all—getting the ink on your hands, drinking in every detail from the baseball box scores, and find out what movies were playing at nearby theaters.

Careful not to wake his wife, Max took Toby's leash off and the two sat on the front porch of the fifty-year-old, recently renovated home. As with many homes in Central Texas, the foundation left a lot to be desired; so Max and Marcia had to dig into their savings to have the entire "undercarriage" of their single-family place repaired.

"So, Toby, only three families have the Sunday paper. Believe it or not, some of the greatest moments of my career took place related to the Sunday paper. Before you knew me—long before you knew me—I was a young newspaper reporter looking to make a name for himself. Sometimes, it got me in trouble. One of those times was 1978 when I got in the middle of two intense investigations.

"I remember those times like they were yesterday," Max said, kissing Toby on the head.

Chapter One

The Carbon County Courthouse is a throwback to a time that never was. It sits on the corner of Lehigh and Susquehanna Streets, a building sturdily withstanding time with last-forever burnt clay bricks and what, a century and a half ago, represented state-of-the-art diamond-shaped leaded windows.

Max Rosen carefully walked down the four steps at the courthouse's Broadway entrance and looked both ways. Max, shaken to the core, had to make a phone call. It was early November 1978, twenty-nine years before the first iPhone, so finding a working payphone was in order. Looking to the right, he found a sparkling new phone booth in from of the Dreidelback General Store two doors down from the courthouse.

Tall and formerly thin with wire-rimmed glasses, Max was twenty-five years old and had just lived through one of the worst days of his life. As an entry-level newspaper reporter for the *Chronicle*, the area's newspaper of record, Max had made his second blunder in as many weeks. The first one was an honest mistake: at Jim Thorpe High School's annual athletic awards banquet, the young reporter misidentified the most inspirational teammate winner on the women's basketball team. Keep in mind, it was twenty years before Vice President Al Gore coined the term *Information Superhighway*. There was no Facebook or Instagram for Max to use to verify the school's honored junior point guard's name and spelling.

Even then, Max never carried money. He did find a dime at the bottom of his briefcase. He had a shopworn, faux-leather standard-issue one, common to insurance salesmen and would-be junior executives who shopped at discount places such as Leh's and H. L. Green's.

Hands shaking, Max slipped his lone dime into the middle slot of the payphone and hit "0" for the operator. A few rings and a kindly female voice said, "Operator. How can I help you?"

"I'd like to make a collect call to Harold Rosen, area code 215, 676-4192. Please say it's Max on the line."

Exactly ninety-three miles from where Max stood, his father answered and accepted the collect call.

"Is it okay if I come home to live? I am going to get fired." Max's voice trembled.

"This is your home. You are always welcome here. I am sure whatever happened is not nearly as bad as you think. You know my motto: 'This too shall pass.'" His father's words were comforting but not overly realistic.

Harold Rosen, now retired, was a wonderful man whose dreams and drive were not always aligned. Before marriage, Harold still had an interesting, generally elaborate business scheme that would never reach fruition. Needing to provide a stable home for his wife and two kids, he torched his dreams and worked thirty years for the US Government in middle management.

In the division of parental labor, Harold oversaw inspiration and undying support for his two children. At this moment, however, even the sincerest words at the other end of a long-distance call could not provide Max the guidance he needed. The reporter, whose career was twisting in the wind, thanked his father and hung up.

Max turned around and walked past the courthouse, crossing the street where Broadway turned into Lehigh Avenue. *Lehigh Avenue*, Max thought. *Wow. That takes me back.*

Lehigh Avenue was the ultimate safe place for the twenty-five-year old reporter as a child. In his mind, he was transported to 21st Street and Lehigh Avenue in Philadelphia. This was where Connie Mack Stadium stood, a stunning, grimy, glossy cathedral to baseball in the 1960s. It was a solemn sanctuary for Max, a place where time stood still and where all worries—even those that can burden a child—vanished for a few hours. It was a place Max, as young as six, went hand in hand with his father, who would tell tales of Babe Ruth, Jimmy Foxx, Lou Gehrig, and other ballplayers of his youth. Every fan will tell you that its players were the best in the decade in which he followed the game. For Max, who saw in their prime Mays, McCovey, Koufax, Brock, Gibson, Seaver, and Clemente, he knew his era was nonpareil.

With a half chuckle, Max thought of the old baseball adage: *Three strikes, and you're out.* With two significant blunders in as many weeks, Max was anxiously standing on a busy corner in Jim Thorpe, Pennsylvania on a cold mid-November afternoon, pondering his next move. To save his job, it would have to be something spectacular as a means for redemption, or this washed-out reporter would be back to sending out resumes with cover letters and freelance clips in hopes of landing something. Somewhere. Anywhere.

Max worked at the Carbon County bureau of the local newspaper of record in the Lehigh Valley. Its headquarters was thirty-two miles away and served as the hub for its many bureaus and staff or reporters, editors, photographers, and support infrastructure. Headquarters took over a city block in downtown Allentown, Pennsylvania. Allentown was a prosperous, thriving town with such major industries as Mack Trucks, Air Products and Chemicals, Alpo (the dog food company), and Bethlehem Steel. It also was home to the earliest days of professional wrestling, with matches held at the Allentown Fair Grounds.

Max's suburban office was in Nesquehoning, a borough that once prospered during the days of anthracite coal mining. Anthracite is known for having the fewest impurities among coal classifications and is preferred as a fuel source over such types as lignite and bituminous. That said, Nesquehoning's coal mining days were a thing of the past, given the health concerns that came from heavy mining in the area. Unlike Allentown, Carbon County's economy was, at best, stagnant with an air of quiet desperation hanging over the area's streets and sidewalks.

Max was dreading going back to the office. He pulled the generic Dodge sedan that served as a company car into an angled parking spot on Catawissa Street one long half-block from the office. His car, a brand-new Volvo he bought to appease his mother, was parked two spots away. It was time to face the music which, Rosen thought, might very well be "Taps."

The newspaper's Carbon County bureau was in a storefront on Nesquehoning's main street. It sat between a pharmacy/general store and the local Elks Club. While understated in location and appearance, the office was one where serious business was conducted. From time to time, some not-so-serious business as well.

Max walked in the front door and made his way past the counter, which ran across the office's front about twenty feet from the door. In addition to writing about the news of the day, the office also handled the business of advertising and circulation. A petite woman with a somewhat reddish beehive named Tanya sat at a machine that punched out linotype rolls of paper that contained the news and features written at the bureau.

The brightly lit office was about sixty feet long from door to back wall. It was configured where pairs of reporters sat at desks facing each other with IBM Selectric typewriters squarely placed in the middle of each work area. It was early afternoon with just a few reporters around prepping for their evening assignments, which usually included covering a local government or school board. Major events that happened on the fly, such as a car crash, fire, or even a bank robbery, were handled by whoever was around no matter what was scheduled later in the day.

Max saw Ray Tomjanovich, bureau chief, at his desk, which sat at the end of the long rectangular office space. Ray was a big man who, courtesy of the GI Bill, played offensive line for UCLA after World War II. The young reporter enjoyed Ray's stories of playing football in college, especially those that included the team's student manager, Paul Tagliabue, a former NFL Commissioner.

As Max approached Ray's makeshift office, the bureau chief pointed to the chair next to his desk without glancing up from his newspaper. The latest edition of a small, local competitor sometimes scooped its larger rival on big stories. Ray generally dismissed the weekly rag for what it was—a gossip-filled paper that thrived on rumor and innuendo.

In his late fifties, Ray still had the physique of a former football player, but he never used his size to intimidate others. The chief's reputation as a solid reporter and excellent writer garnered respect and provided him a steady rise up the editorial ladder to bureau chief. While an editor position at the company's Allentown headquarters could have been more prestigious, Ray was a devoted family man with a married son. The suburban office was a few miles from his home in Coaldale.

Max sat a few feet from the hulking newspaperman who put the area's weekly rag down and took off his wire glasses and spoke with a tone somewhere between anger and utter frustration.

"So, you told me the story about Jim Thorpe getting a new Wawa on River Street was solid, and you had two credible sources. We ran it on the front page of the local edition. And now, we have a shitstorm."

Max had no response. It was plain and simple: in his brief time working out of the Nesquehoning bureau, he came to know how protective the locals were of long-standing family businesses. Even if it was a regional franchise (which Wawa was at the time), even the threat of an outsider would send folks in Jim Thorpe into a frenzy.

It was at a town council meeting that Max had heard the rumor. Two prominent officials—the school board president and the head of the local Rotary—were sitting in front of the reporter and speaking more loudly than they realized. Mike, the school board president, went into detail about a real estate option the outside company had taken for a large parcel on River Street. Carl, the guy from the Rotary, said that he had heard that Wawa had already solicited bids from local contractors to get started once the permits had cleared.

Nothing gives a new reporter a bigger thrill than to be behind a scoop. For Max, who had no formal training in journalism, hearing concrete facts from two of the town's leaders meant the info was solid. A front-page story presented itself as a gift from the newspaper gods.

That day Ervin Swan was the night editor at the bureau, which meant he went through every story scheduled to run in the *Chronicle* the next morning. After editing the paper sheets that came across his desk, Ervin would walk the paper down to the linotype operator, Tanya, who would punch the tape that would then be sent to a desk editor at the main *Chronicle* office in Allentown.

Max handed Ervin two stories: one, an inconsequential wrap-up of the Jim Thorpe town meeting; the other, a headline-grabbing piece about a Wawa invading Jim Thorpe's precious, closely guarded local business community. Ervin took the five sheets of paper from Max, quickly looking up with his usual menacing glare. As it turned out, Ervin was a major anti-Semite and bristled at having an outsider—especially a Jew—at his place of business.

Max's two stories went through Ervin's review, which led the night editor to shuffle his way down the long aisleway and stop at Max's desk. Ervin's waddle was the result of two hip replacements and a BMI of 42. Given his seniority, few had the guts to make fun of his wacky walk.

"You sure about this?" Ervin asked, knowing that even if Max verified the sources, the information was probably wrong.

"Yes. I heard it from Mike and Carl," Max replied, certain that Ervin knew these men by their first names.

Ervin said nothing more, made his way to the linotype operator, and handed her the edited copy.

This brings Max back to his meeting with Ray. He apologized for a major error, one which required the *Chronicle* to print a retraction—a weak response to his blunder. Max just sat, eyes beginning to well up, staring down at the blue linoleum floor.

"Max, I have to put you on a two-day suspension, after which you will be facing a three-month probation," Ray said in a forceful yet forgiving tone. "During that time, you will need to show us why we hired you in the first place. We took a chance on bringing in someone with no newspaper experience, but you showed us a quick mind and a head filled with great ideas."

All Max could muster was a quiet thank you. He wanted to thank Ray for the chance to redeem himself, but there was one important lesson he had learned so far in his brief time as a reporter: it is better to show than tell.

After this conversation, which turned out to be more of a light scolding mixed with a minor vote of confidence, Max walked toward the front door. Halfway down the narrow corridor between desks, Tex, a skinny guy in his late thirties, reached out and put his hand on his younger colleague's arm.

"Let's you and I go get a cup of coffee," Tex said. In contrast to his name—well, nickname—Tex was not from Texas and had no direct association with the Lone Star State. Max discovered that his older friend and colleague was called "Tex" because that was his call sign way back when he was a long-haul trucker. If Rosen remembered correctly, the CB name had something to do with the way Tex spoke slowly, a trait commonly associated with heavy Southern drawls.

Tex was the *Chronicle's* long-standing writer/reporter who once worked out of the paper's Allentown office. After winning several state and national awards for his writing, the paper graciously allowed Tex to work out of the bureau, which was only twenty minutes from his home in New Philadelphia. Tex had a colorful past. In addition to being a former trucker, he had lived on a commune in Tennessee and painted houses in Alaska. There were rumors that Tex once worked for the CIA, but that was never confirmed.

Max and Tex left the office and walked up Catawissa Street a few blocks to a family-run coffee shop, Nuggles. Nuggles was a popular local hangout that was popular long before Starbucks made its way to Carbon County, and a decent coffee cup was difficult to find. Years later, when Max's reporting career would take him to Seattle, his appreciation for coffee would expand. But for now, if it was hot and not instant, it was fine.

"So, here's the problem," Tex mumbled between sips of his piping hot caffeine fix. "You had the right idea by trying to keep your ear to the ground and impress everyone with a scoop. I get it. What you need to do is refine your technique and not get ahead of yourself."

"Wait," Max replied. "Are you saying that what I did was not as big a deal as everyone says?"

Tex chuckled and put his mug down. "No, you shit the bed, my friend. What I am telling you is that your instinct is right on. You also don't know the people in these parts; folks here can be dense, both inside the office and outside. And because you are an outsider, you have to tread lightly and go the extra mile to prove your worth."

Max Rosen's head spun with Tex's words of counsel.

"To put it simply," Tex said in his elongated delivery, "you were in the right church, but the wrong pew."

The pair left Nuggles and Max headed home. At this time, his home was a recently renovated second-floor one-bedroom apartment a few blocks north of the office in Nesquehoning. His conversation/pep talk with Tex lit a fuse in Max, and the suspended reporter had two days to bring some genius scheme to fruition.

And Max knew just the right person to consult for help to bring the scheme to reality.

Chapter Two

Memorial Day, 1978: six months before Max's career crossroads. Max and Barrett Fine stood outside a side entrance to Resorts International Casino in Atlantic City. After decades of political chatter, Atlantic City, once a proud summer escape for working-class Philadelphians, was about to open its first legal gambling joint—Resorts International.

Friends since age seven, Fine was eager to demonstrate to Max one of his newly discovered passions, that of a card counter at blackjack. Barrett was prone to developing various challenging skills such as performing elaborate memory tricks and becoming a nationally ranked table tennis player. At the time, Fine was an out-of-work attorney who had made a killing buying condos before AC legalized gambling, and reselling them for a handsome profit after the controversial bill was passed.

The front entrance to the hotel/casino faced the famed Atlantic City Boardwalk. Decades earlier, Fine and Rosen's families would vacation at the shore—Fine's at the luxurious Sheraton Deauville; Rosen's at a rooming house or thirty-dollar-a-night motel a block away from the beach. The Boardwalk was different this Memorial Day weekend as a sea change took place when such icons as Steel Pier, Captain Starn's, and the 500 Club were shoved aside for slot machines, video poker tables, buses of seniors, and all-you-can-eat, artery-clogging buffets.

None of that mattered to Barrett Fine—he wanted to play blackjack and impress his friend with the ability to outsmart the house and win big. The crowd at the Boardwalk entrance to Resorts showed no sign of thinning out as the muggy late-May midafternoon became early evening. Fine grabbed Rosen by the arm and said, "Let's head around the side and see if we can sneak in."

The oddly mismatched duo—Rosen, five inches taller than his friend, tended to dress down for any occasion—walked toward Pennsylvania Avenue to the workers' entrance. A few stragglers hung around outside the side door when Fine walked up to a bored Hispanic security guard and offered him twenty dollars to let the two men into the building.

The casino was straight ahead from the side door. The garish décor and overpowering smell of cigarette smoke was the perfect tableau for a once-vibrant city fallen to hard times. Fine, eager to become a blackjack legend, found the closest five-dollar table and proceeded to lose five straight hands. Not accustomed to losing, Fine got up, motioned Rosen that it was time to leave, and they left the way they came in. The trip back to Philadelphia was only ninety minutes, but Barrett Fine's stone silence made it seem longer.

Barrett Fine grew up in a two-story modest row home across from a large Catholic church some twelve blocks from Max Rosen in Northeast Philadelphia. Barrett was a rare prodigy whose diverse talents ranged from playing the piano to an accomplished athlete in multiple racquet sports. Few folks know that Barrett was polydactyl, which meant he was born with six fingers on his left hand. Occasionally he bragged about this physical anomaly, which was an asset in athletic endeavors. At other times, he did his best to hide his extra digit inside his pants pocket.

Max met Barrett in second grade when elementary schools in Philadelphia had thirty kids in a classroom with three separate teachers for each grade. Even at age seven, because of their rare, yet distinctly different, intellectual gifts, Max and Barrett realized there was a predestined force that would forever connect them. Both had older sisters, mothers with unrealistic academic demands, and sympathetic fathers. Theirs would be an off-and-on brotherhood that would have its peaks and valleys for the next more than a half-century.

At the time of Max's work troubles, Barrett was living sixty miles away in a fashionable condo in a part of Philadelphia overlooking the Delaware River that was supposed to be the next big thing. Returning from an afternoon of hustling wannabe tennis pros at a nearby court, Fine saw the blinking light on his answering machine.

"Call me when you get this," the familiar voice said.

Max Rosen placed the phone back onto its cradle on the wall outside his apartment's small kitchen. It was ten thirty in the morning on day one of his suspension from work, and the day was dragging. He was not much for daytime TV, and the radio reception for his favorite stations in Philadelphia was fuzzy at best. Too antsy to read the free newspaper he had delivered every morning, Max took a folding chair, opened the sliding door to his balcony, and sat.

The view from Rosen's second-floor apartment was nothing to write home about. Miles and miles of desolate farmland were dotted with houses in disrepair and other reminders of a region that went downhill after unregulated coal mining took its toll on the local economy and health of its citizens.

Max stared off into space, losing his sense of place in the cool autumn air. He appeared to be in some sort of trance, but it was what others might call an intellectual coma. The young reporter had an inexplicable ability to remember things from his past very closely and personally. He was not much for predicting the future, but when it came to remembering precisely how the furniture was laid out in his family's home in 1965, Max was uncannily prodigious. It was the same native skill he used to successfully win bar bets over trivial matters, especially when they were related to sports. Max's associative memory was akin to how internet search engines would work in the future, matching keywords to related content in nanoseconds.

As Max's mind wandered, going in varied self-charted directions, he thought back to an eventful day thirteen years earlier, which triggered the brainstorm that might lead to a spectacular comeback.

It was November 1965. Walking home from junior high school, Max was stopped at the corner of his street by a tall, rugged-looking man holding a shiny badge who asked Max his name and address. What followed was a series of questions that were unusual to be fired at a twelve-year-old. Max Rosen later found out that his neighbor, Harry Gold, had been released from jail on good behavior. The FBI wanted to make sure everything was in order before allowing the accused Cold War spy, a man instrumental in the conviction of Ethyl and Julius Rosenberg, to take up residence in his family's crowded home in Northeast Philadelphia. Sadly, Harry Gold, let out of prison due to bad health, died a few years later.

Here is the thought process that took Max Rosen from the notorious Harry Gold to his dilemma. Tex mentioned that the idea of surreptitiously getting tidbits of gossip could lead to a career-boosting scoop. As Max did at the Jim Thorpe town council meeting, overhearing conversations had a kernel of viability. But, as the currently suspended reporter later figured out, the two local men took advantage of the reporter's inexperience and gullibility. Instead of discussing a matter of great importance in their just-loud-enough-to-be-overheard chat, the school board president and his buddy decided to deliberately feed Max a line of bullshit that would be a nice welcome gift to the area. Max's ah-ha moment involved eavesdropping without being present, catching the local powers that be unaware of their most vulnerable moments.

And that is where the ghost of Harry Gold came into play. If Max would learn and master the techniques that Cold War spies used to gather secrets, he could use that prowess to gather scoop-worthy nuggets and regain his footing on his tenuous career. He called Barrett back and arranged to meet for coffee in Quakertown, a city twenty miles outside of Allentown.

Max had a thing for Dunkin' Donuts dating back to his childhood when his mother would take him and share a powdered sugar cruller along with a coffee that was 80 percent milk. Memory lane was a tricky, chilling trip for the twenty-five-year-old man. Many of his earliest years were pocked with times of sadness and vulnerability that continued to haunt him and would for another quarter-century. There were great times, too, that, in retrospect, cushioned the blow of bad memories.

As he sat at a cramped table by the window, Max saw his friend's silver BMW pull up in front of the donut shop on West End Boulevard in Quakertown. Barrett called his friend in need back and agreed to meet Max. The message on his answering machine intrigued Barrett, who was always up for a challenge.

Max, not fussy about his coffee, stared into his cup, swirling the grounds that sat at the bottom as Barrett sat down. It was fifty degrees outside, and the heat was on full blast at the Quakertown DD, so Barrett removed his imported cashmere jacket and folded it across his lap to be sure it didn't come anywhere near the possibly dirty floor.

"You want anything?" Max asked his friend.

"Do you know if they have anything other than drip coffee here?" Barrett said smugly, knowing the answer.

For the first time in several days, Max smiled and let loose what amounted to a semi-chuckle. "Yeah, right," he said.

"Okay, so you tell me you fucked up royally, and you're looking for my help to follow people and learn their secrets?"

"No, that's not what I said," Max responded, irritated over his friend's typical obnoxious comment. "I said I need help in figuring out a way to secretly eavesdrop on important people to get information for award-winning new stories."

"Award-winning." Barrett laughed. "From what you told me, you need to prove your worth or send out your resumes. Again. I'd say you may want to settle for coming up with the news that will keep you employed."

Ignoring most of what Fine said, Max went in for the kill, which meant stroking his buddy's massive ego. "The Cold War. Didn't you write your master's thesis at Penn on the Cold War?"

Barrett nodded with a curious look that made him close one eye and scrunch up his brow. He wondered what the favor would be and whether it would be something that would pique his intellectual curiosity and be worthy of his time.

"I need some Cold War spycraft ideas. I remember you told me that the Soviets planted a bug in a replica of the Great Seal, which they had as a gift to Averell Harriman when he was ambassador. I need something like that."

Ever the wiseass, Barrett responded, "You want a replica of the Great Seal? Or do you want to know more about W. Averell Harriman?"

"No," Max responded. "I want to eavesdrop on people using some sort of bugging device that we can plant somewhere out of the way and listen in on private conversations."

Barrett listened intently while he turned and stared out the window into the distance as the August afternoon turned into the early evening. Barrett got up in one motion, walked to the door, and gave an insignificant wave goodbye.

Max knew his friend well enough to know that he was not getting the brush-off. When faced with a challenge, Barrett liked to go off and let the idea rattle obsessively in his brain. The results were almost uniformly on point; the method was idiosyncratic. Rosen figured he would give Fine a few days to ponder.

There was one day left in Max Rosen's suspension from the *Chronicle*. He used that day to briefly visit his family in Philadelphia and ready himself to return to battle. Max decided he would take any assignment he was given and dive in headfirst, but with extreme caution to avoid blunders. He did not want to get the boot with a third strike before implementing his new plan—whatever it would be.

After a dinner with his parents in Philadelphia, Max returned to the office. His suspension had ended, and he tried to act as if nothing out of the ordinary had happened. Still, ten sets of eyes were on him as he walked to his desk. After putting his briefcase down by the side of his well-worn faux leather chair, Max walked to the board that sat behind whoever was on duty as night editor. Luck not being on his side, it was Ervin, and the young reporter was assigned to cover the Coaldale Pysanky Egg Festival. It was the bottom of the barrel for even an entry-level reporter. Such social events were generally farmed out to freelancers, but Max smiled and told Ervin he would head over to Miner's Memorial Park where the event was being held.

Not being a major news event or breaking story such as a fire or plane crash, reporters were expected to take their photos, putting one in the win column for Max. His mother was a would-be professional photographer, which meant she had a darkroom in the basement but had never sold any pictures. Still, Max learned everything about photography and bought a Nikkormat camera in 1975 with his savings from working in a chain shoe store for two summers.

Since Miner's Park was only a few miles away, Max decided to take his car. On his way over, he fiddled with the Volvo's car radio. Being too far from either Philadelphia or New York to get their radio stations, he had to settle for whatever would come in with minimum static. Between Philadelphia's WFIL and New York's WOR, Max found an odd station that was unusually clear for the area between Nesquehoning and Coaldale.

When the song "My Best Friend's Girl" by the Cars ended, an amateurish voice introduced the next song. There was a weird commotion in the background mixed with some high-pitched giggles. *Holy shit,* Max realized. *I found a pirate radio station.*

At that point, Max's associative memory kicked in. When he was eleven, Max's older sister, Nancy, had a group of friends who devised a pirate radio station in the basement of one of their homes. Nancy's friends gave themselves DJ names such as Steve Diamond (né Steve Polansky) and Fred Kay (né Fred Rabinowitz) and operated their illegal broadcast operation every weekend evening. While Nancy went on to medical school and became a respected ear, nose, and throat doctor, her radio friends never amounted to much.

While Max was never invited to join the fun, he became somewhat—well, more than somewhat—of a radio nerd. He learned everything about pirate radio stations, including their rich and storied history, as well as the rudiments of setting one up. It was, as Rosen learned, as simple as taking, or building, an FM transmitter and directing its signal via an antenna to a set spot on the FM dial. You could play music or talk or, if the mood strikes, do nothing, and fill the airwaves with silence.

Max arrived at Miner's Park just as the awards were being announced. While the concept of decorating eggs in some intricate pattern escaped him, he wanted to knock this assignment out of the park. Claire Remington won for the best overall design, and she proudly spoke of her family's Ukrainian heritage, which made for a nice piece of news fluff. Remington's picture was holding her multicolored egg made for a colorful story buried on page three of the local zoned edition of the *Chronicle.*

Typical to morning newspapers, regular reporter shifts ended at 10 p.m. unless there was a breaking news story. Skipping the practice of joining his colleagues for a beer after work, Max headed home and called Barrett, going into detail about his brainstorm on how to eavesdrop on local bigwigs and gather worthy news nuggets that could become great stories. Barrett was quiet as he sat in his favorite reading chair sixty miles away, and Max took his silence to mean Barrett hadn't come up with a better idea, and he was on board with the plan. They agreed to meet at the Carbon County Courthouse on Friday afternoon.

The men's room in the Carbon County Courthouse is empty at 5 p.m. on Friday. The last regular daytime cleaning crew leaves at 4 p.m., and the overnight crew reports to work at 7 p.m. The coast was clear for Max and Barrett as the building was empty, with the front and side doors locked. All that remained as an escape route was a fire door in the back that was easily sabotaged to stay partially open.

Barrett shook his head in disbelief. His friend of eighteen years had asked for some favors over the years, but this one was close to a request too far. "So, you are Q, and I'm James Bond," he whispered to Max.

With a nervous smirk, Max replied, "Whatever you say."

The execution of the Rosen-Fine gambit—or Fine-Rosen if Barrett had any say in the matter—included hiding a small FM transmitter in the courthouse's main elevator. There were two creaky old self-service lifts in the building, but the county officials used the larger one. There were three floors, with the top floor being the judges' chambers and the county treasurer's office. The second floor housed county records, meeting rooms, and the office of the sheriff and district attorney.

The plan was an homage to the scheme called "The Thing" that the Soviets used to spy on the US Embassy in Moscow in 1945. The modern twist was, instead of planting a sophisticated listening device as the Soviets did in the Cold War, a small FM transmitter would be surreptitiously placed underneath the ashtray in the elevator. The transmitter would emit a broadcast signal to a nearby radio tuned in to a specific FM frequency.

At lunchtime and when offices closed, Max would casually lurk on a bench outside the courthouse with an earphone plugged into his Zenith transistor radio. This special news broadcast aimed at an audience of one would come in loud and clear at 93.4 on his radio dial. As with any reporter worth his keep, Max would have a reporter's notebook—a five-by-nine spiral pad—on his lap to take appropriate notes.

Max peeked outside the men's room to make sure the coast was clear. He and Barrett walked over to the elevator and pushed the up button. The doors popped open, and the freshly cleaned ashtray was attached to the far wall near the back left corner. The faint smell of ammonia and furniture polish overwhelmed them as the door opened to the forty-three-square-foot enclosure.

If either Max or Barrett felt like dozing off or were overcome with anxiety, the fresh smell of pungent cleaning fluid would keep them awake. Max pushed the stop button, which held the elevator in place.

Of the pair, Barrett was better with his hands than Max. His special talent was due, in part, to the extra digit he had on his left hand. In addition to being able to tie his shoe with one hand, Barrett could manipulate small objects into tight spaces.

Max handed Barrett the FM transmitter, purchased that day as part of a Heathkit from Radio Shack. The unit was a two-inch square device to which the reporter had soldered a small antenna and three volt battery. Max then took a soldering iron from his briefcase and placed it gently in his buddy's left hand. Two minutes later, the bug was planted underneath the ashtray, in a location that was unlikely to be detected by the cleaning crew. The two men walked briskly toward the fire door and out onto the alleyway that ran the length of the building.

"And so, that's that," Barrett said, quite proud of his role in the caper. He then turned and walked down the alley toward the front of the building. Some ten steps before he reached the front of the courthouse, Fine let loose with some prophetic words.

"What goes up could come down with some great headlines."

Chapter Three

It rained pretty much straight through the weekend after Max and Barrett put the finishing touches on their scheme. Before going their separate ways, Max stood next to his friend's shiny new BMW and took a transistor radio from his briefcase. Nervously, almost in a full tremble, Max plugged the earpiece into the 3.5 mm hole of his Zenith transistor radio. The goal was to see if the selected FM frequency would deliver static or a quiet hum of elevator silence.

With anxiety in full bloom, it took Max longer than it should tune the radio dial. Barrett was tempted to grab it from his co-conspirator but hesitated. A long two seconds later, with eyes closed, Max gave the thumbs-up sign.

When Max had an entire weekend off, he usually made the trip to his parents' home sixty miles south and east. With almost too many threads jockeying for space and time in his conscience, Max knew that sleeping in the single bed of his early twenties was a bit incongruent with the daring feat that was put in motion. To top it off, at twenty-five and sort-of living on his own, Max was not in the mood for twenty questions from his parents—well, his mom, for sure. He also knew that his father did not share any of their son's recent work disaster with his mother—a woman who was uncannily skilled at reading her son and would have put him in a guilt-inspired headlock to reveal his job suspension and probation.

Facing an entire weekend with no plans and a bit anxious, Max spent Saturday cleaning his place and going grocery shopping. College football season was winding down but living in a hotbed for Penn State football made him a surrogate fan of a team on its way to an undefeated season. More than anything, Max loved listening to the games on the radio where he could dive headfirst into Ray Scott's play-by-play. Scott was one of the nation's best football announcers, and his account of the Nittany Lions win over Pitt on that rainy Saturday allowed Max to sit back and enjoy a lazy afternoon.

Sundays were the bane of Max's existence. While it was seven years since Max simultaneously attended both public high school and religious school, the sadness that enveloped him on Sundays remained palpable. True, staying home and watching the Eagles limp their way to another horrific season was not anyone's idea of fun. But sitting in a classroom studying the minutia of Jewish law and customs was equally torturous. Leaving religious school at 6:30 p.m. on Sunday, when it was dark at that hour from late October to May, was a feeling that would follow Max for the rest of his life.

This rainy Sunday, the blues were in full bloom. The sheer illegality of what he and Barrett had cooked up, and its implications moving forward, was slowly sinking in. Not one for any sort of daring escapade, Max wanted to hop in his car, drive to the courthouse, sneak in and rip the transmitter from its hiding place in the main elevator. Stopping himself in a moment of panic, Max reflected on some recent life changes.

Since beginning his newspaper career three months earlier and achieving some form of independence from his family, Max was going through the slow, painstaking process of building confidence and self-esteem. After parking his new Volvo in the lot adjacent to his office on his first day of work, Max had stood next to his car and thought about what lay ahead. He realized his generally passive and shy approach to life would have to change dramatically. The psyche of a young man who always lived in fear of the reaction to less-than-stellar schoolwork and exemplary behavior would have to be pushed to the side to make room for someone whose career goals required equal amounts of courage and talent. So far it was a work in progress, with a few baby steps here and there.

The unease that Sunday morning brought began to fade. Max caught the tail end of the Eagles game on the radio, and what a meaningful game it was! Captured by NFL Films to be part of team history, the Eagles beat the New York Giants 19–17 on a play that would later be called "The Miracle at the Meadowlands." For the lifelong Eagles fan, now sixty miles from his home, the radio broadcasts were a nice antidote to a miserable Sunday afternoon.

Max's mood ultimately changed to one of anticipation for the week ahead. An early dinner and a few hours of listening to Dr. Demento on WMMR was the perfect end to a day that started with far too much introspection. He slipped into bed shortly before 10 p.m. and fell asleep to the sound of his downstairs neighbors' TV playing the theme to "Dallas" at a decibel level fit for the hard of hearing.

Eager to get the week started, Max walked into the newspaper bureau office's front door at 10 a.m. Monday. The *Chronicle*, a morning paper, created odd working hours for reporters. Primetime was from 7 p.m. to 10 p.m. when the local cities, towns, and boroughs conducted their public-facing business. The news deadline was 11 p.m., which required a reporter to return to the office after these meetings had adjourned and bang out a quick, precise account of the event.

High visibility news events such as crime, fire, car accidents, and the like did not adhere to any set schedule. Whichever reporter was in the office when a fire broke out would be sent to the scene to report and most likely take pictures. In his first week, Max was sent to a two-alarm blaze in Lehighton. As a green reporter, he excitedly gathered the facts, took some horrifically beautiful shots of a rampaging blaze, and wound up with his byline on the front page of the *Chronicle*'s local section.

Max stopped dead in his tracks when he reached his desk. There were two notes jammed into his IBM Selectric roller—one from Ray, his boss; the other from Ervin, the night editor. Both men separately told Max he had done a nice job on the pysanky egg piece, especially liking the picture that accompanied the feature story.

Nothing builds one's confidence like an attaboy from the boss, along with the man in charge of handing out assignments most weeknights. Max made his way to the board where that night's activity was posted and saw he was assigned to the Carbon County Executive Board's monthly meeting. It was not much of a thriller as the matters discussed did not draw many citizens. There was time at the outset of the meeting for locals to ask the five-person board questions and air their grievances. The interchange between the board and people from Jim Thorpe, Lehighton, Nesquehoning, and other area boroughs and townships rarely had any newsworthy gems. The public back and forth after the public forum was about as exciting as watching paint dry.

Even after a few months as a reporter getting a first-hand lesson in civics, Max learned about executive sessions—closed-door meetings that often took place before the public part started. Colleagues at the *Chronicle* told Max that these private sessions are where the serious business took place, and the open forum was just for show.

With Max and Barrett's clandestine surveillance in place, it seemed possible that some of the executive board members might discuss their private talks in the elevator after the meeting. This assignment may provide a test of the viability of the hidden transmitter trick and whether it could yield a juicy piece of news or even gossip. Max had just enough time to have a quick dinner before the open executive board meeting, after which he would try and tune in to his new favorite FM channel.

As expected at the meeting, a few locals stood in a line about twenty-five feet from the large, several-inch-thick semi-circular mahogany desks behind which sat the five board members. A woman from Jim Thorpe complained about her neighbor who worked on rusted out cars day and night in his driveway. The noise kept her from a good night's sleep. She was followed by a man from Coaldale who wanted to know why the county changed the trash pickup day from Tuesday to Thursday. The head of the executive board, Mike DeFranco, said he would take the two issues to the appropriate authorities and thanked the pair for coming to the meeting.

There was only one order of new business: to announce that the bid for a replacement water storage tank for the county's correctional facility had been awarded to Kevin's Water and Heating in Jim Thorpe. Other matters were equally mundane, including hashing out the details of the local Thanksgiving Day parade. The meeting was adjourned after one hour.

It was showtime for Max. He had roughed out a plan to sit on a bench outside the courthouse and pretend he was listening to a local high school basketball game. The Jim Thorpe High men's basketball team played for the state title, so a reporter jotting down notes with an earpiece plugged into his radio was unlikely to cause suspicion. Max hopped in the magic elevator before the board members dispersed and quickly made his way to his surveillance spot. His pen and pad came out, and Max was waiting for the show to start.

And start it did. Tuned to 93.4, Max heard the elevator doors open with voices mid-conversation stepping inside. Max was excellent with remembering voices, and he heard Mike DeFranco make fellow board member John Cleaver laugh. It seemed DeFranco, who fancied himself a cutup, was telling one his patented jokes—no doubt minted in fifth grade—which brought laughter to the pair.

"I want to thank you for backing me on awarding that bid to my brother-in-law. Ever since that big HVAC repair chain from Allentown opened shop here, his business has gone to hell in a handbasket," DeFranco said.

"Hey, it was my pleasure," Cleaver responded. "I'm sure we'll come up with a way to pay me back."

Shocked at what he heard, Max dropped his pad on the ground in front of him and nearly crashed his transistor radio into the sidearm of the bench. He scribbled notes as fast as he could so he could capture every word of the conversation between DeFranco and Cleaver. Max also roughed out the news story he would need to write for the morning edition.

Driving back to the office, Max could easily have run off the road, given his level of distraction. He was armed with information that could be the basis for an investigation with serious repercussions, not to mention the kind of reporting that would put him back in the good graces with the powers that be. Two men, considered by their peers to be beyond reproach, appeared to be caught with their hands in the cookie jar.

As Max wheeled into one of the *Chronicle*'s assigned parking spots in the lot down the street from the office, he contemplated his next move. While he was anxious to jump into this story of possible corruption, Max's experience over the past few weeks began to wave a major red flag of caution. Unlike the rigged conversation he overheard that got him in hot water, the interchange between Cleaver and DeFranco took place in the elevator, where there was an expectation of secrecy. There was no way the two men could be aware their conversation was overheard by a reporter sitting outside the courthouse.

Baby steps. That is what Max decided he would take. He first sat down and put together a summary of that night's executive board meeting. The content was dry, and there was little room for analysis or a need for elaboration. A bid for a new water tank was announced, and plans for decorating key spots throughout the county with holiday lights were discussed before getting tabled for later approval.

Max walked his two typewritten pages up to Ervin and placed them in the editor's inbox. The young reporter did not expect much in the way of Ervin's questions and walked back to his desk, stopping at the desk directly across from him. Tom Monahan, a reporter a few years older than Max, was finishing up a feature he had been working on regarding repurposing some of the area's vacant coal mines.

At a young twenty-nine, Tom Monahan had already become a reporter's reporter known for his excellent writing and detailed approach to his craft. Tom graduated from The Ohio State University with a degree in journalism and was editor of the *Lantern*, the school's prestigious newspaper.

Tom and Max were not exactly friends—more of friendly colleagues. Other than their place of employment, they had nothing in common. Tom was married with a child on the way. He wore a three-piece suit to work while Max was prone to open-collared shirts and slacks that resembled what later would be called Dockers. Occasionally, Max did ask Tom a question or two when he got stuck on a story or advice on approaching an interview.

Max asked Tom if he could interrupt for a minute. Tom lifted his head from his Selectric and smiled. "Sure," he said. "What do you need?"

"I know you've talked about the Sunshine Law, and business conducted at civic meetings has to be made public. Is that right?" Max asked.

"Well, yes, but it's a bit more complicated than that," Tom replied in a tone that sounded more like a professor than a fellow reporter. "Why, what do you have?"

Leaving out the part that included the illegal surveillance, Max told Tom about the bid announced at the board meeting and how it seemed a bit suspicious. Max added that there had been an executive session before the general meeting, which is when he thought the bid was rigged.

"Explain to me why you think it was shady," Tom asked Max about the award to Kevin's Water and Heating. "From what you have told me, I'm not sure why you are concerned."

Not an especially good liar, Max had to think fast on his feet. Fortunately for Max, his remarkable associative memory did a quick scan with some excellent results.

"So, do you remember the finals for the AA State Football Championship? I remember covering the event, and Jim Thorpe High School was playing some team from Carbondale. I distinctly remember DeFranco and his family making a big deal when Steve Doll, Kevin's son, made a spectacular catch to win the game. In fact, after the game, I took a picture of the Dolls and the DeFrancos together with Steve in the middle."

"Yeah, I know where you are headed, and it's a little thin if you ask me," Tom said with great skepticism. "I'll tell you what. The Sunshine Law is a bit iffy on executive sessions, but if there was business discussed at the closed-door meeting that was then brought to the general meeting, the details of that business should be available to the public."

"I'm not exactly in the position to make such an inquiry," Max said, nearly pleading with his colleague to dig into the allegation. "Can you make a few calls?"

Tom stared at Max with a mix of sympathy and annoyance. The more senior reporter was doing an investigative piece on abandoned coal mines, but he had a soft spot for Max, especially considering the newbie's nearly tragic mistakes. A few seconds passed, and Tom nodded. "Yeah. Give me a few days."

Max kept his head down, and Monday night turned into Tuesday, Wednesday, and Thursday. During that time, Max was sent to school board meetings in Palmerton, Lehighton, and Nesquehoning, where nothing out of the ordinary took place. Max played things close to the vest and wrote succinct reports from his nightly assignments, patiently waiting for Tom to get back to him. A few trips to his listening post outside the Carbon County yielded nothing of significance.

Friday, Max walked into the office toward his desk, where he saw a small envelope with the words "Max Rosen" typed across the front. Fearing the worst in the form of a pink slip, Max opened it as his heart pounded. For a moment, Max was taken back to the frantic days when he would bring home a report card that he knew would not pass muster. That cocktail of fear, panic, and anxiety was a drink he had hoped was in the past.

Call me at home, the note read. Tom signed it. Tom's day off, but he made a special trip into the office to leave the note.

With hands trembling, Max called Tom, who answered on the first ring.

"You were right," Tom said. "They rigged the bid. Three other bids were lower from companies that had great reputations for service. How about we meet Monday before work to talk about the next steps?"

Max was speechless. In a way, he secretly hoped Tom would come up empty, putting an end to the hidden FM transmitter scheme. With a big win under his belt, Max wondered what secret he would uncover next. And how long would this scam go on before it either put him back in the *Chronicle*'s good graces or found him out of a job? Or worse.

Chapter Four

Max met with Tom the following Monday, and the more senior reporter agreed to take the lead on the story, giving the more junior of the pair a "... contributed to the reporting" byline. That was satisfactory to Max as it led to Ray's praise, as well as from others in the office, including Ervin, who was far from his biggest fan. Once the story ran, there was a shakeup at the county executive board, and while no criminal charges were filed, the governing body lost two key members.

As the case may be, the high Max felt from his victory—or co-victory—was short-lived. It was Max's custom to worry more about what was next than his recent accomplishment. He knew he was still on probation with the *Chronicle*, dwelling that his story on county corruption came by employing illegal surveillance. Max thought of this tactic that he cooked up with Barrett would be like training wheels; once he got back in his boss's good graces and the brass in Allentown, he would remove the transmitter and rely solely on his skills.

Max was not good at compartmentalizing with so much going on, allowing his emotions from one part of his life to bleed onto another. In college, his first time living away from home, any distraction, whether it was family drama or social issues related to dating, clouded Max's focus. Just as he had made a vow to become more extroverted for his job, Max knew he needed to be able to keep his eye on the ball even when he faced an occasional bump in the road. It was time to take some deep breaths and bravely move forward.

A few days after he met with Tom, Max was back to his regular civic meetings and school board elections with a deadly car crash thrown in for good measure. Such was the life of the low man on the reporting totem pole. Looking ahead, Max set his sights on his next reporting opportunity at the Carbon County Courthouse. Friday, a trial was set to start for a Jim Thorpe man accused of arson. The word from the County District Attorney was that they had the guy, Chris Albrecht, dead to rights. Nonetheless, Max had a passion for trials and looked forward to the case. Somehow, he knew his hidden FM transmitter would play a role in the story even though he could not predict how or why.

During Christmas Vacation, when Max was in his early teens, his father took him and his sister Nancy to City Hall in Philadelphia to watch actual trials. Yes, it was cheap entertainment, but from his first visit to the superior court in 1965, Max was hooked and wanted more than anything to become a lawyer. The courtroom looked nothing like it did on *Perry Mason* or *The Defenders*; there was an air of mystery and intrigue in those wood-paneled chambers that Max found intoxicating. His dream of becoming a lawyer did not come true, but Max relished any opportunity to watch the law in action.

The day before the trial over in Jim Thorpe, the bureau in Nesquehoning had a new addition. Sue Reinhard, a news intern and recent graduate of Shippensburg State, was assigned to the team's support role. Tall, with dirty blonde hair and somewhat thick glasses, Sue looked like a cross between an aging hippie and school librarian.

Ray took Sue around to meet the reporters, stopping to talk at length with Tex, who, although happily married, was a serious flirt. It went with his personality, and everyone who knew him took it as part of his charm. After making the rounds, Ray plopped Sue down at an empty desk behind Max. It was a swing-spot of sorts, in that it was shared by the news staff and the circulation department. Often, the circulation folks were out in the field in the afternoon, talking to newsstand operators and delivery boys and girls. It was a tough job: dealing with kids who thought delivering newspapers would be easy money, but when their alarms went off at 5 a.m., they thought otherwise.

Sue reached over and tapped Max on the arm. "I'm hoping we get a chance to talk," she said with a warm smile. "You look like someone who knows his way around the office."

"I am only a few months more senior than you," Max replied with a hint of nervousness. "I came here with very little reporting experience, so I am learning as I go."

"Well, maybe we can learn the ropes together," Sue said with the slightest hint of flirtiness in her voice. "Can I go with you tonight on your assignment?"

"If it's okay with Ray, I guess it's fine," Max replied, nearly stumbling over his words.

Max had little experience working with women and even less experience with women on a social level. In college, Max lacked the self-esteem to have a successful female relationship, always believing he was not good enough for whatever woman he was dating at the time. While classmates drank, smoked, and freely slept around, Max was on the outside looking in. His four years on a beautiful, idyllic campus would never be a fond memory for him.

In a study of contrasts, Max exuded confidence in areas that relied solely on his inborn mental acumen. Three years before working at the *Chronicle*, while still a grad student, Max decided to go on a popular TV game show to pay some of his grad school tuition. His criteria for selecting the right game show were that it needed to be a show taped in New York and relied on intelligence rather than luck.

It proved to be a success, with Max doing exceptionally well and walking away with $5,000. Later in life, Max would appear on another popular game show, this one in California, where he would win big and walk away with a VHS tape of his appearance to show off his celebrity. In reality, Max rarely spoke about his game show success, feeling it made him look like a braggart or egotistical super-nerd.

Sue got the go-ahead from Ray to go with Max to the Coaldale borough council meeting. It was sure to be a dull evening with the usual citizen complaints, but Max was determined to prove himself no matter how lame the assignment. On the ride over, Sue did her best to get Max to loosen up. Born in Easton, Sue told Max about her family and time at Shippensburg State. In her senior year, she became editor of the *News-Chronicle*, the school newspaper, earning her an internship at the *Chronicle* in 1977. A year later, after graduation, she was offered an entry-level position at the Allentown paper, and she hoped to attack the new job with great passion. According to Max's quick math, Sue was twenty-three or twenty-four.

The meeting of the Nesquehoning borough council was as big a goose egg as Max expected. There were a few nuggets that, with a generous helping of light analysis and some extra adjectives, could yield a five-hundred-word news story that would be buried on the back page of the local edition of the *Chronicle*.

Sue sat quietly next to Max at the meeting, scribbling away in her reporter's notebook. Max was concerned that she would want to take over the assignment. But, when they returned to the office, Sue politely asked if she could read his story before it went to the editor. Without outside help or criticism, Max knew it was in his best interest to welcome Sue and have her give his work the once-over.

"This is good," Sue said with the proper amount of enthusiasm. "I like how you made the borough's decision to repaint all the crosswalks sound a lot more important than it was."

Max nodded and walked his two pages of copy up to Ervin, who looked up from editing a feature set to run over the weekend while simultaneously devouring an oversized ham and cheese sandwich. "So, how's your new girlfriend?" Ervin smirked. "I see how she chose to go with you tonight even though you had the shittiest assignment on the board."

The remark caught Max by surprise. He became a shade of Alabama crimson, turned, and walked away. Back at his desk, he saw Sue writing in her notebook. Max wasn't sure what she was working on but thought it would be wise not to ask too many questions.

"Do you want to use my Selectric?" Max asked Sue. "I'm going over to the Elks with some of the other reporters for a beer."

"Can I join you?" Sue fired back almost before the words came out of Max's mouth.

"Umm . . . Sure . . . I guess . . . It's on the corner, three doors down from here."

Sue grabbed her coat and purse and was eager to go. Max didn't know what to make of the bureau's latest addition but figured the best course of action was not to interpret Sue's behavior after knowing her for only seven hours.

Not a big social drinker, Max left the lodge and headed home after his usual six-ounce glass of beer. Sue was busy talking to Tex and Al Hickey, a twenty-year veteran of the *Chronicle* who could drink his colleagues under the table—a talent Al exercised regularly. Tex waved good night, and Al, in customary fashion, slapped Max on the back and said, "See ya tomorrow, kid."

Max drove the four blocks to his apartment, thinking about the upcoming arson trial, hoping Sue would not ask to tag along. He also decided to give Barrett a call in the morning, before work, to update him on their scheme's fruits—so far.

Since joining the *Chronicle*, Max had trouble sleeping. Newspaper work was not the sort of job you could forget once the dinner bell rang, especially when that bell rang at 11 p.m. Max would relive every moment of his workday in slow motion like watching the rerun of an old TV show except in this drama, he was the star. That night, Max had a new character to add to his replay: Sue.

After a fitful night, Max woke up later than usual and made a beeline for the cupboard to get going on a cup of instant coffee. Max ate out of necessity at this stage of his life, not for pleasure or health, so breakfast and lunch blended into one sloppy meal generally consumed standing up over the sink. Dinner was catch-as-catch-can, rotating between a greasy burger, a bowl of chili, or a can of Chef Boyardee spaghetti. His best meals came after family visits, where his mother, an exceptional self-taught cook, packaged up leftovers for Max to take back to Nesquehoning.

Lukewarm coffee in hand, Max's first order of business was to call Barrett with an update. Not what you would call gainfully employed, Barrett's days included hustling self-absorbed tennis players for a few extra bucks or playing backgammon or chess at a park near his home in Philadelphia. Barrett was between girlfriends, his last one being his secretary at the District Attorney's office. When Barrett walked away from his life as a crusader lawyer, so too did he leave Sheena, his assistant and occasional date. Women were not a priority in Barrett's life. Like Max, Barrett lacked in self-confidence with the opposite sex. In most other matters, his ego could fill the Grand Canyon.

Barrett picked up on the third ring. "Yo, Max, what's up?" he answered. He liked to start his conversations with Max by saying "Yo" because it was an unflattering stereotype associated with Philadelphia people. The coarse greeting was especially in vogue due to *Rocky*, the film that had taken the country by storm three years earlier. Barrett, interested in trivia few others cared about, knew that Sylvester Stallone's lone connection to Philadelphia was the few years the movie star went to Lincoln High School in the city's Mayfair area.

Max waited for a few beats and went into a recap of the past few days, relaying his success with their FM transmitter ploy and the secret conversation that led to a front-page story in the *Chronicle*.

"Okay, so what's next?" Barrett asked, barely waiting for Max to finish. "Oh, wait. I thought of something. Have you thought about sitting outside the courthouse on a regular day? I mean a day when there are no meetings scheduled?"

"Hmm. That is interesting. The only issue is if I sit outside and hear something and can't identify the voice, I'll have to dash into the courthouse and see who it was talking to."

"I say try it once or twice," Barrett said. "I'd try it on a Monday. That seems to be a day when there could be many people going to apply for permits and such or look up weird things like property records. Who knows what sort of chatter you'll pick up?"

At this point, Max could intuitively tell that Barrett was ready to get off the phone. Knowing someone for so many years allows a friend to pick up nonverbal cues or tells that keep a long-term relationship running smoothly.

"Got it. Thanks for your advice," Max said, ready to end the call. "Take it easy on those tennis pigeons at the playground. One of these days, you will meet your match."

After a quick shower and a leftover sandwich that passed for brunch, Max was out the door and on his way to the Carbon County Courthouse for his assignment to cover the local arson trial. As he searched for his keys, Max grabbed his briefcase, which held his transistor radio, two notepads, several pens and pencils, and a box of Mike and Ikes.

Max planned to stop at the office for a few minutes before zooming off to the courthouse for what he hoped would be an exciting day. Taped to his Selectric was a note from Ray that told him the trial was postponed until the following Tuesday. The state's key witness—the Carbon County Fire Marshall—had a conflict and could not make it for the opening arguments.

Remembering his conversation with Barrett, Max thought it would be a good time to head over to the courthouse, sit on the bench outside, and listen in on Radio Free Carbon County. At best, he would uncover something worthwhile; at a minimum, it could be good for a laugh. The winding road that led from Nesquehoning to the center of Jim Thorpe never had much traffic, but on this Friday, cars were lined up from Nesquehoning to just outside Jim Thorpe's city limits. Max saw flashing lights ahead with a county sheriff directing traffic. It was nothing too serious—a car drove off the road and into a barrier, and while the damage looked significant, those inside the gray Nissan seemed okay.

Max breathed a sigh of relief. Had the accident been more serious, he would have felt obligated to get out, talk to the deputy in charge of the details, and snap a picture. For some ghoulish reason, locals loved reading about car accidents in the paper. It was not a reporter's job to question what sold papers, only to feed those hungry for local news.

A parking spot opened across the courthouse on Broadway, and Max's trusty bench was unoccupied. The sky was dotted with ominous black clouds, so Max thought it would be smart to get his umbrella from the trunk.

Instead of looking both ways when crossing Broadway, Max looked both ways before assuming the bench's position. He took out his pad, pen, and then transistor radio and earphone. Tuning in to 93.4, all Max could get was static, but after jiggling his antenna around, he heard the voices of a man and woman.

"I think my parents will be pissed," a woman with a young, coarse voice said. "I promised them they would be at our wedding. I don't want to be there when you tell them we eloped."

"We're married, so they will just have to learn to live with it," the man replied, not quite shouting but certainly amped up with anxiety. "And what about my parents? They hate you and made me promise I'd break up with you."

When the elevator reached the ground floor, the pair walked out of the front door. Maybe nineteen years old, the woman was wearing a long flowing dress while her newly minted husband wore a button-down flannel shirt and jeans. Max could not help but stare, connecting the elevator eavesdrop with this couple on their way to at least three weeks of marital bliss.

And then someone tapped Max on the shoulder. He turned, and there stood Sue. She smiled, holding a bakery box in both hands. She eased her way onto the bench only a few inches away from Max.

"I love the cupcakes from Blended Bakery," Sue said, noting Max's shocked look. "My favorite is their Twister Pretzel ones."

Max sat speechless, scanning his generally reliable smarts to come up with a plausible response.

"Might I ask, what are you doing here, and what are you listening to on that radio?" Sue said, smiling.

No logical answer popped into Max's mind. At least one that would not require a fifteen-minute explanation. He put down his radio and simply said, "I'm not sure why I'm here. It's nice to see you."

Chapter Five

Realizing Max was tongue-tied or perhaps emitting garbled speech from a sudden stroke, Sue reached out and gently put her hand on his forearm. Her hand was soft and warm, while Max's entire body felt like one giant icicle. He truly was at a loss and close to a full-blown panic attack.

"I have these cupcakes, and there's a coffee place down the street," Sue said as she turned to the side to speak face-to-face. "Let's go over, and we can get to know each other better."

Max appreciated the gesture, and without saying a word, he got up and followed Sue—who was a good head shorter than him—to Last Drop, a small coffee shop mostly frequented by tourists. Max started by walking alongside Sue, but the narrow sidewalk forced him to move a pace behind her. As they neared the coffee shop, Max took a couple of deep breaths to regain his composure. He didn't want Sue to think he was a babbling idiot or social misfit, so Max quickly thought of a few conversation starters.

"I notice you wear a Delta Zeta pin?" Max asked with as much charm as he could muster as the pair sat at a table midway toward the back of the coffee shop. "Did you belong to a sorority in college?"

"No, actually, it's my sister's." Sue smiled. "I am not the sorority type. She just got married, and her husband asked her to stop wearing it. He thinks it will give guys the wrong idea. I think it's kinda cool."

A waitress, no doubt a local high school student, came and took their order. Sue surreptitiously took one of the pretzel-topped cupcakes from its box. She cut it in half and pushed a piece of the pastry Max's way.

"So, you're wondering what I was doing sitting on a bench outside the courthouse, listening to my transistor radio," said Max, diving right into the subject at hand. "It's sort of weird, but I do my best thinking out of the office, and I like the hustle and bustle. It may not be the sort of people watching at Times Square or the Champs-Élysées, but it's all we have. As far as the radio goes, I listen to WGPA, a local station that plays elevator music, so it's like white noise to tune out all the background chatter," Max said, suddenly realizing he was talking fast.

"I get it," Sue said. "I grew up in a large family, so I cherish some alone time."

As they continued to chat, the folks behind the counter at Last Drop cleaned the counter and started to rinse out the giant carafes that sat on a table alongside the far wall. Without realizing it, they had been sitting at the coffee shop for an hour. Since it was a few minutes before closing time, Sue and Max got the hint. They grabbed their coats and made their way up Broadway back toward the courthouse.

"I'm parked across from the courthouse," Max said. "Where are you?"

"Right here," she replied, pointing at a VW Rabbit desperately in need of a car wash. She took out her keys and opened the door with her back toward Max. Sue climbed into the driver's seat and turned on the ignition. "Don't Look Back" by Boston came blaring out of her car radio. Blaring could be an understatement; Max felt the entire car shake once the radio came on.

"I enjoyed this. To be continued." Sue closed her door and pulled away, heading west toward Nesquehoning.

Max's time with Sue went by quickly, leaving him with a warm feeling he was not accustomed to. With limited successful social experience overlaying years of self-doubt, understanding his emotions was not Max's strong suit. Getting into his car, also in need of a good wash and wax, Max thought about Sue, the weekend ahead, the arson trial taking place the following week, and, most of all, the FM transmitter that sat idling over the weekend.

Not much happens newsworthy in Northeastern Pennsylvania on a Friday night in the fall. It was the end of high school football season, and one of the rookie reporter's jobs was to take calls from stringers with football scores. Those scores were then compiled and passed on to the sports desk of the *Chronicle* in Allentown. The other job the newbies were asked to handle was obituaries. Funeral directors would call in with death notices of recently deceased. Max learned his first week on the death desk that obituaries, being a public record, had to be written in exact detail. With his turns taking obit calls, Max learned more about various religions and their funeral procedures than he ever did in his Comparative Religions of the World class in college.

With Max working high school football scores—a task which included answering calls inquiring who won the Marion Catholic-Coaldale High game—Sue was working obits. New to that task, Tex was more than willing to show her the ropes. Luckily, it was a slow night on the death desk with only one call from the Ovsak Funeral Home.

Max again passed on the opportunity to head to his parents' house for the weekend. He wanted to take the next two days to learn as much as he could about household fires and arson. A thirty-seven-year-old Jim Thorpe man, Chris Albrecht, would face charges of second-degree arson for not only burning down his home but also the neighbors on either side. Albrecht had many run-ins with the law, including a few DUIs, assault and battery, and two domestic abuse charges. In short, Albrecht was last in line for Carbon County Man of the Year.

Arson can be challenging to prove. Experienced fire marshals and arson investigators have, at most, a 60 percent chance of proving the crime and an even more difficult time finding the perpetrator. Max wanted to follow the trial closely, so he knew it was time to get the lowdown from an experienced fire investigator.

Max's sister Nancy had a high school friend, Gene Watson, a twice-decorated firefighter at Trevose Fire Company, Neshaminy Falls Station 84. Max knew Watson in passing, so he asked his sister for Gene's number. The plan was to call Watson on Saturday afternoon, compile notes and then go into the office on Monday to read all the past clips related to Albrecht and the Jim Thorpe fire.

The day Max dreaded most, Sunday, would be for tidying up and trying to prepare something for dinner other than a Stouffer's frozen lasagna. If things went well, Max might have leftovers for a few days, which would keep him away from greasy hamburgers and the canned chili served at most of the local diners. His lack of desire to cook had little to do with his ability to cook; as odd as it seemed, Max had a large collection of food magazines such as *Gourmet* and *Bon Appetit*. He had neither the time nor inclination to treat himself to a fancy salad or gourmet stew. At least for now, Max stuck to meals he could eat over the sink while listening to sports talk shows on the radio.

Max reached Gene Watson on the first try. Watson was an avid golfer and had just come in from a round at Middleton Country Club. The lieutenant from his fire station was a member of the country club and periodically invited Watson to reward his heroic efforts. Gene was in a good mood, shooting 74 for the day, besting his boss by three strokes, which earned him a free lunch at the country club's famous buffet.

"My sister gave me your number," Max said warmly. "I hope it's okay that I called on a Saturday."

"Sure, Nancy is great. I think my girlfriend at the time and Nancy were in the same art classes in high school," Gene said, still in a good mood from his morning on the links.

"So I have this arson case I am covering here in Carbon County, and I would like to do a great job with it, so can you give me a few tips on arson? Like, how difficult is it to prove, and are there things I should look for from the investigator's report to know whether he did a thorough job on the case?"

Gene paused for a second. He took a long sip from his victory beer and wondered how much he should tell this reporter—someone he never met and knew third hand. After what seemed like a long fifteen seconds, he responded.

"Well, here are a few things. Was it an easy cause to determine whether it was arson, or was it complex? What I mean is, was there more than one point of origin, and if so, were they close to one another? Was there anything suspicious, like was a window left open? An open window gives the fire more oxygen to spread. And was there property loss? I'm not sure if you can find out, or even if this comes up in a trial, but do they have a record as to whether the guy accused of arson recently took out an insurance policy worth more than the property?"

There was a delay as Max was busy scribbling down notes. "I do know this," Max told one of Trevose's Bravest. "The guy is a scumbag who is hated around town. I think he may be going through a divorce and was fired from his job."

"Yeah, that's all circumstantial," Gene replied. "Facts matter here, so pay close attention. Hey, listen, the Penn State game is about to start, so let me know if you have any more questions once the trial starts. Okay?"

"Thanks so much. Nancy sends her regards. Enjoy the game."

Max replayed the conversation in his head, trying to pick out the key things to look for and not prejudge the trial because the accused was an asshat.

Saturday bled into Sunday, and this weekend Max did everything he could to avoid falling into his usual case of the blues. The Eagles played the St. Louis Cardinals away, so Max tuned in to Charlie Swift's play-by-play on WCAU and busied himself cleaning up the kitchen and bedroom and did something that passed for wiping down the bathroom. The game was a nail biter with the Birds prevailing 14–10, making the team 8–5 for the season, a far cry from those miserable seasons the team had when Max was in high school. The team began its slow turnaround in 1976 when they brought former UCLA head coach Dick Vermeil on board. After a 4–10 season in '76 followed by a record of 5–9 in 1977, the Eagles were making their way up the NFC East's rankings.

When Max decided to get into newspaper work, most who knew him assumed he would be a sports reporter. While in grad school, Max interned at Philadelphia's leading sports-talk station, where he picked up his writing talent. He would write the scripts for the nightly sportscasts and realized the words came easy. Pete, the on-air talent, was impressed with Max's work and encouraged him to do more writing and branch out to topics other than sports.

Monday was slow at the Carbon County bureau of the *Chronicle*, so Max focused on going through all the newspaper clips related to arson cases in the area. In 1974, a Tamaqua man was accused of arson when he neglected to update the wiring in his attic. A short in the wiring made a spark that quickly ignited and set ablaze the family's decades of photographs stored in the small room at the top of their home. Those color photographs emit a toxic particle, which not only is a health hazard but also can clog up a chimney, trapping smoke inside the building.

In that case, the homeowner was found guilty of criminal negligence as opposed to arson. Lewis Erbe, the perpetrator, was sentenced to seven years at the State Correctional Institution in Chester, Pennsylvania. Ironically, he was scheduled to be released in one month on good behavior after serving four years.

Max was well-prepped for the trial, fueled by equal measures of ambition and bad instant coffee when he arrived at the courthouse an hour before the trial was scheduled to start. Waiting outside the courtroom on the top floor of the building, Max nearly forgot that the elevator he used to reach the top floor was the one in which he and Barrett had planted an FM transmitter. He chuckled, wondering if someone driving by would accidentally tune their car radios to 93.4 FM and hear the chatter coming from inside the building.

Being well-versed in many of the upcoming trial particulars, Max was able to identify the key players: Mark Tobias, the county district attorney; Michael Wolf, the defense attorney for Chris Albrecht; and Albrecht himself. Tobias was a world-weary sixty-two-year-old legal fixture in the last months of his service to the county. Tobias, a three-term DA, lost to Mary Englehardt, a forty-five-year-old native of Jim Thorpe who went to Penn State for undergraduate school and earned a law degree at Pitt. It was a close election, and to be honest, Tobias was glad to be moving on to private practice.

Wolf was well known in Carbon County for being a master at getting DUIs overturned on small technicalities. In his early fifties, Wolf tipped the scales at 285 pounds, which is a lot for a man a shade under six feet tall. Nonetheless, he wore a beautifully tailored suit that underplayed his significant girth.

Chris Albrecht was unaccustomed to wearing a coat and tie. Constantly tugging at his collar, Albrecht had a smug look as all eyes silently gazed at him from across the narrow hallway outside the courtroom. Albrecht squirmed on the wooden bench while Wolf spoke sternly to his client. Max took out his notepad and scribbled a question—*How could Albrecht afford a lawyer as costly as Wolf?*

This being a jury trial, an exercise in justice in front of twelve of Albrecht's peers, there was a day of *voir dire*, which is the process of selecting prospective jurors. From what Max gathered from speaking to various courthouse officials, things went smoothly, and the result was seven women and five men with two alternates.

Shortly after 10 a.m., the courtroom doors swung open and a small crowd entered. This hall of justice had handsomely paneled walls flanking two sets of twenty rows of gallery seating. The DA and defense teams were already at their respective seats at tables between the audience and the raised platform where the judge would preside. The defendant's twelve peers were seated in the jury box, anxious for things to get rolling. As Judge Kasmir Schantz entered the room, the bailiff rose and all stood while the diminutive jurist took his seat and lowered the microphone in front of him.

Schantz was a controversial appointee to the court in Carbon County. With little experience as a prospector or trial lawyer, Schantz specialized in Allentown's real estate law before taking a seat on the bench in Jim Thorpe. His predecessor, Glen Heffelfinger, died the year before from a sudden heart attack on the fifteenth tee at Olde Homestead Golf Course thirty miles south of Jim Thorpe, leaving a spot open on the district court. Pennsylvania governor Joe Wharton appointed Schantz to fill the remainder of Heffelfinger's term. An election in 1979 would put Schantz's seat up for grabs, so every trial under his jurisdiction would be closely watched and evaluated by the court of public opinion. With so much on the line, the *Chronicle*'s coverage would be carefully followed by curious voters throughout the county.

The three hours of the morning session of the trial were filled with procedural discussions, many of which were done with the DA and Wolf standing directly in front of Judge Schantz out of earshot. The seven women and five men doing their civic duty were losing patience and appeared ready for a break to eat lunch, smoke, or use the bathroom.

Tobias and Wolf walked back to their respective seats. Wolf whispered something to his client, and the DA looked at his watch and nodded to the judge. Schantz positioned his microphone, turned it on, and tapped it to ensure it was on.

"Let's take a ninety-minute break for lunch and resume at 2 p.m.," Schantz said in a voice barely audible to those in the courtroom.

Without missing a beat, Max jumped up from his seat in the last row and bolted toward the stairs, racing down to the first floor. He found the men's room where he and Barrett plotted their eavesdropping plan, opened the door, and found an open stall. Max then opened his briefcase, took out his transistor radio, and spun the dial until he got to 93.4. Initially, there were ten seconds of static, which Max attributed to him being in an enclosed room with thick, cement walls. As the signal got stronger, Max recognized the voices of Wolf and his client, Chris Albrecht. It was obvious they were alone as Albrecht spoke:

"Now, you're sure they won't find out about that secret insurance policy, right?"

"I'm sure we covered your tracks, but I have to tell you that was a really stupid thing to do," Wolf angrily responded.

"No way will I be found guilty," Albrecht continued as the elevator reached the ground floor. "Not only will I have more than enough to pay you, but I will be on my way to Mexico by the end of the week."

A cold shiver crashed across Max, less-than-elegantly seated on a toilet fully clothed. He had a suspicion that proved to be accurate. Given Albrecht's reputation, it was a deliberate arson case, but Max never figured there was a big payday lying in wait. Max knew this could be the story that not only would put him back in the good graces of his editors but boost his reputation at the *Chronicle* as a star on the rise.

Nothing in this illegally obtained information was of any use without legitimate corroboration. Max knew he had his work cut out for him.

Chapter Six

Max knew nothing about insurance of any kind. He had car insurance, but his parents paid for it as part of their auto and umbrella policy. He was certain his parents had life insurance policies through their jobs, but he was unaware of the details. The *Chronicle* offered health insurance, but Max had an inherited fear of going to the doctor, so premium healthcare coverage was wasted on him. Not only did Max need to learn the basics about how insurance worked, but he also had to investigate what sorts of scams can be used to cash in on deliberately set fires.

The afternoon of the trial's first day dragged on. The county brought the county fire chief, Bill Yaich, to take the stand. He outlined the facts reported on in the news and discussed over the back fences and taprooms of Carbon County. Max gave the county half a point for the testimony.

The day in court ended with testimony from Ray Schwab, a state arson investigator. Schwab was far too matter-of-fact in his assessment of the fire to project authority. He pointed to a large amount of property loss, noting the fact that several points of origin could indicate an amateur arsonist who went overboard in his attempt to cover up his crime. Schwab droned on for an hour before Michael Wolf gingerly rose from his chair and took to cross-examination.

"So, Mr. Schwab, you say there was a huge property loss," Wolf said, standing unusually close to the state investigator. "Isn't that common in many fires?"

"Well, yes, but I have a hunch. There was significant destruction that made it difficult for investigators to find the cause."

"Is there ever so much damage that you cannot find the cause of a fire?"

Schwab paused, clearly caught off guard. "Well, it's rare, but it happens."

"When was the last time it happened to you, Mr. Schwab? Do you remember?"

"I'm not sure. I'd have to look through my records."

Wolf turned and slowly walked back to his seat at the defendant's table. He paused midway and looked over his shoulder. "That's all I have for that witness."

The defense attorney could not believe the county attorney did not ask the arson investigator whether Albrecht had a fire insurance policy. The trial was a long way from being over, and the jury appeared confused after Schwab's testimony, so things were somewhat going in Albrecht's favor.

Like a boxing match, Max was awarding points for each round, and he begrudgingly awarded that round to Wolf and Albrecht. Max, too, was bewildered that the topic of insurance was not raised. He remained hopeful that the details of Albrecht's secret policy would come out in the trial.

Max returned to the office distracted from the first full day of Albrecht's arson trial. Sue was seated at Max's desk, writing in her notepad as Max walked by on his way to tell Ray about his day in court. Sue reached out and grabbed Max's arm as he came by.

"I hope it's okay that I am sitting here. Ray wasn't sure you'd be coming back here after the trial."

"It's totally fine. Listen, I need to go to talk to Ray."

Ray was on the phone when Max approached his desk. Clearly in the middle of a personal call—probably with his wife Maxine—Ray motioned for Max to take a seat. A minute later, Ray hung up the phone and took off his reading glasses.

"So, how was court?"

"It dragged on for a bit, but the county did a crappy job with the state arson investigator. The defense attorney—I think you've heard of Michael Wolf—picked apart Schwab's testimony. That's the state investigator, and if you ask me, he's not long for his job if that creep Albrecht gets off."

Ray nodded. "Listen, I don't want you to spend all of your time on the trial. There are a couple of other stories I need you to work on. Tom and Ervin both have vacations scheduled next week, so we need to cover for them. Why don't you go to court tomorrow for the morning and then come in, and we can talk about another assignment you can do at the same time? Before you go," Ray added, "why don't you put together a quick piece on the opening day of the trial. Just a description of the players and a recap of the fire. There are lots of clips from when it happened."

Max agreed to the assignment but also didn't want his disappointment to show. He needed to cover as much of the trial as possible to find out about Albrecht's insurance scam. Still, he was only a few weeks into his probation period and in no position to argue with the boss.

"Sure, Ray. I'll write up a short piece and turn it in before I go. I will come to see you right after lunch tomorrow. By the way, I was planning on going home this weekend to see my family. Do you think you'll need me Saturday or Sunday morning? I'll be back by five on Sunday for my regular shift."

"That's fine," Ray said, clearly ready for the conversation to be over. Max noticed his boss sneaking a peek at his watch while they talked.

After a long day in court, Max was ready to go home but stopped at his desk and asked Sue to move so he could bang out an overview of the opening of the arson case. Working from memory, it did not take more than fifteen minutes. Sue picked up her things and moved across the room to an empty work spot.

Before leaving, Max remembered that he needed a new reporter's notebook. He was terrible at shorthand and was getting the hang of taking detailed notes in high-pressure situations. Max always marveled that his aunt, who worked for a court reporting agency, could touch type seventy-five words a minute and operate one of those cryptic Stenotype machines used to take verbatim dictation at trials.

"Are you sticking around?" Sue asked from across the room as Max opened a drawer on the left side of his desk. "I'd love to get a cup of coffee if you have time."

"Raincheck. I am gassed. This trial is exhausting, and I have some research to do before I go back to the courthouse tomorrow."

Sue was disappointed. Lacking any understanding of women, Max wasn't sure what was going on with Sue, putting him on edge. Was she trying to pick his brain for ideas or just looking for a friend in a new work setting? Throughout college, graduate school, and now in his chosen career, Max couldn't imagine any woman finding him interesting or attractive. Given that assumption, he was sure there was no romantic interest on her part. Whatever her interest may be, it would have to wait for another day.

Max had a restless night overcome with far too many moving parts competing for space in his brain. Since joining the *Chronicle*, he had been having sleep issues, mostly due to an inability to shut down after intense days of work. The need to have at least eight hours of sleep had been impressed upon him when he was young; even now, Max was not sure why he lived in fear of what would happen if his sleep bank wasn't filled to the brim.

The excitement of the trial got Max's adrenaline going. A lot of those seated around him in the gallery looked at him as he made his way to a seat on the aisle near the back of the courtroom. The summary of the arson trial's progress made the front page of the Carbon County section of the *Chronicle*, so folks—many of whom were Albrecht's friends and family—figured this unfamiliar face was likely the reporter who wrote the news story. The story was straightforward, although Max's description of the defendant was not complimentary, saying he was "callous in his appearance at the trial."

Judge Schantz appeared forty-five minutes late and appeared harried as the courtroom rose upon his arrival. The judge motioned both attorneys to the bench to discuss some business related to the trial. Wolf was doing most of the talking, so the discussion may have had something to do with whether Albrecht would take the stand on his behalf. The impromptu meeting ended, leaving about thirty minutes before lunch, at which time Max had to return to the office.

Bennett Krause, a local car dealer and neighbor of Albrecht, took the stand. His home suffered damage from the fire, and was scheduled to testify that he had overheard Albrecht boast at a local bar that he was about to come into some big money. It was a thin heap of gossip, but the county didn't have much in the way of witnesses aside from the fire investigator and a few of the defendant's neighbors.

Krause was uneasy on the stand. Tobias did his best to lead the witness through his story of what he heard in the bar, but the Jim Thorpe auto jockey stumbled through his answers, giving the appearance of being carefully coached. Wolf then put Krause away with a few simple questions:

"Who else was in the bar when you heard Mr. Albrecht talk of this alleged plan?"

"I don't exactly remember," Krause mumbled.

"Did you have anything to drink that night, Mr. Krause?"

"I had a few," he muttered, barely audible.

"How many is a few?"

"Two or three beers, maybe."

"Was it two or three? Or more. What if I told you the bartender that night could testify you were drunk on the evening in question?"

"I guess I had more than two or three."

Wolf looked at Krause and then the judge. "I've had enough of this witness, Your Honor."

With that, the court was in recess for lunch, and Max needed to head back to the office in Nesquehoning. There was a drizzle, so Max flicked on his windshield wipers at low speed. He reached for the radio, and much to his dismay, the local station was playing "You Don't Bring Me Flowers," a duet from Barbra Streisand and Neil Diamond. Max was indeed thankful he reached the parking lot by the office just as the chorus "Well, you just roll over . . . And, you turn out the light . . . And you don't bring me flowers anymore . . ." came on. He was quick to shut the engine off so he could end this musical misery.

As Max entered the office, he was surprised to find his desk chair was nowhere to be found. He looked around and asked one of the circulation department staffers if he had seen it. Tim, a balding guy of about forty-five who worked in circulation and enjoyed yelling at young newspaper delivery kids, shook his head no. Max was about to go back to Ray to talk about his assignment and ask about his chair when he spotted his chair through a crack in the door of the open men's room.

That's weird, Max thought to himself.

Max opened the door to the restroom and immediately recognized his chair. It was relatively new with the sticker "Property of the *Chronicle*" on the bottom of the backrest. Not sure what was going on—was it a rite of passage or hazing or something else?—as he wheeled the black leather office chair the thirty feet back to his desk, he heard a familiar voice behind him.

"Oh, you found it, Jewboy."

There stood all six-foot, four inches of Stan Raidler, a disheveled man with a broom in one hand and a giant smirk across his unshaven face. Raidler was the office gofer, doing odd jobs and janitorial work such as cleaning the bathrooms and mopping the floor. A native of nearby Lehighton, Max had heard—but never confirmed—that Raidler recently was released from a state prison where he served three years of a five-year sentence for statutory rape. Whether or not the rumor was true, his presence gave Max the creeps and he had as little interaction with Stan as possible.

Growing up in a Philadelphia neighborhood that was north of 90 percent Jewish, anti-Semitism was new to him. In college, someone did ask him where his horns were, believing that Jews had horns. A year later, someone in Max's Sociology 101 class asked him why he was wearing a shirt and tie to class. When Max said that he taught religious school at a nearby synagogue after class, his fellow sociology student's reaction was alarming yet predictable.

"You're Jewish?" the guy declared rather loudly. "You don't look Jewish?"

Raidler's chair prank was far more serious as he was a rather large dude who possibly was recently released from the hoosegow. Max had never been in a fight in his entire life, and squaring off against a rough-hewn bully was not the place to start.

"I don't like what you said about my friend Chris," Raidler said as Max pushed his chair under the desk. "Neither do a lot of other people around here, so you'd better watch your step. Maybe you should go back to your mommy and daddy in Philly."

"Thanks for the warning," Max replied, rattled from the exchange with this menacing weasel. Max looked down at his briefcase, rummaging through it, pretending to look for a pen. He was waiting for Raidler to walk away, and after another minute of glaring, the bully and his broom walked out the front door.

It took Max a good ten minutes to stop shaking and regain his composure. After his fight-or-flight trembling eased, Max walked back to meet with Ray. In his quick walk to the back of the office, Max decided not to mention the incident with Stan. Instead, Max would seek the counsel of Tex, a level-headed guy whose worldly experience gave him crisp insight into other people.

"How was court this morning?" Ray asked, pushing his reading glasses up to the bridge of his nose.

"Not much happened since the judge was late."

"Okay. I have an assignment for you. The newspaper in Wilkes-Barre is on strike, and I want you to drive up there and talk to the head of the union. It seems the reporters and pressmen who are out picketing are considering starting a rival paper."

Ray knew that Max's grad school studies covered all sorts of media companies and their business models, so the bureau chief saw the young reporter as the perfect choice to cover the story. Ray also thought it would be a nice change of pace for Max to get out of the area for a day and tackle something different from his usual assignments. Wilkes-Barre was forty miles north of Nesquehoning, so Ray instructed Max to take his car and turn in an expense form for his mileage.

Max spent the early part of the afternoon reviewing his trial notes before heading home to pick something out of the freezer for a late lunch or early dinner. He wanted to get an early jump on the day by leaving for Wilkes-Barre before 9 a.m. for his meeting with Ray Chorba, the union president representing the reporters. The assignment was different than any other Max had covered in his short career. Still, he had a keen understanding of how media companies work and was ready to utilize that knowledge.

Before heading home—which was less than a mile from the office in Nesquehoning—Max needed to take a detour which was way out of the way. He headed toward the Carbon County Courthouse with the intent of quickly tuning in to his hidden FM transmitter in hopes of catching some juicy gossip. Max figured it might be time for an afternoon break or early recess, at which time a juror, witness, attorney, or even Albrecht might be caught spilling some secret beans.

A young man in his thirties and an older woman, perhaps in her early sixties, were seated on Max's bench smoking when he reached the courthouse. Max's memory scanned the pair and remembered them from the jury, which meant they were on recess. Max parked his car across the street from the courthouse and waited for the pair of jurors to head back inside. As they flicked their cigarette butts on the ground, Max took out his transistor radio and tuned to 93.4.

49

Max kept time in his head, and after what seemed to be two minutes, the voices of a man and woman came in clearly. They were in the middle of a conversation:

"I think you'd like my daughter," the woman said, taking a deep breath. "She just got out of a bad marriage and is taking classes at Penn State's Hershey Campus."

"If this thing is ever over," the man responded, clearly wishing he were anywhere else, "maybe I'll give her a call. I wish they would move along and let us deliberate."

"I'm with you because my boss isn't happy about this prolonged jury duty. I do have one question that is bothering me. Have you heard anyone mention whether Albrecht had fire insurance for his crappy house? It seems he had to have some, right?"

With that, the elevator reached its destination.

Max's nascent reporter's intuition was heating up. *I've got to get on that fire insurance question. And I better do it fast.*

Chapter Seven

Max left early the next day for Wilkes-Barre and decided to take the Pennsylvania Turnpike instead of local roads to expedite the trip. Radio stations came in and out on his journey until he landed on WKRZ, a rock station in Forty Fort, a Wilkes-Barre suburb. As he entered the town, Max spotted the picket line along Market Street in the center of the city and grabbed a parking spot across the street from the newspaper entrance.

Ray Chorba was easy to spot. Chain-smoking Chesterfields with a cup of coffee in his right hand, Chorba looked like his picture, which Max found in an AP story from the start of the strike. Like many who grew up in the hardscrabble of Pennsylvania's coal mining district, Chorba looked to be in his mid-fifties, but, through his research, Max learned the union president was thirty-eight.

The two reporters sat at a card table that acted as a desk/gathering spot for the men and women on the picket line. Chorba, a senior metro reporter for the *Times-Bulletin*, was an easy interview on the asking side of the questions for close to a decade. Max listened to Chorba, who explained the paper had not offered a wage increase in five years, despite a 7 percent cost of living increase for most of Northeastern Pennsylvania.

The entire session took less than an hour. Max snapped a few pictures of the hearty souls on the picket line and was on his way, wishing Chorba good luck. A few months into the job, Max had not thought much about pay increases and other personal finance issues. His time with the union boss gave him pause to think about those considerations for the future.

It was only 11 a.m. when Max pulled out of Wilkes-Barre and onto Exit 105 of the Pennsylvania Turnpike's Northeast Extension. Heading south, he figured he would get to the Carbon County Courthouse just before recess. Max might catch a stray comment from a juror or attorney making his or her way down the elevator with any luck.

Traffic was moving quickly, and forty-four minutes after getting on the road, Max was parked in front of the Carbon County Courthouse. Having bolted from home with only time to make a cup of instant coffee, Max rifled through his briefcase, looking for something to eat. His choices were a half-empty box of Mike and Ikes, a crushed package of Lance peanut butter crackers, or hard candy. With little regard for dietary concerns, Max ate all three food scraps, which would tide him over until he got to the office.

A few people came out of the front door, but Max did not recognize them from the jury. They could have been in the building for anything from getting a marriage license to filing for a permit to get a new septic tank. Max turned the key to start the engine so he could listen to the radio while he waited. Max forgot that when he parked the car, he left the radio on top volume, listening to "You're the One That I Want" from *Grease*. He nearly jumped out of the driver's seat when "Y.M.C.A." came blaring out the car's speakers at ninety decibels. Just as he hit the radio's power button, Max saw a juror he recognized leave the courthouse.

Max grabbed his transistor radio and tuned into the secret courthouse elevator station.

After some static, Max heard, loud and clear, Albrecht speaking to another male whose voice he did not recognize.

"That was a close call," Albrecht said to his elevator companion. "When they asked me about the fire insurance on the house, I nearly shit a brick."

"Look, I know we had an agreement about this second policy, but I'm getting nervous they might find out," the other man said.

"One more day. All we must do is get through one more day. The policy they found was for less than the house was worth. That should be enough to throw them off."

"Okay, if you say so. I am putting my life and my family on the line here. This better be worth it."

Max watched as the two men left the building. Albrecht went right and sat on the infamous bench and lit up a nasty looking cheroot cigar. While Max was not necessarily a cigar aficionado, his days sitting in the grandstand at baseball games with his father gave him a tutorial on cigars. The smell of most cigars—cheroots aside—brought Max a wave of warm nostalgia.

The other gentleman, who Max speculated was an insurance agent, walked left out of the courthouse. Tall and slender, Max could not get a good look at his face, but the man had the gait of an athlete, walking on the balls of his feet with long, smooth strides. As Max dubbed him, "Mr. Insurance Man" was quickly out of sight, no doubt parking his car around the corner out of plain sight. If he was indeed an insurance salesman, he was probably off on another appointment.

Max returned to the office by 1:30 p.m., stopping to pick up a hamburger and fries at Carbon County's lone McDonald's. Sitting at his desk, the young reporter ate with one hand and typed with the other. He batted out twelve hundred words on the Wilkes-Barre newspaper strike and handed both the story and the film from his camera to Al Hickey, who was manning the editor's desk. Al had been nice to Max from day one, and Al's knowledge of both the art and science of reporting impressed everyone in the bureau, as well as at the main office in Allentown.

The insurance issue related to the arson case became an intellectual itch that Max needed to scratch and understand its role in the trial. With an hour to kill, before he was given an assignment for the night, Max went to the Panther Valley Library in Coaldale to find out what he could about insurance policies. On a hunch, looking through some reference books on insurance, he was able to confirm that one person could have more than one policy on a home, car, boat, or whatever. What if Albrecht bought a standard policy that would not raise suspicion but somehow got a second high-value policy under another family member's name?

Max headed back to the office, remembering he wanted to talk to Tex about the incident with that scumbag Stan Raidler. As Max was pulling into the bureau's parking lot, Tex was just getting out of his car. Besides being a superb writer, Tex was a car buff and took pride in his spiffy new BMW 6 Series sedan. He loved showing off the sleek automobile, taking Max on the occasional ride during which he would gleefully ramble on about the features of the car: the powerful six-cylinder engine; the metallic paint imported from Italy to the BMW factory outside Munich; the ability to go from zero to sixty in three seconds; and a cool, in-dash cassette player with four surround-sound speakers. Max would politely smile, as he viewed cars as merely a way to get from one place to another. Max did like the cassette player since he felt the car radio and stereo were any automobile's best accessories.

Max intercepted Tex along the sidewalk outside the coffee shop and told his older, wiser friend he needed to talk for a minute.

"What's up?" Tex said with his ever-present grin firmly in place.

"It's that Raidler guy. He's harassing me by moving my desk chair into the bathroom and made a nasty, anti-Semitic remark."

Tex stopped and leaned against the wall between the coffee shop and the cleaners down the bureau's block. "Well, that sucks. I've heard lots of rumors about the guy, but I know he's still angry from being sent to prison. I wonder if there's more to it."

"What do you mean?"

"I know he's friends with that guy whose trial you're covering, and he probably wants to stick up for his buddy. What you said about Albrecht was none too flattering. Still, that is no cause . . ."

"I take it you think the best course of action is to let it be, right?"

Tex smiled. "Yep. That's my advice. The thing about bullies is that if you ignore them, in most cases, they go away."

As Max entered the office, he noticed Ray a few steps from Max's vacant desk. Ray had a look on his face that did not radiate warmth and support, so Max feared the worst.

"What the hell took you so long?" Ray probed. "I expected you back an hour ago."

"I made a quick stop by the courthouse just to catch up on the morning news from the trial." Max felt that being direct and honest was the best course of action.

"Listen, I want you to put that trial on the back burner for now. You can go back when the jury deliberates, but other than that, I have plenty of stuff for you to work on."

Max was a bit startled. The trial, especially with his eavesdropping tips, would be a step to get him back in the newspaper's good graces. He felt his stomach drop. Challenging Ray, however, was not a wise move if Max wanted to remain employed. "Yes, sir. I'll ask the clerk to call when they wrap up closing arguments. Till then, I am ready for anything you need."

Ray turned around, and without saying a word, walked to the back of the office and sat down at his cluttered desk. While only on the job for a few months, his reporter's intuition was beginning to grow; something about this whole trial thing didn't add up.

Max sat and poured through the papers stacked on his Selectric. On top was a school board meeting in Lehighton that night. Attempting to get as much background as possible, Max pulled some clips from recent school board meetings to acquaint himself with the players and issues. There was some discussion on a bond to pay for the high school gym's renovation, but not much else newsworthy. All things pointed to the assignment being a snoozer.

Raidler walked through the front door, mop and bucket in tow, and made his way up the aisle between the two rows of reporters' desks. He slowed down at Max's desk but didn't say a word, instead conveying his feelings with a look that could kill and leave no evidence. Thinking about his chat with Tex, Max applied the "ignore the bully" idea and smiled back at the creep.

Dealing with Raidler was the furthest thing from Max's mind. His boss implored him to stay away from the trial until the jury went into deliberation, yet something about the arson case nagged at Max. He had a few hours before his school board meeting and decided to take a low-risk, yet bold, step that could hopefully confirm what he heard on his radio earlier in the day. While Ray told him to stay away from the trial, his boss didn't expressly say to not go to the courthouse.

Max typed a brief letter that he would take to the Mark Tobias, the county DA:

Dear Mark,

Have you checked as to whether Chris Albrecht had a recently filed second fire insurance policy (maybe under another name) that was for a large amount? It might be worth looking into.

Sincerely,
A Concerned Citizen

Traffic was light between Nesquehoning and the courthouse in Jim Thorpe. Taking the lead from the mystery insurance salesman, Max parked around the corner from the center of all things legal in Carbon County. Relatively new to the *Chronicle*, there was little chance of anyone on the street recognizing Max, but he nonetheless walked briskly. He also didn't want to dawdle in case Ray was keeping track of his movements.

Max entered the building and took the elevator to the second floor. The DA would be in the courtroom, so the only person in his office was an assistant whose job was to answer the phones and keep track of Tobias's appointments. Max gently placed his letter in the inbox that sat toward the front of the assistant's desk and quickly headed out. On his way out of the building, Max got in the elevator, in a bit of luck, in which he and Barrett had planted their FM transmitter. Alone in the closed space, Max reached behind the ashtray and felt the device still firmly in place. *How long do we have to keep this thing here?* Max wondered. For now, though, its purpose was to ensure a local scuzzball didn't get away with a heinous crime.

As Max headed back to his car and then back to the office, his focus changed from giving the DA a gentle push to figuring out Albrecht's accomplice's name and background. If the DA took the anonymous note seriously, the truth should come out as well as the name of Albrecht's partner in crime. Max contemplated a scenario that would put the two men together in this plot to escape justice. Also, what would be the motivation for Mr. Insurance Man to get involved in something that could cost him his livelihood, not to mention his freedom?

Max had a lot to learn.

Max returned to the office and kept a low profile before heading out to the school board meeting. Sue was sitting at desk of the reporter on vacation, offering Max a smile and a wave when he returned to his regular perch. He had about thirty minutes to get ready for his assignment, figure out what he was going to eat on the way, and, most importantly, whether Tobias would get his note and act on it.

Sue got up, walked over to Max's desk, and gently put her hand on his shoulder.

"I haven't seen you in a few days. How have you been?"

"I'm okay, but I have been busy with a few assignments Ray pointed in my direction. How have you been?"

"Frankly, a little bored," Sue whispered. "I thought getting to work in a big newspaper would be more exciting."

Sue sensed Max was preoccupied. She took her hand off his shoulder and walked back to her desk. "We should get together next weekend outside of work," she said, walking away. "Is that okay with you?"

"Sure," replied Max, taking the path of least resistance.

With that personally nerve-wracking exchange concluded, Max headed out and decided to again make a quick stop at McDonald's on his way to the Lehighton. Lehighton had just opened the county's first Pizza Hut, but a pie seemed like a messy choice as an "eat while you drive" dinner.

Lehighton was not on the top of Max's favorite places to go. The city had nearly as many bars as people, and there were always drunks wandering around either looking to panhandle or start a fight. Even at 6:30 p.m., when Max pulled into a parking spot near the high school, there were plenty of derelicts wandering about.

The school board meeting came in under an hour with barely enough news to warrant a three-paragraph story. The topic of renovating the high school gym sailed through without a discussion. The details, Max learned, would be ironed out during an executive session. Max's mind went into full eavesdrop mode: *I wish the high school had an elevator. I'd love to plant a bug to find out what's going on.*

Max drove back to the office and banged out a recap of the meeting in Lehighton. Ray left a note on his Selectric that he had another feature idea for him and to come in early to discuss. Max was puzzled by Ray's attitude, given the jury was likely to go out for deliberation the next day. Ray agreed that Max could head to the county courthouse once the jurors went into decision mode. Something about Ray and these assignments that could conflict with covering this important trial made no sense. For a moment, Max believed his boss was doing his best to keep him away from the arson case.

The timing was perfect. At 11 a.m. the following day, Max walked into the office to meet with Ray and learn what hot story loomed on the horizon. As he walked by his desk, Max's phone rang. He stopped to answer.

"*Chronicle*, Max Rosen speaking."

It was the courthouse clerk informing Max that the jury left their seats in the courtroom and was headed into a conference room to determine the fate of Chris Albrecht. The courthouse was close enough that there was little chance the verdict would come down before he reached Jim Thorpe. Max walked back to Ray's office as he prepared to leave, but the big man was nowhere to be found. Max left a note saying the jury was out, and as agreed, he was headed there for the verdict.

The next thirty minutes became a fragment of time Max would relive and retell for decades to come. It was a turning point for Max as a reporter, being part of a spectacle he would write about, and people in Carbon County would read about in the *Chronicle* for a week.

Max parked in his new secret spot around the corner from the courthouse. He walked with purpose the one block to the entrance and took the six steps two at a time. Max's adrenaline was pumping, although he wasn't entirely sure why. As fate would have it, the Max and Barrett Memorial Elevator was waiting on the ground floor and was ready to take him to the courtroom level.

The jury was still in deliberation. Max took a seat on a long backless bench outside the courtroom. It was difficult to be patient in these situations, but Max closed his eyes and took deep breaths. When he opened his eyes, a surprise was waiting; seated a few feet away was Chris Albrecht. Albrecht appeared jumpy as his attorney stood twenty feet away on a payphone. The defendant in the arson case turned and faced Max.

"You're the guy from the *Chronicle* who has been covering the trial, right?" Albrecht said with more than a hint of sarcasm. "So, do you think I'm guilty?"

Max was stunned. "Uh . . . I don't know," he meekly responded. "Does it matter what I think?"

"Honestly, I don't give a shit what you think. I was just curious as to what you might say."

Michael Wolf, seeing this tête-à-tête take place, hung up from his call and strolled over. The defense attorney whispered something in Albrecht's ear, and the pair walked away down the hall toward the restrooms.

The next fifteen minutes took place in slow motion for Max. The clerk appeared and proclaimed that the jury was done and would be returning with a verdict. Courthouse personnel and a few folks who had been in the gallery were told they could reenter. Among those making their way into the wood-paneled room of jurisprudence was Mr. Insurance Man. More than a head taller than Max—who stood at six-foot-two—Mr. Insurance Man looked familiar to Max in some way, though he couldn't put his finger on it.

As Albrecht, his lawyer, and Tobias stood, the judge returned, and the jury foreman handed the bailiff a piece of paper. In turn, the bailiff handed it to the judge, who glanced at it and, expressionless, handed it back to the court officer. The bailiff walked over to the jury box and passed the note back to the foreman.

The judge then asked the foreman to read the verdict aloud. "In the case of Carbon County versus Chris Albrecht, we the jury find the defendant not guilty."

Albrecht pounded the desk and hugged Wolf. Those in the gallery were shocked at the ruling. Most sat motionless, mumbling and shaking their heads. It was infuriating to them that Albrecht got away with setting fire to his home. Little did they know there was a kicker in a big payday in the form of a secret insurance policy.

Max was scribbling away in the last row of the courtroom as Albrecht and Wolf walked by. "How do you like that, asshole?" Albrecht sneered. "Go write that up in your shitty paper." Wolf grabbed his client by the arm and ushered him out the door. Three steps behind him, Tobias followed with a mile-wide grin.

"I know it was you who left me that note," the county DA said to Max. "Follow me. I think you'll enjoy this."

Max and the DA took the stairs, and waiting between the elevator and front door was the Carbon County Sheriff and three deputies. Standing on the bottom step, Tobias reached out to hold Max in place. "Sit tight," he said. "The fun is about to begin."

Albrecht, Wolf, and Mr. Insurance Man left the elevator. Midway between the elevator and front door, the sheriff approached the men and uttered a statement Max could barely hear over the commotion.

"Chris Albrecht and Tim Tomjanovich, you are under arrest for fraud."

Max did not hear the name of Mr. Insurance Man over the gasping crowd, which was getting the rare privilege of watching two crooks get nailed. The big man crouched and hung his head in shame. Max would get the man's name from the DA later.

Two deputies approached and put the pair in handcuffs. Their expressions went from exuberance to terror in one minute. The deputies ushered the men out a side door to a waiting car, presumably on the way to county jail.

"Your note did it," Tobias told Max. "I always felt something was missing from the investigation. Honestly, the local cops did a lousy job digging into the case. And after the two witnesses for the county shit the bed, I assumed it was a lost cause. Thank you, and I'll be more than glad to give you an exclusive interview for your efforts."

Max was on cloud nine. He wanted to find a payphone and call his dad and tell him the good news. He left the courthouse and walked to the right to his car. Three strides away from the building, Max felt a hand grab his arm from behind. Max turned, and there standing in front of him was the giant of a man he called the boss. Ray stood, tears streaming down his face. His grip tightened on Max's arm.

"I wanted to personally thank you for getting my son arrested," Ray barked. "Tim is a good man, and now he's on his way to jail."

Chapter Eight

Captain Lou Albano stood on the apron of the squared circle hugging the top rope, spewing epithets at the crowd. Sweat dripped from the salt and pepper beard of the greasy, forty-five-year-old wrestling legend as he taunted the five thousand rabid fans at Allentown's Ag Hall. As one of pro wrestling's most colorful icons, Albano sparked fury in the arena when he danced around the outside of the ring, tugging at his wild mop of hair adorned with multicolored rubber bands.

Max, Barrett, and two of the *Chronicle's* sportswriters sat ringside at a World Wrestling Federation championship night. That particular evening, Larry Zbyszko and Tony Garea defeated the Yukon Lumberjacks, managed by Captain Lou, to win the WWF World Tag Team Championship in the shade over nine minutes. Garea applied a Figure Four Leg Lock to Yukon Eric to end the match and secure the title.

Max had been to Ag Hall years before. On a memorable night in 1975, Max and one of his best friends in college, Sandy Klein, stood on rickety wooden chairs in the rundown venue and watched Ali beat Frazier in The Thrilla in Manila on closed-circuit TV. That night remains one of Max's fondest memories of his years in college.

As the crowd headed for the exit, one of the sportswriters, Nick Bednar, grabbed Max by the arm. "Hey, Max, you wanna meet one of the wrestlers?"

Bednar, one of the *Chronicle's* senior reporters, covered Lehigh University football and Lafayette University basketball, two of the area's collegiate programs. His years at the paper, plus his contacts with promoters and PR flacks, provided carte blanche to any backstage access.

The four men were ushered into a dingy locker room in which the men on that night's fight card were in the process of nursing wounds suffered from their night as theatric gladiators. Bednar introduced Max to Tony Garea, a personable grappler from New Zealand, and Ernie "the Big Cat" Ladd, a six-foot, nine-inch, 290-pound former lineman for the San Diego Chargers of the old American Football League. Max and Barrett were wrestling fans dating back to an era when matches were shown at off-hours on UHF TV stations. Along with their new sportswriter buddies, the pair left Ag Hall, grinning from ear to ear.

In the three weeks since the Carbon County arson case hit the fan, Max had newfound popularity at the *Chronicle*. A four-part series on the trial, along with interviews from Tobias, the DA, and the county sheriff, made for great copy. The feedback from readers of the *Chronicle* was rewarding, but his colleagues' respect was worth more than any raving letter to the editor.

Among Max's new friends was Bednar, who was not only impressed with the reporting and writing, but he had also discovered his co-worker's passion for sports. He called Max a week after the series ran and arranged for them to meet for coffee. The two men hit it off, spending more time talking about Max's days as a play-by-play announcer for his college football team than the arson case that grabbed the paper's headlines.

The outcome of the arrests after Albrecht's acquittal took on a life of their own. Wolf and Albrecht were convicted of insurance fraud and sentenced to five years in state prison in Chester, with each one getting a $50,000 fine. Tim Tomjanovich agreed to turn state's evidence against the lawyer and his client, and in return, had to serve two years' probation and pay a $25,000 fine. Ray, Max's boss and Tim's dad, did not suffer any punishment from his attempt to block Max's coverage, but did put in for early retirement.

There was some additional fallout from Ray's departure: Stan Raidler never returned to the office. It wasn't clear whether he was fired or just stopped showing up for work. In Ray's absence, the *Chronicle* didn't feel ready to name a replacement, so Al Hickey and Ervin Swan rotated in as managing editor for the bureau. The newspaper business in the late seventies was turbulent, filled with mergers, Joint Operating Agreements, and flat-out failures, so the tremors caused by the events surrounding the arson case did little to disrupt day-to-day business.

For Max, after receiving praise from peers and management, work settled into its customary routine. Civic meetings, fairs, celebrations, and the occasional car crash or robbery became standard issue tasks for the young reporter. The most memorable assignment was one when a bank about fifteen miles east of Nesquehoning was robbed. It was the fourth holdup for the bank in as many months due to its prime location at two major interstate roads. Getaways were a piece of cake.

Taking a different approach to the story, Max led with the robbery facts but ended with a tongue-in-cheek remark that it might be time for Bank of America to rethink such a vulnerable location. That is, unless it likes giving away free greenback souvenirs.

The weekend plans Sue suggested never materialized when Max decided to go home to Philadelphia for a family visit. He promised to make it up to her but wasn't quite sure what that meant at the time. Sue was getting to understand Max's fragile personal existence, and while she wasn't sure what she expected out of their relationship, taking things slow was her only recourse.

Max's weekend with his parents started with him driving to Philadelphia after work, late Thursday. From personal experience, he knew his mother would be waiting up no matter what time he arrived. The good news was that she would have some of his favorite food waiting in the fridge when he pulled in to the driveway. Sure enough, as he turned the corner onto their street, Max spotted his mother peering out the front window. "Nothing has changed," Max muttered to himself.

Max made small talk with his mother as he devoured the egg salad sandwich waiting in the fridge. He was careful with his topics, wanting to avoid anything that would lead to serious questioning. After far too many talks in which his mother "spoke like a Dutch Uncle," Max was in no mood for anything but a restful night. He finished his meal, kissed his mother on the cheek, and went off to bed.

Most of Friday, Max hung around the house, tacking a few solid naps onto a decent night's sleep in his old bed. With his mother off playing mahjong, Max went into great detail about his work on the arson case with his father, leaving out the hidden FM transmitter and the fact that his boss was forced into early retirement.

After dinner, Max drove over to Barrett's condo to talk strategy regarding their successful eavesdropping caper. Barrett did not read the *Chronicle*, being out of its circulation area, but a few of his friend's stories ran on the AP Wire and were included in one of Philadelphia's daily papers. Secretly,

Barrett felt as if the entire scheme was his idea, but could not take credit lest he admit to being part of a criminal conspiracy. The former attorney and part-time tennis hustler had an ego that needed constant nourishment.

"So, should we take it down?" Max asked his friend/co-conspirator.

"Ya know, I have a feeling about this. I think there's one more story that will go up with the elevator and come down with a front-page item." Barrett paused and took a swing from his bottle of Frank's Black Cherry Wishniak soda. "Let's give it one more week."

"I never knew you had such psychic powers to predict breaking news?"

"Take it out, smartass, if that's what you want. I just feel there could be one more story that could get you out of that hick town bureau and behind a desk in Allentown. You're riding high, man . . . leave the money on the table and roll the dice."

"By the way," Barrett added with his trademark smirk, "You forgot to thank me for helping you land the story of your career. I take cash, Visa, and MasterCard. No American Express."

Max got back to his parents' home long before his mother could worry about him staying out too late. She did have a plate of her famous meatballs waiting for him, which made Max miss her cooking, but not the usual side of guilt and sadness. It was a rare occasion when he was able to go to bed before 11 p.m. Even if the solid night of rest ahead was on his lumpy old mattress, Max looked forward to making a major deposit in his sleep bank.

Alongside his meaty nighttime treat was a note from his mother that Max's friend from college, Dan Hersh, called asking his former roommate to call back if it was before eleven. It was ten fifteen, so Max took the kitchen phone, a long cord, and went into the living room. The streetlight outside shone brightly through the front window, enabling Max to sit in the dark and make his call.

"Max, I heard you were coming home this weekend," Hersh blurted out. Nothing about Max's junior year roommate was subtle. "A bunch of us are going to the Sixers game tomorrow night, and we thought you might want to come."

"Let me check my busy schedule," Max joked. "Sure, what time?"

"The game is at eight, but we thought we'd all meet at the Rusty Scupper around six. Does that work?"

"Yeah, why not? Who else is coming?"

"Aside from you and me, there's Steve, Norm, and Marc Stein."

"Okay. See you then."

Max relished the chance to be with some people who had nothing to do with the newspaper business. Because of their all-encompassing careers—two were in medical school, and one just joined a prestigious law firm—the talk would be fairly superficial and friendly. Of the four, he was the only one who knew anything about sports, so it gave him a chance to show off his pro basketball knowledge in general, the Sixers in particular.

The Rusty Scupper was a bar and restaurant near Philadelphia's waterfront. It wasn't exactly the hippest place in town, which made it ideal for five men who, between them, had been on six or seven dates in their lifetimes. After some hellos and watcha-been-up-to's, the quintet of young professionals ordered some drinks and appetizers.

Norm Weiss was seated to Max's left, and with the din of the Saturday night crowd beginning to take over, the two launched into a timely conversation. Norm Weiss graduated from the University of Pennsylvania Law School and was recruited by top firms in New York and Philadelphia. Wanting to stick close to home, Weiss chose Fogel-Rothchild-Hess, a practice that specialized in injury law. F-R-H was not a team of ambulance chasers; instead, they went after egregious malpractice cases and the emerging field of protecting people who had information about dangerous business practices related to their employers.

Norm mentioned that he was impressed with his friend's reporting on the arson case and was sure to save the clippings and pass them around to others in his office. Max was impressed, given that Norm not only finished in the top ten in their high school class but also made law review at Penn. Additionally, he won the Professor C. Edwin Baker Award for advancing social justice. Norm was not a talkative sort, usually observing his surroundings more than jumping in mouth-first—a trait Norm and Max shared.

"I think you'd be interested in the firm's new direction, which is to attract and protect citizens who want to report illegal practices with the government or Fortune 500 companies."

"I think I heard something about that during Watergate, right? Didn't it have to do with the release of the Pentagon Papers?"

"Good knowledge." Norm grinned. "It's covered under a statute that is over a hundred years old, and primarily it relates to people who turn in government wrongdoing, but we're also looking for cases in which big companies can be held liable for not releasing information such as product recalls."

"How do you find these people?"

"At this point, we hope they find us. We've gotten some publicity from one case in which a defense contractor was selling faulty helicopters to the Army. Someone in engineering came forth because, in advanced testing, the mast of the copter's rotor system had a 20 percent failure rate."

"That would have made a great story."

"Part of the settlement," Max's friend added, "was to keep the details sealed. Still, within government and legal circles, it created a buzz."

The discussion turned on some lightbulbs for Max. Such cases would make for great investigative reporting. He made a mental note to follow up with Norm to find out more about these cases.

The three others in Max's group got up. It was thirty minutes to tipoff, and they were taking a cab down to the Spectrum, leaving their cars parked at the restaurant. Hersh's mother worked as a concierge at one of the city's bigger hotels, and she was able to score five seats behind the Sixers bench. It had been a year since Max went to a Sixers game; the team's sickening loss to the Blazers in the 1977 NBA Finals was enough to send even the most loyal fans reeling.

The Sixers came out flat but limped along to be only two points behind Seattle at halftime. Jack Sikma, the center for the Sonics, was having a career night while Philadelphia's heralded bench contributed only 24 points to the visitors' 41. At the buzzer, the final score was 100–97, with Philadelphia on the short end.

The concessionaires made little profit from the five friends who had one beer and one Coke between them. Max bought a soda for the souvenir cup, which showed Dr. J in full flight. He wasn't sure who bought the beer, but Max was certain whoever it was complained about it being five dollars.

After taking cabs back to the Rusty Scupper and some brief goodbyes and see-ya-soons, each man took off. Max had a thirty-five-minute drive up

I-95 and calculated that he'd reach the front door of his parents' house around eleven. While he had no way to explain it, when Max went out with his friends, his mother never waited up. But then again, on those occasions, he rarely got back after eleven thirty.

Sunday lunch was a nice sendoff for Max. His mother prepared a corned beef with some homemade potato salad, packaging up her son's leftovers to take back to Nesquehoning. The kitchen conversation was light with little grilling about his job and whether he was seeing someone. Talking about Sue would have been awkward. Max suspected his father told his wife of twenty-seven years to cool it. Around 2 p.m., Max took off, timing his departure to the Eagles game kickoff at Minnesota. Charlie Swift's play-by-play would make the tedious ride go more quickly in this all-important game for the Birds as they competed for a Wild Card playoff berth.

Max got back to his one-room apartment just as Ahmad Rashad caught a 20-yard TD pass from Fran Tarkenton to beat the Eagles 28–27. The loss dropped Philadelphia to an 8–6 record with only an outside chance at making the NFL Playoffs. At least the close game and the exciting action made the ride go quickly despite a slowdown on the Pennsylvania Turnpike. Max usually took the turnpike, despite the toll, which was a contrast to his mother, who would drive miles out of the way to avoid paying tolls. At least gas was twenty cents a gallon.

Somewhat refreshed, he got to the office an hour before his scheduled six o'clock start time. One reporter each night would be asked to begin his or her day an hour late and stay an hour after the official business close at eleven thirty. That night was Max's turn to work the graveyard shift.

Waiting on Max's Selectric was a letter that looked to be an invitation. The letter asked Max if he would be gracious enough to attend the monthly meeting of the Carbon County Chamber of Commerce. The event was scheduled for the following Thursday at the Country Inn and Suites by Radisson, which sat halfway between Jim Thorpe and Lehighton. He was not being asked based on his recent celebrated reporting; the goal was for county leaders to get to better know the man whose job it was to write about all things Carbon County.

Max knew little about the chamber or the venue but didn't see any harm in getting out in public. He had heard that the hotel, which was all of two years old, had an excellent meeting room on its top floor, which was in great demand for weddings and other celebrations. It might be a good time for him to drag out his one suit and display his sartorial majesty. He also wondered if it might be worth asking Sue to come with him—not necessarily as a date, but to make up for him canceling their recent plans and boost his confidence going into this event.

On this slow Sunday evening, the monotony was broken by a call from the Blavosky Funeral Home. A local World War II vet had passed, so a special ceremony was to honor Steve Nalesnik, a winner of the Purple Heart for his heroism at the Battle of Anzio in 1944. Max took the call, wrote up the details for the funeral and wake, and batted out a brief story about Nalesnik's life.

Done with that task, Max combed through clips in search of information about whistleblowers. With all past articles on individual pages of newsprint folded in small envelopes in a large file cabinet, the job was like finding a needle twisted around another needle in a haystack. Just by happenstance, he did find out some interesting things about one of his current interim editors, Ervin Swan. Swan, it seemed, had a lawsuit against St. Luke's Hospital in Allentown for damages after he got an infection from his first hip surgery. The case was settled out of court, but Swan made it very public that he didn't get what he deserved from the case.

That explains a lot, Max thought to himself. *It could be one of the reasons he's an anti-Semite.* According to the four-year-old story, the lawyer representing the hospital was Joel Wiener. In addition to being a top legal mind, he was also president of the synagogue where Max taught while in college.

The week went by quickly. Max RSVPed to the invite from the Carbon County Chamber of Commerce. He began digging into information about some of its biggest members and came away with a list of who's who in business and politics in the area. Standouts included Juniper Letterpress, a printer and publisher that specialized in corporate newsletters; BLM Inc., a manufacturer of machine parts; Genesco, Inc., an owner of the local Falk's

Supermarkets; and Andersen Trucking, a short- and long-haul logistics company. Many accountants, lawyers, and real estate firms were also members, as was the *Chronicle*, despite having its headquarters in Allentown.

Sue was given her first major assignment related to school overcrowding. Her job was to conduct a series of interviews with teachers, students, and administrators to get varied takes on the problem. When other reporters in the bureau asked her about the opportunity, Sue said that her mom was a junior high school teacher in Macungie, so it was a topic near and dear to her heart. Despite all the work on her plate, Sue was excited and surprised at Max's invitation to attend the chamber of commerce event.

It was always wise to operate on the theory that it's better to overdress than show up at a gathering looking like a ragamuffin, Max believed. His one suit, purchased with his parents' assistance at B&G Silverman, a discount clothier in Philadelphia, looked fresh since Max had worn it twice—once to a friend's wedding and again to a college classmate's party celebrating his graduation from med school. To go with the suit, Max had the choice of two dress shirts—both white—and one tie that may or may not have gone out of style. He was certain that no matter how he looked, Sue was bound to look better.

General anxiety set in after lunch when Max realized that he would be at a meeting where he knew only a few people, but the idea of bringing a *date* along would make the situation more complicated. He wasn't sure how to introduce Sue. As a friend? A fellow reporter, or maybe just someone he met in the parking lot? As far as to how Sue felt about the evening, that was too much for a socially inexperienced man to process.

Max and Sue left the bureau together in what could be described as their Sunday best. The other reporters were far too busy with their work to notice or care, which was simply fine for the couple. Sue laughed on the ride over as Max nervously fiddled with the car radio jumping from station to station when a song he didn't like came on. Now being somewhat of an expert in elevators—or least where to hide things in them—Max was impressed with the hotel lift's modern design. He stood looking at the back of the unit, wondering what Sue was thinking about his visual scan of the motorized bucket.

As they arrived at the top-floor meeting room, the *Chronicle* reporters were greeted with a beautifully decorated space with an open bar and twenty round tables with bright tablecloths and vases filled with roses and carnations. Max and Sue split up, shaking hands with local leaders wearing name tags for easy identification. John Andersen, head of the area's largest trucking firm, was the guest speaker for the meeting, which was close to starting. Max and Sue met at their assigned table and introduced themselves to the six other guests at table five. Sue had grabbed a white wine from the bar and brought one over for Max, realizing he might be nervous in such a social situation.

Andersen delivered a fifteen-minute commercial about how his trucking firm has been the county's backbone for two generations. He rambled on about how his company has been responsible for hauling the large components used to build most of the area's bridges and roadways. Andersen loved the sound of his voice.

Bored with this self-aggrandizing soliloquy, Max looked around the room, hoping to find someone or something to distract him from Andersen's endless prattle. At the main door to the meeting room stood a short, grubby man in his late thirties wearing overalls, furiously shaking his head. His hands clenched at this side; the uninvited guest appeared angry and distraught. If smoke could come out of his ears, he'd fill the room with carbon monoxide.

Max elbowed Sue and nodded his head in the direction of the man in the door. Sue returned the poke with a look of bewilderment as if to say, "What's going on?" His curiosity getting the better of him, Max got out of his seat, trying not to attract attention, and walked toward the rather peeved bystander.

"Is everything all right?" Max whispered to the visitor.

"No, it's far from all right," Dan replied. Below the left shoulder, the man had a patch that said *Andersen Trucking* along with his name, Dan Bigelow.

"Something bothering you?"

"Who the fuck are you?"

"I'm a reporter with the *Chronicle*. I'd love to hear what you're so mad about."

"Okay, but not here. Let's go down to the bar, and we can talk there. I have a story you won't believe."

Max motioned for Sue to leave. She softly and politely said her goodbyes and joined Max and his new acquaintance by the elevator. Max introduced her to Dan just as the elevator arrived. The three got in, and Dan hit B, which was the lower level that housed the bar.

"That guy up there sounding like a hero for the county is a murderer," Dan said matter-of-factly. "I can't wait to tell you more."

Chapter Nine

Sue held her breath for the three-minute elevator ride to the first floor. In her life as a reporter, she had never heard such a horrific story. Sadly, Max was rarely shocked by man's inhumanity to man. A student of the Holocaust, nothing surprised a man who grew up in a neighborhood filled with those who lived through demonic places such as Auschwitz and Bergen-Belsen. Still, Dan's recounting of the previous year of his life made the hair on the back of Max's neck stand on end.

"For the past year, I have been driving a flatbed up Interstate 81 to Central New York, collecting barrels of gunk, and driving them back here to Pennsylvania." Dan continued as if speaking in a trance. "I was told to take the barrels and dump them in an abandoned coal mine near Tamaqua. I was never told what was in the barrels, and many of them were rusty with some serious wear and tear. When I lugged them to the front of the empty mine, there were often many spillages. I will tell you one thing—it stunk. And it burned the hell out of my eyes."

Max got his wits about him. As the elevator doors opened, the conversation moved to the hotel lobby. Max and Sue sat on a small sofa while Dan sat in an overstuffed chair, angled to face them. Talking about the sordid details of his last twelve months lifted a weight from his shoulders. Dan rubbed his eyes, hiding the fact that he was beginning to cry.

"I hear what you've been through, and I know it's been terrible, but why did you decide to show up tonight?" Max asked.

"Well, Mr. Rosen. Today I got some bad news. A few months ago, I was getting these awful headaches that would come and go. Eventually, they got so bad that I went to a neurologist down in Allentown at St. Luke's. They ran some tests, and it appears I have migraines and, believe it or not, early-stage Parkinson's Disease. Jesus Christ—I'm only thirty-five.

"I wanted to see that bastard who ruined my life stand up at that meeting and tell all his lies about what he's done for this county." Dan paused, bending his head as he began to weep uncontrollably.

Max looked at Sue as she reached into her purse for a tissue. Despite all the emotional shortcomings of his own life, Max had the innate ability to push his personal feelings aside and think clearly in such high-stress situations. He gave Dan time to unburden himself of this built-up dread while he opened his briefcase and pulled out a notepad.

Max inched closer to Dan, so their conversation could remain as private as possible. There were several routes the reporter could take to bring this story to light, but Max felt it was equally important for Dan to be taken care of. The uncertainty of Max's recent weekend with his buddies offered at least one immediate solution.

"A lot is going on here," Max said softly to Dan. "I think there are a few paths we can take. First and foremost, I have a friend who is an attorney in Philadelphia who, I am sure, would love to hear your story and take the necessary legal action. We want to ensure that you get the best medical care possible and that Andersen Trucking pays for it.

"Also, we need to find out exactly what's in this crap that is being dumped in empty mines. I seriously doubt you are the only trucker working for Andersen that is being harmed by this. I will look into that, and I need to speak to the managing editor of the *Chronicle* to get the resources needed to put this on the front page. I cannot guarantee you anything, but we will give it everything we have to bring these people to justice and get you the care you deserve."

Max was determined to kill three birds, and if it took several stones, he was up to the challenge. First up, he needed to get Norm Weiss involved. Even if Dan didn't fit the exact profile of a whistleblower, the ailing truck driver was desperate for someone with the legal prowess and resources to come to the aid of the thirty-five-year-old truck driver. Recalling his conversation with Norm before the basketball game, Max remembered the passion with which his friend spoke of his firm's commitment to this new area of practice.

While Max was loath to give Norm any advice, he imagined there were other truckers—from Andersen and other companies—in the same boat as Dan. Growing up with a father whose favorite TV program was *Perry Mason*, Max felt he earned a telelaw degree from CBS. With that less-than-rudimentary knowledge, he thought there could be something he had heard of called a class action lawsuit. Whatever the proceedings, Max knew Norm Weiss and his firm were up to do battle.

Leaving the hotel, Max and Sue walked to his car and headed back to the bureau. The ride took longer than normal, but Max was silent as he thought carefully about the steps that lay ahead to make this front-page news. After getting to Nesquehoning, his first task was to write down everything he remembered beyond the frantically scribbled notes he took. He needed to not only get the attention of the *Chronicle*'s editors but also wanted to ensure that every fact was checked and checked again. Even though a lot of time had passed professionally, he was still on the clock for his probation period based on earlier mess-ups. Max's big series on the Carbon County arson case was yesterday's news; he knew it was time to add to that success. And if Max could do it without secretly bugging a county elevator, so much the better. Even though, in this situation, a memorable elevator ride played a major role.

After typing up several pages of notes, Max asked Sue if she could come over to his desk to look over what he put together. She walked over from a desk across the aisle and grabbed a chair from the desk behind Max's. As she pushed her chair up to see his work, Max noticed she had a heavenly smelling fragrance that he had not noticed before. The scent was flowery, like lilies, with a touch of spice that threw Max off his game as a warm feeling of flush took over his body. He hoped that she put on this delicious perfume for his sake, but this was neither the time nor place to ask.

Sue made a few notes on Max's typewritten sheets that added some color to the evening's events. For one thing, she recalled that Dan had a prescription bottle in his shirt pocket and that his hands shook when they said goodbye. Those insights told Max that, no matter how the reporting moved forward, he needed Sue on his team. He already realized the *Chronicle* was likely to assign a more experienced staffer to the investigation.

Max's good fortune was that Al Hickey was on the editor's desk at the bureau that night. Before jumping the gun and talking to an editor in Allentown, Max wanted to go through proper channels, and he knew Al was a great place to start. He would take Al's direction on who to contact next and include himself in whatever conversation.

Al Hickey was a man who had seen and heard it all. In his twenty-plus years at the *Chronicle*, he covered murders, prison escapes, raging fires, and even a kidnapping. At least those were some of the stories Al was willing to share over a few cold ones at the bar next door. Listening to Max's retelling of Dan's story of illegal chemical dumping, Al wrote down a few notes and asked Max a few follow-up questions. He then told Max to sit tight, and he would call the managing editor first thing in the morning. While Jack Devlin, the paper's managing editor, didn't exactly work banker's hours, he would not be at his desk at nine thirty on a Thursday night.

Max tossed and turned all night. The waiting room in his brain was overcrowded with people and issues wanting attention. He did the best to put them at bay, but the net result was less solid sleep than what his mother would have approved. Around four in the morning, Max got up and went over to the makeshift office he set up in the living room. The workspace consisted of a bookcase with a fold-down shelf and a kitchen chair. To clear his mind, Max drew a diagram with the names of the people and companies involved and played connect-the-dots to determine how to approach the investigative reporting that lay ahead. Max felt the drawing would be a great tool to bring to whatever meeting Al Hickey arranged in Allentown.

Over a microwaved cup of leftover Folgers instant coffee, Max shook off the cobwebs and got ready to jump in a hot shower. Just as he was ready to turn the water on full blast, the phone rang. Max grabbed a towel and dashed out to the kitchen to answer.

"Hey, Max, it's Al Hickey."

"Hi, Al. I was just about to get in the shower. What's up?"

"That's an image I'll try and forget," Al said with an oversized laugh. "We have a meeting down at the *Chronicle* at eleven thirty. It's with Devlin and a few other people."

"Wow, that was fast. I appreciate you pushing this through. How about I meet you in the parking lot a few minutes before?"

"Sure thing, kid. See you then."

Max got ready in record time and boiled some water for another cup of instant coffee. He looked through his fridge for something to eat on the run. On his last trip home, Max brought back marble rye from Don's Bakery. A quick pop into the toaster and a piece of sweet Muenster cheese on top, and it's a somewhat hearty meal to go.

With traffic light on a late Friday morning, Max made to Allentown in record time. He was at least twenty minutes early, so he drove by the Allentown Fair Grounds, the site of some of his best memories from college. Driving past the farmer's market toward the newspaper, Max remembered all the great ethnic food he loved from his college days—especially pretzels. Not the soft pretzels they sold on street corners in Philadelphia, but the hard ones that were common in Pennsylvania Dutch areas of Reading, Lancaster, and Allentown.

By the time he imagined going through the samples at the Tom Sturgis pretzel factory, Max had pulled into the *Chronicle* parking lot. Al Hickey was waiting there next to his green Chevy Impala. Standing next to Al was Tom Monahan, Max's colleague from the bureau. His presence made sense; with Tom's experience and great reporting skills, he was a natural part of the team.

The *Chronicle* was not big on devoting space to large conference rooms. Max, Al Hickey, Tom Monahan, Jack Devlin, and Tim Daniels, publisher of the newspaper, jammed into a 175-square-foot room short of two chairs. Al and Jack Devlin stood as Daniels started the meeting.

"This is some story you have on your hands, Max. Tell me how you came about it. Don't spare me the details."

Max pulled out his notebook and the papers he typed at the office after meeting Dan at the Carbon County Chamber of Commerce event. Remarkably poised, Max rose to the occasion, speaking with confidence and purpose. Devlin and Daniels, the paper's top dogs, scribbled notes on legal pads as Max went on for a solid twenty minutes.

The managing editor and publisher were passing notes back and forth while Max spoke. Their exchange was far from a grade school exercise of sending around giggling slips of paper that said the teacher smelled like vegetable soup. The high-powered newspaper execs compiled a list of next steps, including speaking to the *Chronicle*'s lawyer and contacting state and federal agencies such as the EPA.

Max concluded his soliloquy, and for a moment, there was silence in the room. Devlin and Daniels looked at each other as if to determine who should act as spokesman. Devlin, twice a Pulitzer Prize finalist for the newspaper's work in covering local politics, took Max's place at the front of the small conference room. Devlin was a former offensive lineman and punter for Lehigh University in the mid-sixties. His punting was the talk of Division 1-D back in the day, and there even was a rumor he had been offered a tryout with the New York Jets. Devlin looked more like a football coach than a former player in a three-piece suit and power red tie undone at the collar. Still, his presence and reputation commanded respect by his peers and direct reports at the *Chronicle*.

"So, here's the plan," Devlin said with authority. "We're going to work as a team, reporting to me. For the reporting, I want Tom to take the lead, but I want Max to play a major role.

"I understand that Max has a legal contact in Philly, and that's perfect. If you can give me his name and number, I'd like to give him a call after the meeting and tell him about our course of action. We want to ensure we don't do anything that would interfere with any investigation the state or EPA will do into this chemical dumping. Let's be clear: our goal is to tell the story that not only digs deep into this calamity but inform and educate our readers. We want to make it personal. Let's find out how many others were impacted by this. We should do what we can to see if this dumping did any harm to area farms or bodies of water. I want Al to supervise Tom and Max. And Max, I want you to know this is the kind of work that turns rookie reporters into MVPs," Devlin concluded, using a sports metaphor he knew Max would appreciate. "You will get a co-byline for everything we publish."

As the room emptied, each attendee knowing his part moving forward, Al asked Tom and Max to meet him at Trivet Diner for a quick lunch. The venerable restaurant was about ten minutes from the *Chronicle*'s HQ and on the road that led back to Carbon County.

Max and Tom walked to their cars, and as Max opened his door, Tom called out and hustled over to his colleague.

"Wait up a sec," Tom said, running out of breath as he double-timed it across the parking lot. "I just wanted to tell you how great it will be to work with you. I just wanted to let you know that it's important for us to share everything we find. We must trust each other."

"I wouldn't have it any other way," Max replied with the utmost sincerity. "Even though we don't know each other all that well, I think we share the same goals. See you over at the Trivet," Max said as he worked his way into the front seat.

As he started the car and turned on the radio, he thought about the times he went to the Trivet during college. It was a late-night spot for early breakfast after a night of drinking. Wisely, Max ended his trip down memory lane right there. No point in digging up the past when the immediate future looked bright.

The three men sat at the Trivet Diner, waiting for their lunch orders. It was noon, and they were lucky to get a booth when several workers from nearby Whitehall Mall came in during the midday break. The booth faced Tilghman Street, which ran several miles from Allentown's heart through Macungie to the start of the Carbon County line. Traffic was especially heavy with the new entrance to the Pennsylvania Turnpike a few miles north of the restaurant. Motorists can quickly and easily get on the popular toll road north toward Wilkes-Barre or south toward Philadelphia, Valley Forge, or head west at the turnpike interchange and pull into Pittsburgh in four hours.

After the waitress delivered their food, Al Hickey launched a discussion on his approach to the investigation. Al had no issue talking with his mouth full, which caused Max and Tom to hide their laughter. Neither of the younger reporters dug into their meals while Al held court.

"Here's how I think we should divide things up," Al said after taking a bite of his overstuffed burger, "Tom, I'd like you to meet with the folks from the EPA. I know they have an office here in Allentown. If they cannot help, you're going to have contact with the Philly branch.

"Max, I want you to speak with Dan and get the names of other truckers—either one with Andersen or other local companies—and talk with them. We need to approach this from several angles—the truckers who got sick, area farmers who may have crops that failed from the chemicals, and even pets that may have gotten sick. Also, Max, follow up with your lawyer buddy, whatever his name is. I know Devlin is talking to him, but he's your friend, so I'm sure he can share some points that may be slightly off the record.

"As for me, I've lived the Carbon County my entire life. I will check with some doctors I know and see if they have had a bunch of patients with illnesses related to this poison. I know they can't give me names, but general information will help."

Al dipped into his side of french fries and took a breather. Before speaking, Max gulped down a few spoonfuls of the soup of the day. It could have been vegetable or navy bean, he couldn't tell. He hadn't visited the Trivet before midnight on his previous trips to the local late-night destination. The food didn't matter much this time; Max's adrenaline was pumping, and he was ready to dive into the work ahead, not the watered-down bowl of canned soup on the table before him.

"One thing I wanted to ask," Max said to Al and Tom. "Do you mind if I ask Sue to help me contact the people affected? She has a great bedside manner, and that would be valuable in many of these conversations."

Al looked at Tom, and the two men shrugged their shoulders to say it was fine with them.

"Just make sure her helping you doesn't take away from other assignments she might get," Al said as the men got up from their booth. "With what happened to Ray, we're shorthanded, and we can't put another body from the bureau on this full time."

Al, Tom, and Max got in their cars and pulled into the traffic, heading up Tilghman. Max flipped onto the radio, and the song "I'm Every Woman" by Chaka Kahn blared through the Volvo's stereo speakers. Max laughed at the song, thinking about the conversation he was going to have with Sue when he got back to the office.

At two o'clock on a Friday afternoon, traffic from Allentown to Nesquehoning was heavy. People making their way to the Poconos for skiing or just R&R took over the highway. After the day's intensity, Max enjoyed the time to decompress and focus on the music on WAEB, Allentown's only pop music station. Afternoon jock Guy Randall Ackley mixed in pieces of cornball humor between songs, doing his best to keep those stuck in their cars from serious road rage.

Max pulled into the bureau's parking lot and made his way to the office. As he opened the door, Max brought with him a blast of cold air this late November afternoon. Everyone turned around when a loud whooshing sound accompanied Max as he made his way to his desk. As he hoped, Sue was sitting at his desk frantically pummeling on his Selectric as if it were fighting her words.

"You want me to move?" Sue asked as Max stood next to his desk. "I'm just typing up some notes from a meeting I went to last night."

"No, it's okay. Listen, I have some great news to share. We had a meeting with the managing editor and publisher this morning about how we're going to handle the work on the chemical dumping story. I suggested to Al, who's running point, that we could add you to the reporting team. If that's all right with you?"

"All right? Are you kidding?"

Sue jumped out of Max's chair and hugged him. Her familiar flowery scent nearly made Max weak in the knees. He closed his eyes and held on for dear life. While in an embrace that was north of pure friendship, Sue finally let go, reached over, and kissed Max on the neck.

That warm, familiar flush came back, and Max opened his eyes. Sue was standing there smiling, hoping her boldness might be the start of something special. And, as if on cue, Max's phone rang.

"Saved by the bell," he whispered, still overcome from the kiss. "Let's talk later."

Chapter Ten

Max had called Barrett over the weekend and gotten him up to speed with his new assignment. Barrett was proud of his friend—well, as proud as rivals since second grade could be— and his success. Barrett raised the issue of the FM transmitter hidden in the elevator outside the stately governmental building in Jim Thorpe.

"I almost forgot about it," Max told Barrett. While that wasn't true, he hoped Barrett would have an idea that might include removing it from its current resting spot.

Barrett didn't buy it for one second. He chuckled and told Max that he had a slow week and would be willing to extricate the device from its perch in the courthouse. Barrett didn't say that he had a desire for a Yocco's hot dog, so any excuse to head in the direction of Allentown was fine. A Yocco's hot dog, an order of Mrs. T's Pierogies, capped by an A-Treat grapefruit soda to wash it all down was enough to go a hundred miles out of your way.

One issue Barrett had to deal with was the fact he didn't own a transistor radio. He knew of only one store that might have it, and that was Silo. He checked the yellow pages, and there was a location in Quakertown which was on his way. The day was shaping up.

Barrett parked across the street from the courthouse and took out his brand-spanking-new Emerson nine-transistor P3751B long with a nine volt battery. He dug into the box and found the earphone, and put everything together. He futzed with the dial until he found 93.4, and that's when he heard a pair of would-be restaurateurs perform their comedy act in the elevator.

"I think you're nuts."

"No, I think it will work. Jim Thorpe is crying out for a Thai Fusion restaurant. I checked, and there isn't one within sixty miles of here."

"Did you ever think about why? This is meat and potatoes country, pal."

"Look, it's my money, and all I'm asking is for you to do the build-out. I'll take care of everything else. We got the permits, so there's no looking back."

As two somewhat urban looking chaps emerged from the elevator at the Carbon County Courthouse and onto the sidewalk, Barrett Fine was in his snazzy BMW laughing his ass off. He never thought listening to people in an elevator could be so amazing. *I'm wasting my time taking dates to the Bijou. I can drive up here and hear a better show on a transistor radio.*

With two Yocco's dogs, three pierogies, and a sickly-sweet can of soda under his belt, Barrett was ready to get this over with. It was 3 p.m., meaning the courthouse closed in two hours, which was about an hour and fifty-nine minutes longer than the former-attorney-turned-tennis-hustler could wait.

"Oh, what the hell," Barrett said as he got out of his car and headed toward the courthouse. It wasn't very crowded, and he was quick with his hands—that extra digit and all—so it should be a piece of cake.

A few folks were in the lobby, and Barrett did his best to ignore them. He walked over to the Fine-Rosen memorial elevator and hit the up button. Upon arrival, two men and a woman exited, and Barrett made his way, quickly pushing the door closing button. He reached behind the ashtray and felt the transmitter but suddenly realized it was soldered to its base. Barrett wanted to scream at his carelessness by forgetting to bring a file, small saw, or anything that could cut through the solder. The transmitter had been there for several weeks, and it was going to take more than a quick yank to pull it off.

Barrett went up and down the elevator five times, thinking of a way to get that damned device from its clandestine spot on the ashtray. He thought about ripping the entire ashtray off, but he had neither the strength nor time to do that. It didn't help that folks got on and off the elevator the entire time he stood there staring at the FM transmitter. Barrett ignored their curious looks as that would break his concentration.

After enough rides up and down the courthouse to make an average person nauseous, Barrett got off on the top floor and looked for a janitor's closet. He wasn't sure whether he'd find anything to solve his dilemma, but at this point, it was worth a look-see. In reality, Barrett could have left the secret unit stuck to the ashtray, and no one likely would find it, but he was a man on a mission. It was his nature to tackle what he believed to be impossible.

Barrett found the room that said *custodian* on it and gently opened the door in case someone was going about his business inside. On one of the shelves, Barrett found a possible solution—industrial steel wool. He presumed it was used to remove rust from window jams and other surfaces that got wet and then, with age, began to decay. He took two large pieces to be safe.

By this time, it was thirty minutes until the building was set to close, so Barrett went down and hid in the bathroom just as he did with Max weeks before. He followed the same plan, and when the building appeared to be empty, he made his way to the designated elevator, closed the doors, and hit the hold button to keep it in place.

In ten minutes, Barrett scrubbed off enough solder to loosen the transmitter. He was careful not to harm it, as he had no idea what plans Max had for the surveillance device. Barrett put the transmitter in his pocket, released the stop button, and opened the doors.

Just outside the now infamous elevator stood a security guard with a serious scowl. "Excuse me, sir, what the hell were you doing in there?"

Barrett, who considered himself lightning fast on his feet, paused and calmly said, "I lost my girlfriend's engagement ring in there, and I waited until everyone left to hunt for it."

"What?"

"Yeah, I was talking to my lawyer an hour ago, and on the way down the elevator, I must have dropped the ring. It was in a small box marked Littman Jewelers on it. Is there a lost and found here?"

"I think you're fulla shit, buddy, but I can't imagine you'd be doing anything illegal in an elevator. Just get the hell out of here before I change my mind."

Barrett walked quickly out the front door, which was not yet locked for the night.

On a cool December night, Barrett's underlying nerves led to enough perspiration that the back of his shirt clung to his back. While he was calm and, in his opinion, rather slick in his exchange with the guard, there was no way to turn off his fight-or-flight mechanism. As he drove back home to Philadelphia, Barrett decided to leave his confrontation with one of the county's security forces out of his report to Max.

It took Barrett a few days to speak in person with Max on the phone. He left a few messages on Max's vintage answering machine, but the young reporter was working at full speed, burning the candle on the top, middle, and bottom.

Max returned Barrett's call on a cold December Saturday on a rare day off. He had worked twelve days straight on the investigation into the chemical dumping. The progress that Al's team had made was impressive. Al was the sort of leader who didn't need to yell or prod; he commanded respect and handed out praise when justified and gave constructive criticism when such was relevant.

Max's call with Barrett was deliberately brief, but they had a good laugh about the entire caper from panicked installation to harrowing removal. Barrett knew Max well enough to understand his friend needed to hang up and move on with his day. The nature of their friendship was such that after eighteen years, they had an unspoken bond that allowed each one to detect the other's behavioral signals, no matter how subtle.

Max had fallen behind on personal and household chores like cleaning and shopping as the intensive interviewing with victims of the chemical dumping took up most of his time. Max's process was to speak with the folks in the homes, starting with an assurance that what they said would be kept confidential. He would add that he had a contact in Philadelphia who was preparing a class action lawsuit against Andersen Trucking and two companies in upstate New York responsible for the hazardous waste. Max also asked for permission to use his small Sony microcassette recorder to ensure he had their words on the record. Sue offered to help him with the tedious transcription of the conversations that often lasted an hour.

Jack Devlin called for a major update meeting for Monday in Allentown for all involved with the investigation. Max suggested it was wise to include Norm Weiss to get an update about the class action lawsuit. Devlin agreed and added that the newspaper's lawyer, Stacy Eidelman, should attend.

With two days before his command performance and forward marching orders, Max took the day to relax. He had a lengthy call with his parents, telling them the broadest brush strokes about his current assignment. His mother asked if he was eating properly and getting enough rest. After more than two decades, Max knew the best answer was to simply say, "Yes."

On Friday afternoon, after Sue had finished typing up an interview Max had with a farmer in Lansford who was suffering from a suspicious cough, she slid her chair over to his desk and asked if he had any weekend plans. As usual, Max fumbled for an answer and offered a cop-out excuse that he was tired and needed Saturday and Sunday to get back on his feet and take care of stuff around the house. Ever patient, Sue slid her chair back to a desk across the aisle without saying anything.

There was a cold chill on in the air Monday morning as Max got into his car to drive down to the *Chronicle*'s main office. Never knowing how to rid his windshield of frost and condensation, he played with the heat, defroster, and air conditioning buttons before giving up. Instead, he went back into his apartment, grabbed a ratty T-shirt, and wiped the inside windows clean.

On his way down to the *Chronicle*, Max looked for a distraction and began to think about the likely top songs of 1978. It was a good way for him to clear his mind while keeping it engaged with an interesting topic.

With the popularity of the movie *Saturday Night Fever*, he guessed two or three Bee Gees songs would make the year-end list of hits. Keeping on the same path, Max figured *Grease* also would score, even though the film was putrid. His two favorites of the year, "Use Ta Be My Girl," by the O'Jays and "Peg" by Steely Dan, may make the top twenty but were not considered blockbusters.

Max pulled into the *Chronicle* parking lot exactly forty minutes—and nine songs—after leaving his apartment in Nesquehoning. He was twenty minutes early for the meeting, so he decided to duck into the Little Apple Market for a cup of coffee. Max's taste in coffee had not progressed from those funky crystals that make up instant but relished the opportunity for someone else to do the preparation.

Tom Monahan was standing at the counter reading the *New York Times* as Max walked in. Dressed, as always, in a three-piece suit, Tom was downing a can of Diet Rite soda, wanting to get a shot of caffeine without having to drink coffee. Max noticed that Tom never drank coffee at the bureau, far preferring caffeine-rich green tea or Diet Pepsi based on mood and the time of day.

Tom's back was to the door when Max walked in, but the door chimes rang out, causing the mustachioed senior reporter to turn around. Max eased his way to the counter, stood next to Tom, and asked the older man behind the counter for a cup of coffee, black. Max had an intolerance to all things dairy, so he wanted to play it safe before the big meeting.

"We haven't touched base in a while," Max said.

"Like you, I have been swamped. Untangling the governmental mess as to which agency oversees chemical dumping is a challenge. It's almost as if they want to ignore its existence."

"I hear you. My last two weeks have been gut-wrenching talking to truckers, their families, and some farmers whose lives have been impacted by toxic waste. There are times I find it hard to keep my emotions in check during these interviews."

Tom looked at his watch and suggested they walk over to the newspaper building for the meeting. The Wells Fargo Bank clock showed the time to be four minutes before the hour and the temperature to be a balmy thirty degrees. Not too terrible for a December day in the Lehigh Valley. Tom wisely wore a wool overcoat while Max had a sweater underneath his faux leather jacket, which did little to stop the wind from chilling him to the bone.

Jack Devlin stood at the head of the long table in the main conference room—easily twice the size of the room for their first meeting. He brought along a whiteboard on which he wrote each reporter's name. The day's goal was to write underneath each name the progress that the person had made and what tasks were left. Devlin's goal was to get a handle on timing—how much was left for fact-finding and when the writing started. The managing editor would have to go through a process for each piece of the series that would run in the *Chronicle*; the work would have to be reviewed by the publisher and the company lawyer before it could be fit to print.

Exactly eighty-five minutes later, Tom, Max, and Al were clear on the next steps. Devlin had been in touch with Norm Weiss, and things were moving ahead with the class action lawsuit against Andersen Trucking. There was, however, a hitch: the companies responsible for the chemicals were difficult to pin down. The toxicity at each dumping site could have waste from one or more companies, so determining the precise culprits might be challenging. It was theoretically possible that the sludge byproduct from one of the companies in upstate New York did no harm, while others potentially did the bulk of the damage. Devlin emphasized that it was a small part of the overall story and more of a legal matter that had a minor impact on their reporting. Harmful or not, chemical dumping is illegal any way you slice it.

The week that followed the meeting at the *Chronicle* headquarters was intense. Max interviewed three more victims of the chemical dumping, including a farmer whose flock of sheep died at an alarming rate. He feared that the grazing pasture somehow had been contaminated, but the cost of doing the proper soil testing was out of his ballpark. Max assured him that, at some point, the EPA could come and do the work, which would allow him to potentially be compensated for his loss.

Tom was having a more difficult time with each governmental agency passing the buck to the other. Because the chemical dumping took place over state lines, it was a federal case. Still, the various bureaucracy pieces were not sure as to who should file suit against the toxic polluters and determine which laws were being broken. Over the years, Tom had developed contacts at the EPA, Justice Department, and several state offices, including the attorney general and the Department of Environmental Protection. Toward the end of the week, Tom's luck changed when he reached the county's congressional representative, Earl Dent. Dent knew of Tom's earlier reporting on laws involving juvenile justice and was happy to help. Suddenly, the wheels of justice spun at warp speed.

One week later, Jack Devlin brought his team back together at the Chronicle's main office. The meeting intended to begin the process of outlining how many articles his reporters would produce and when the first one would be ready to be reviewed by the paper's attorney.

Before the meeting, Max and Tom arranged to get together again at the Little Apple Deli. While Max sipped a cup of overly strong brew, the two decided that they would take a shot at writing the series together. They agreed their styles were complementary, with Tom being great at delivering cold, hard facts, while Max would add his lyrical touch to the pieces.

Devlin asked Tom and Max to write the series at the main office. Al, who once worked as a copy editor in Allentown, would directly supervise their work. The agreed-upon stories would begin with Max's encounter with Dan Bigelow and then segue into how the chemical dumping started, which companies were responsible for the travesty, the impact on the people of Carbon County and the environment, responses from state and federal authorities, and the class action lawsuit. Norm Weiss also asked to review the articles before they hit the printing press.

Since it turned out that Max and Tom lived almost across the street from one another, they carpooled to Allentown, with each taking turns driving. Max was less manic with his car radio when it was his turn to take the wheel. Tom had a Toyota Corolla, which was roomier than Max's Volvo, and Max came close to dozing off a few times on the forty-minute trip.

During the next week, the two reporters, working in concert, produced a five-part story scheduled to kick off on the following Sunday on the front page. Max was far too exhausted and involved with the task at hand to realize the impact the series would have. After the series ran, there would be time to enjoy the fruits of the collaboration and analyze how he went from nearly being terminated to star-on-the-rise in a ridiculously short amount of time.

Max slept in on Saturday before the first story would make the headlines. After a quick cup of instant coffee, he called his parents to update them about the investigatory work and its outcome. Max could feel his father beam through the phone while his mother joined in with her praise. Making his mom and dad proud was the icing on the cake. Max promised to save copies of the papers and bring them on his next visit.

"When *are* you coming home?" his mother asked.

"Soon, I promise. Give me time to recover from this last month, please."

Later on Saturday, Max called Norm to thank him for his help. The call went on for twenty minutes as the attorney gave Max a blow-by-blow of the class action case, which would likely net the fifteen people named as plaintiffs more than $100,000 each. That is, Norm added, depending on how the appeal process went.

Max decided to go gourmet for dinner after his obligatory calls, popping a Stouffer's frozen lasagna into the toaster oven. A lettuce wedge was considered a salad, and a can of Del Monte green beans rounded out this luscious meal. The timing was perfect: just as the frozen lasagna finished, the puck dropped for the Flyers-Penguins game.

The one-sided affair was all Flyers with a 4–0 shutout of their Pennsylvania rival. Left-wing Bill Barber was one goal short of a hat trick, and goalie Bernie Parent stopped all twenty-eight shots that came his way. After the post-game show, Max called it a night, anticipating a big day on Sunday.

Since one of the perks the *Chronicle* offered was the free home delivery of the paper, Max hopped out of bed at 7:30 a.m., put on his robe, and bolted down the steps outside his apartment. There at the door was the Sunday paper. Max unfolded it and stared at the headline: *The Invisible Enemy* while the subhead read: *Out of State Poison Brings Horror to Carbon County*.

Max's hands shook as he stared at the byline: "Part one of five-part series by Max Rosen and Tom Monahan." The two agreed to swap the order of the names each day the stories ran. As if walking in a dream state, Max slowly walked up the steps to his apartment. He sat down on his sofa—a used piece purloined from his parents' basement. Max was used to suppressing his pride, especially when it came after he achieved great success. He sat, staring at the window, and drank in the great glory of his work.

Engrossed in his achievement, Max initially ignored the fact his phone was ringing. He looked at the clock, and it was only eight fifteen, so Max wondered who was calling so early on a Sunday.

"Hey Max, the *Philadelphia Inquirer* ran your piece today after the AP picked it up. That's amazing work." The voice was that of Norm Weiss. Since Max spoke to him the day before, he wondered what the call was about.

Weiss took a deep sigh and began to speak. "Listen, I hate to ruin your big day, but I have some bad news. I just got a call from Dan Bigelow's wife. He died, Max. I am so sorry."

Chapter Eleven

Max stood in the shower and wept, thinking of Dan Bigelow and his young family. The hot water cascading down did little to drown his tears and the sorrow he felt deep inside. He was too young to remember his grandfather's funeral. Max's memory of an uncle's death was hazy other than the fact that in his waning days, Max sat with him most afternoons while his aunt went to work.

While the accolades poured in from *Chronicle* colleagues and friends who read the series in their local papers, Max did little to accept the praise. He was deeply sad Dan Bigelow was not able to share in the success. He realized that he, Tom, Al, and Jack Devlin put in a lot of hard work, but Max did not overlook that he and Sue happened to be in the right place and the right time. Again, it all started with an overheard conversation in an elevator ride.

Midafternoon, Max got a call from Tex, who was concerned about his young colleague's wellbeing. Tex had been involved in a major story about a cut in funding to some school districts in Carbon County and had been out of touch for most of the past two weeks. Even with a heavy workload of his own, Tex closely followed the chemical dumping saga.

"I wanted to make sure you were okay after hearing about Bigelow's death," Tex calmly said. "I know it's a crazy cup-half-full thought, but without you, his family would be shit out of luck."

Max and Tex agreed to meet away from the office for a beer later in the week. Tex was anxious to hear all the details about Max's recent work and share a few tidbits about Sue. It seems she was a big help in Tex's school district reporting, during which time they became good friends.

After taking a day off, Max returned to the office on Tuesday, hoping for a few low-key days. Al was on a well-earned vacation, taking his wife, Betty, to Gettysburg. Ervin manned the bureau editor's desk, and, to Max's shock and delight, he found a gift from the usually grumpy Ervin on his desk with a note of congratulations. There it was—wrapped in a copy of the Sunday paper—a Phillies scorebook made for the 1964 World Series with a card from Ervin and his wife, Mary. Given this piece of sports memorabilia was made for a series that never materialized, its value was priceless

Anyone who knew Max knew that the 1964 Phillies was the team that stole and later broke his heart. It was a team that sat on top of the National League for seventy-three consecutive days, hit a ten-game losing streak, and finished second to the St. Louis Cardinals when all was said and done. During the ten-game disaster, Max would become sullen after the losses to the point where his mother forbade him from listening to the radio broadcasts.

After two days of deep sorrow about the Bigelow family, Max felt a smile come to his face when he looked at the cover at his new treasure. On a flagpole, there were three pennants: the Stars and Stripes on the top, followed by a Phillies banner with a blank pennant at the bottom representing the team's American League TBA opponent.

Max walked up to Ervin's desk to thank him, and the overweight editor said he wanted Max to know how much he admired and respected the hard work he put in. Max and Ervin were unlikely to become close friends, but the kind gesture from a man who previously cursed him under his breath was a huge step in the right direction.

The Nesquehoning bureau was still without a full-time editor after Ray's untimely departure. The job was a thankless one located in an undesirable location for anyone accustomed to an urban lifestyle. The *Chronicle* insisted that the bureau chief lives in the area, which significantly limited the potential pool of candidates. It was a lot to ask a junior editor from Allentown to move to the sticks, even if it meant a promotion and a bump in salary.

Growing up in a densely populated part of Philadelphia, Max couldn't imagine spending more than a few years in Carbon County. In his short career at the *Chronicle*, he understood the mentality and culture that goes with a more rural community. Max knew that when his apartment lease ran out, he would move to Allentown even if it meant commuting to the bureau office.

Max spent Tuesday and Wednesday going through the mail and returning messages left during the time he was working in Allentown on the series. Ironically, one of the messages was from the Carbon County Chamber of Commerce with an invite for him to be the guest speaker at their next monthly meeting. Max was not big on speaking live in front of crowds, so he called the chamber's office and politely passed.

Another call was from the *Philadelphia Bulletin* with no message. Max did some freelance writing about music for the city's afternoon paper before joining the *Chronicle*, but he imagined the call was about something else. Remembering some of his concert reviews and interviews made Max recall how much he enjoyed that work, especially interviewing John Edwards. The latter became the lead singer of the Spinners after Philippé Wynne left the group. After the story ran, Max was given two tickets to see the group live, but even with his prodigious memory, he was hard-pressed to remember who accompanied him. The *Bulletin* call was from the entertainment editor Max wrote for and was just another in a series of congratulations.

Wednesday, Max was assigned to cover the Coaldale Borough council meeting. It was the last meeting before the Christmas holidays, so it would be quick and to the point. December was not a prime time for citizen participation in these civic affairs, so it likely would not last more than one hour. Max thought it might be nice to invite Sue since they hadn't spoken for more than a few minutes while he was working on the chemical dumping stories. Sue did transcribe three of Max's recorded interviews and went along on two other face-to-face sessions when the presence of a woman reporter made the in-person calls more relaxed.

After work on Wednesday, Max met Tex for a beer in Jim Thorpe at the Union Publick House, which specialized in having a variety of Yuengling beers on tap. Yuengling, a 150-year-old brewery in Pottsville, experienced a resurgence that many beer lovers linked to the Bicentennial when it was proclaimed the nation's oldest active brewery. Max was not big on beer, so he ordered a six-ounce glass of Yuengling's lightest and sipped it while talking with Tex. Tex talked about his work on the local school district's funding and asked many questions about Max's investigatory work. While downing his second glass of Yuengling dark, Tex reminded Max of their conversation weeks before when Max thought he was on thin ice due to his repeated blunders.

"You've come a long way, baby." Tex snorted, laughing at his joke. His line was lifted from a ten-year-old ad campaign for Virginia Slims cigarettes and, Tex thought, was the perfect compliment for the occasion.

Max's night out did him a world of good, even if the beer was not his beverage of choice. For the first time in weeks, he had a good night's sleep and woke up Thursday with his sights set on a new challenge. What lay on the horizon, he thought, may or may not involve bugging another elevator. The FM transmitter that played a big part in resurrecting his Max's career was resting comfortably in Barrett's apartment, ready, if need be, for a new deployment.

When Max came into the office around eleven, there was a note waiting for him stuck between his Selectric rollers. The message was from Jack Devlin, requesting a phone call as soon as possible. Max decided to call right away before he had the chance to get nervous or excited. He knew Devlin's number by heart after many late-night conversations, during which the managing editor asked for progress reports on the chemical dumping stories.

The *Chronicle* was not the sort of operation where executives had secretaries or admins. The Daniels family owned the paper—a clan that made its money in the department store business and had a reputation for being thrifty when it came to what it deemed extra personnel. After three rings, Jack Devlin answered the phone.

"Hi, Jack. This is Max Rosen returning your call."

"Thanks for getting back to me so soon. I figured you might still be recovering from some hectic times. Listen, I have a few things I wanted to talk to you about."

The managing editor's voice was noncommittal, so Max instinctively squeezed his hand into a fist like he was preparing for an injection. "Sure. What did you want to talk about?"

"Okay. The first thing is to be kept between you and me. I am in the process of building a team of reporters and feature writers that will work on special projects throughout the year. I want you to be on that team. I am also asking Tom Monahan. I have a few others in mind, and once I decide on the other slots, we will have a meeting of what I want to call 'The Sunday Squad.'

"Just like the chemical dumping story, I envision these special reports starting on Sundays," Devlin added. "It's a great way to boost Sunday readership. I'd like to have people read the paper for more than the Sunday coupons and Parade magazine."

"I don't know what to say." Max wasn't speechless, but it took some time for Devlin's words to sink in. "But, yes, I am excited and honored."

"Don't be that honored yet, Max. You have no idea what sort of work is involved," the managing editor said with a medium-sized guffaw. "There's more, though. I doubt that you know this, but our restaurant critic Mimi Raynor is leaving to work for the *Philadelphia Inquirer*. I guess she thinks that's the big time. Anyway, I am not sure where I heard it, but I seem to remember you have some knowledge of and passion for food. Would you be interested in filling in for her while we find a permanent replacement?"

"Restaurant reviews? Well, I have read a lot of them, that's for sure, but I've never written one."

"What I had in mind is for you to put together something about great lunch spots in Lehigh and Carbon County. It will take less time and effort and might be fun. We can call it 'Out to Lunch.'"

"You know, Jack, that could be fun. The guys in the office are always talking about these lunch spots that only the locals know about. Tex was telling me the other day about someplace in Tamaqua he loves. That would be a good place to start."

"Okay, so you're in?"

"Sure, when do you want me to start?"

"Is next week too soon?"

Max didn't tell Devlin or anyone else he knew at the *Chronicle* that he owned a complete set of *Gourmet* magazines dating back to its first issue. In 1977, when he visited a friend from college in law school, Max purchased them from a soon-to-be-closed library in Charlottesville, Virginia. There were more than a hundred issues, and Max paid fifty dollars for the lot. He crammed them into the back of his mother's new car and took them back to Pennsylvania, where the copies of the legendary food publication now lived. On second thought, he realized a *Gourmet* from 1963 with a recipe for *coq au vin* wasn't going to be of any help with a bunch of earthy lunch reviews.

Not knowing what was in store with this Sunday Squad deal, Max decided to give Barrett a call over the weekend to see what additional spycraft tools they might be able to dig up if needed. The FM transmitter might be useful but adding to their bag of clandestine tricks was worth a discussion. There were a lot of elevators in Allentown.

As promised, Tex took Max to a small lunch place in the heart of Tamaqua called Texas Chili Dog. Max figured this wiener emporium was about fifteen hundred miles from Texas by his rough calculations, so there had to be some unseen linkage. Tex took control and ordered two specials: chili dogs with chopped onions and chili on buns that had seen better days. The hot dog was decent, but the chili lacked flavor and punch. What it did have were pinto beans, which, as Max knew, would not be considered real chili by any red-blooded Texan. Max enjoyed the lunchtime crowd that sat on barstools around a 1950s-era green Formica counter talking town gossip. Most of the locals knew Tex and enjoyed poking fun at his new goatee, which made him look more like a carnival barker than a newspaper reporter.

On the ride back to the office after what would best be called an "interesting" lunch, Tex talked about his time working with Sue while Max was fully engaged with the chemical dumping investigation.

"She's a smart cookie," Tex said, glancing over at Max to see his reaction. "I think she's going places."

Max sat quietly, looking out the window at Panther Creek along Water Street, which ran from Tamaqua to Nesquehoning. He was listening intently but did his best not to bite on his colleague's fishing expedition.

Following a sixty second dramatic pause, Tex continued. "You know, she likes you. That said, she can't figure out whether the feeling is mutual. She doesn't know if you are shy, scared of women, or just plain socially awkward."

Max let Tex's words sink in. "Maybe a bit of all three," he said, barely above a whisper.

And without another word between them, Tex pulled into the bureau's parking lot. The two men exited Tex's BMW and walked quietly to the office. While making his way along Catawissa Street, Max replayed the last few minutes of his conversation with Tex, wondering if his reply would be passed on to Sue.

It had been a while since Max visited his parents in Philadelphia, and he was overdue. He left after work Friday and took the turnpike because it was lit much better than some of the backroads he often drove. He pulled into the driveway shortly after 11 p.m. after an hour and a half on the road. To his surprise and delight, Max's mother was not peering out the window waiting for his safe arrival. Max smiled and thought the weekend was off to a good start.

Max showered and climbed into bed after devouring a plate of home-cooked corned beef that his mother left out for him. Less than five minutes after hitting the pillow, he was asleep and was out like a light for eight solid hours. He woke to the sound of something sizzling on the stove, which he knew was a serving of home fried potatoes and a small scrambled egg. *If anyone should be writing about food*, Max thought, *it should be my mother.*

Max spent the day doing his best imitation of a couch potato watching the Pittsburgh Steelers play the Denver Broncos with his father in a rare Saturday NFL game. The Steelers were on their way to a 14–2 Super Bowl season under future Hall of Fame quarterback Terry Bradshaw. The Broncos were headed for a decent 10–6 record but would be knocked out of the playoffs by these same Steelers a few weeks later.

Max and his father talked throughout the game, but it was mostly a recap of Max's last month working on the chemical dumping series. Harold, Max's father, told him how much his Uncle Marty would like to see him on one of his visits home. Marty and Harold loved to sit for hours and tell Max of their days seeing legendary baseball greats like Ruth, Gehrig, Jimmy Foxx, and Lefty Grove in the 1920s and '30s.

The weekend zoomed by, marked by good food and a lot of rest. Max hopped into his car Sunday after dinner to head back to his home in Nesquehoning. As he left, Max's mother followed him out to the car. He rolled down the window as she approached.

"Nancy tells me you met someone at work?"

"She's exaggerating, Mom. There's a new woman who is an intern at the paper. We've become friends, and nothing more."

"Is she Jewish?"

"I doubt it."

With that, Max pulled away.

Max came into the office Monday hours before his scheduled 4:30 p.m. start time. He generally came in way before his prescribed hours, fueled by an eagerness to get started and the fact there was nothing else to do in this rural town.

And like the week before, a piece of paper was stuck between the rollers of his Selectric. It was another note to call Jack Devlin but without the previous sense of urgency. *Why keep the man waiting?* Max thought as he dialed the number he now knew by heart.

"Max, glad you called me back. Listen, I've made progress on the Sunday Squad I told you about. I arranged for a meeting on Wednesday for the four of you to meet. I've already spoken to Tom. We'll get together at 10 a.m., so maybe you and Tom can ride together.

"Oh, one more thing," Devlin added. "I read the copy on your first lunch review. You sure know food and have a way with words—it's hilarious. Sorry, but it may be your last; we hired someone who worked at Rodale as our new food critic."

Wednesday came fast. An early arctic blast enveloped Lehigh and Carbon County. Max searched his closet for a coat warm enough for the day but quickly realized his heavy wool coat was sitting in his closet at his parents' house. He improvised with a long-sleeve undershirt and pullover sweater, which he wore underneath his faux leather jacket. Max was late to meet Tom, so he had no idea how ridiculous he looked.

Tom pulled into the *Chronicle* parking lot with only a few minutes to spare. There was no time to go across the street to grab a cup of coffee, so the two men hoped someone would have the courtesy to bring coffee to the meeting. That hope was quickly dashed when Max and Tom entered the large conference room in the newsroom's far corner.

Jack Devlin was seated at the head of the table. On his right sat a tall, slender man who looked to be in his early forties. In front of him sat a pencil case and a large Big Chief notebook, the kind Max used to keep score for Phillies games. The extra-wide margin was ideal for writing in player names save for those such long ones as Joe Amalfitano or Red Schoendienst.

Seated across from the table was a striking woman with an olive complexion and a smile that lit the room. Her black hair was short and elegantly styled, making her look more mature, but she appeared to be in her mid-to-late twenties. In contrast to the other newcomer in the room, she had a traditional white spiral reporter's notebook and a single Bic pen on the table in front of her.

The managing editor asked Max and Tom to sit down, and Max chose to sit next to the man with the cool notebook, being far too shy to even consider his other option.

"I have coffee coming for those who want it," Jack Devlin said, kicking off the meeting. Behind him was a whiteboard with the words "Sunday Squad" written across the top. "I think it's time for introductions. Tom, why don't you start."

Tom issued a compact bio, which was little more than name, rank, and serial number. He mentioned that he went to The Ohio State University and worked in the Nesquehoning bureau. Max followed with an even shorter summary saying that he was from Philadelphia and joined the *Chronicle* without any journalism experience in August of 1978.

The tall, slender man stood up as if he were reciting the pledge of allegiance and introduced himself as Aaron Grant. He was born and raised in Dothan, Alabama, and graduated from Auburn University's journalism school in 1963. He worked for newspapers in Alabama, Kentucky, and Ohio before joining the *Chronicle* five years ago. After the meeting, Max later learned that Grant had been twice nominated for a Pulitzer Prize for investigative work.

Without any fanfare, the last member of the quartet spoke.

"My name is Ximena Ortiz. I am originally from Arequipa, Peru, but my family moved to Bethlehem when I was five years old. I went to Lehigh University, graduating in 1973, after which I joined the *Chronicle* as a feature writer. I also wanted to say that I loved the series you guys did on the chemical dumping and am excited to be part of this team."

"With that out of the way, let's get down to business," Devlin said, taking charge of the session. "Let's talk about goals, how we work as a team, how we vet ideas, and so on."

Over the next hour, topics were brainstormed, and the four members of the Sunday Squad began to speak casually, peppered with light banter between serious topics. By the end of ninety minutes, Tom, Max, Aaron, and Ximena had a handle on each other's strengths and weaknesses. They also knew where individual interests lay.

The meeting ended when Devlin said he had to get ready for lunch with the publisher and stated the team would meet once a week at the same time. Devlin added that he expected his four stars to regularly call each other to collaborate and bat ideas back and forth before bringing them to the meeting.

Tom and Max decided to stop at the Trivet for lunch on the way back to the bureau. It was noon, and the parking lot was packed. There was a short line out the door, and as the two men approached the diner, Max excused himself to use the restroom inside. Instead, he found a payphone on the wall between the men's and ladies' bathrooms. From experience, Max knew that a three-minute call to Philadelphia from a payphone would cost seventy-five cents. He dropped three quarters into the appropriate slots and dialed.

"Yo, Barrett," Max said in hushed tones to his friend's answering machine. "We are going to have to up our surveillance game. I hope you're up for it. Allentown has a lot of elevators."

Chapter Twelve

Allentown's holiday season did not shine as brightly with cheerful decorations as it did in New York or Philadelphia. Save for twinkling lights and a sparkly fake silver Christmas tree in the window of Hess's Department Store three blocks from the *Chronicle* office on Hamilton Street, the city's "main street" was all business, dressed in December gray. Contrary to the lyrics of the song "Allentown" made famous by Billy Joel nine years later, the economy at that time was robust. The economic decline from the closure of the major factories, such as Mack Trucks and Alpo, would come years later.

Barrett had agreed to meet Max in the lobby of the nearby Renaissance Hotel at two o'clock. This meetup would give Max time to plan the next chapter in their surveillance saga and still make it to the bureau in time. Max got to the city early, scouting for apartments. While he had three months left on his lease, the landlord had offered him an early out. Given the nature of the apartment building's flimsy construction, the second floor's steps caused the lower unit to shake if someone ran up the twenty-five stairs too quickly. At 180 pounds, Max was hardly light on his feet.

Max found a few candidates for his next home. One was a bit too close to the college he attended for four long, challenging years. Another was a half-block from a fire station but close to the fairgrounds, which he found appealing. Max would whittle the choices down and have his parents come and help him decide.

At two fifteen, Barrett showed up in the hotel lobby demanding hot chocolate. Max remembered that Hess offered hot chocolate to its customers during the holidays, and the iconic department store was on the way to their destination.

With his sweet winter treat in hand, Barrett dove right in.

"So, with this new assignment, you want to eavesdrop not just on one building, but two?" Barrett said between sips.

"I'm not saying that I will rely solely on what I hear in the elevators, but I have to admit, those overheard conversations helped get me where I am today."

"And where exactly do you plan on hiding these transmitters?"

"I was thinking Allentown City Hall and the federal courthouse. They are just a block apart."

Barrett shrugged his shoulders. "I guess in for a penny, in for fifty pounds. Wait," Max's friend continued. "How do you plan on listening in on two locations? That will eat up a lot of time."

"I have an idea that takes care of that."

"Do you care to tell me, or should I guess?"

"Later. Right now, let's go to the lobbies of the two buildings and scope out the elevators. By the way, I bought a second FM transmitter." Max pulled a shiny new Heathkit gadget that was still in its factory wrapping.

A cold wind whipped in a circular frenzy as the two men headed east on Hamilton Street toward the two government buildings. City Hall was an old relic that dated back to the 1930s, while the federal building was a more modern glass-and-steel structure from the generic school of architecture. On the way, the two men walked past the old courthouse, where Max stopped and pointed to the plaque out front.

"Did you know that during the Revolutionary War, the founding fathers hid the Liberty Bell here?" Max said, his breath turning into a cold weather cloud with every word.

"Am I supposed to care? I'm freezing my nuts off here, and you're playing history teacher?"

Max and Barrett made their way to Allentown City Hall and scoped out three elevators that serviced four floors. They were older attendant-run elevators that had been updated to become self-service. Small billboards were fastened to the back of the elevators advertising various upcoming civic events such as a Christmas charity drive. Placing a transmitter to the back of the frame that held the billboards was a piece of cake.

Moving on to the federal building, Max knew there were three elevators, but there were five floors. Like the building, the lifts were only a few years old; no doubt built with some pork-barrel money owed to a local, influential congressman. For that matter, a vote in favor—or against—can buy an elected official any number of rewards. In this case, a yes vote on some earmarked military spending was rewarded with a brand-spanking-new federal office building.

The elevators in the federal building had neither billboard nor ashtrays. It would take the team of Barrett and Fine some time to figure out how to hide the transmitter in those up-and-down machines.

Barrett walked Max to his car, which was parked a few blocks west of the *Chronicle*. It was not in the reporter's best interest to be spotted to avoid explaining what he was doing wandering the streets of Allentown in the early afternoon on a day fit for polar bears or reindeer. As they approached Max's car, Barrett reminded him to explain how they planned on surveilling two buildings.

"I have someone we can trust. I plan on asking her to help monitor the federal building while I tackle the city hall. Let's talk in the next few days about an installation plan."

Barrett shook his head in disbelief. "Man, if this goes south, please leave me out of it. This is getting a bit too out there for my taste."

Max had decided to meet Sue the following Saturday afternoon for coffee at Heffelfinger's Coffee and Tea, a few blocks from the campus of Max's alma mater. He planned to confess to Sue why he was sitting on the bench outside the Carbon County Courthouse a month ago when she spotted him after cupcake shopping. Max wasn't going to reveal all the details of his sleuthing, but enough to intrigue Sue into joining the upcoming caper. After his work on the chemical dumping—which was all above board—Sue had to know Max's heart was in the right place and would be willing to give him wiggle room in his tactics.

Sue arrived on time, dressed for the weather. Max still had forgotten to retrieve his winter coat from Philadelphia and was wearing several layers underneath his faux leather jacket. Sue approached Max, kissed him on the cheek, and sat down for coffee and Funny cake, a Pennsylvania Dutch specialty.

With eyes fixed on Max, Sue listened as Max explained using an FM transmitter to nail Chris Albrecht in the arson case and how he planned on using it for his work with the Sunday Squad.

"And that's where you come in," Max offered in a serious tone. "I need your help."

Max spoke deliberately, revealing about 90 percent of his and Barrett's actions related to bugging the Carbon County Courthouse. Sue sat quietly, taking it all in between sips of coffee and bites of cake. She occasionally nodded to let her friend and colleague know she was listening intently. After ten minutes of what amounted to something between a confession and soliloquy, Max stopped.

"So, what do you think?" Max said after taking a deep breath.

"I understand you were in a tough spot because of your suspension, and while I don't generally subscribe to the belief that the ends justify the means, I don't condemn you for what you did. It was ingenious." Sue smiled. It wasn't exactly the face of evil, but it lacked any shred of innocence. "So, why did you want to tell me this secret?"

"Yeah. I need your help. I want to make a name for myself with this Sunday Squad, so my friend and I plan to bug the elevators at Allentown City Hall and the federal courthouse. I hope to use the stuff we hear to verify info we find through traditional methods—you know, good old-fashioned investigative reporting."

"I'm in. What do you need me to do?" Sue said before Max could get his words out. "Who knows? Maybe it will help me somehow. Also, this way, you can owe me one."

Startled by Sue's eagerness, Max hardly knew how to respond.

"Wow. Barrett, my friend from Philadelphia who helped me plant the transmitter in the Jim Thorpe building, is working on a federal building elevator scheme. City Hall is a piece of cake."

"Okay, just keep me posted," Sue replied with confidence. "Listen, while we're out, do you want to do something like go to a movie?"

"If you want to know the truth, I planned on looking at apartments here in Allentown. I am planning on moving here in the next few months."

Max and Sue spent the rest of the day with the *Chronicle* classifieds, crisscrossing the city, looking at a wide range of places. Most of the landlords or those subletting assumed Sue and Max were a couple wanting to move in together. At one place—a two-bedroom near 27th and Tilghman Streets—Sue grabbed Max's hand as a joke when they were being shown the unit.

"Oh, darling, isn't this just the loveliest place?" Sue said in a breathy voice, just loud enough for all to hear. Max turned bright red and looked down at his feet, hoping his size twelve Chuck Taylors had an answer to Sue's joke.

At 6 p.m., Max drove Sue back to Heffelfinger's, where she had left her car. He told her that he had plans for dinner with some college friends, but Sue knew it was an excuse for Max to get his bearings after what was, for him, a confusing day. She kissed him on the cheek and got in her car.

The rest of the weekend was not as restful as Max had hoped. While taking care of his usual chores on Sunday, Max listening to the Eagles beat the New York Giants 20–3, making their first trip to the NFC Playoffs in eighteen years. As the game wrapped up, Max sat at his kitchen table with a yellow pad and made a list of possible investigations and targets he might focus on in his new role. Going back to his first eavesdropping score for ideas, he put "Payoffs" and "City Officials" at the top.

Max set his focus on Mark Donahue, the three-term Democratic mayor of Allentown. Donahue was the most popular elected official in Lehigh County over the past twenty years. He could be the man of the people in a rally supporting equal pay for women. Later that same night, he was a bigwig wining and dining CEOs of companies considering Allentown for relocation. Depending on your political stance, Donahue was either considered flexible or a phony.

Donahue came on the scene quietly in 1968, having moved from Springfield, Illinois, where he was a city councilman and high-profile car dealer. During his official campaign, Donahue, a burly Irishman who proudly wore his heritage, met his wife Margaret, who volunteered in the office. The former Margaret O'Brien graduated from Cedar Crest College in Allentown, but had moved to Illinois to do graduate work in nursing at the University of Illinois Springfield. The two married and decided to move to the Lehigh Valley, where Mrs. Donahue had a prominent family.

After selling his car dealership in Springfield to a group headed by his cousin John, Mark Donahue decided to become a civil servant after he and his wife relocated east. He volunteered at several area shelters and became a deacon at St. Paul's Catholic Church. Always with a friendly greeting, whether it was Sunday after mass or in the dining room at a local soup kitchen, Donahue's magnetic personality led him to pursue political office. After two years on Allentown's city council, Donahue ran for mayor and beat the Republican incumbent in a landslide. He was the darling of the local Democratic Party leaders and union officials.

Donahue's meteoric rise and popularity were further bolstered by his success in bringing new companies to the area. The Royal Typewriter Company was convinced to move its operation from its original headquarters in Hartford, Connecticut, to Jordan Creek in the northern part of the city. The terms of the deal to bring Royal to the city were never made public. The same was true for Radio Flyer, the nation's largest manufacturer of toy wagons. After fifty-three years with its main office in Chicago, Radio Flyer moved to a vacant building on South 7th Street in a rundown part of Allentown. The city, again with deal terms somewhat sketchy, promised the toy company the moon, including renovation of the abandoned site, which once made machine parts for long-haul buses.

In 1974, Donahue ran virtually unopposed in his reelection for mayor. The Republican Party all but conceded by putting a retired judge on the ballot against the incumbent. The margin of victory was the largest in local political history. The celebration that marked his win made the headlines of the *Chronicle* as it brought out political bigwigs from around the state, including Governor Milton Shapp and State Representative James Ritter, a close friend of Donahue's.

Call it instinct or maybe wishing thinking, but Max knew something was not quite right about Donahue. He wanted to know more about those deals that brought two companies to town that seemingly had no intention of relocating. Royal and Radio Flyer brought jobs and prestige to Allentown, but at what cost? Also, there had to be a lot of city money spent on renovating the dilapidated building on South 7th. How was that accounted for, and how were the bids for the construction jobs to do the massive renovation handled?

Al Hickey, the editor with whom Max worked closely on the chemical dumping series, shared a rumor that Mark Donahue was accused of playing footsie with one of his secretaries during his first term as mayor of Allentown. Hickey said there was an under-the-table settlement to keep things quiet lest the church deacon's reputation take a major hit.

As per Jack Devlin's instructions, Max wanted to team up with one of the other squad members to brainstorm how to approach digging into Mark Donahue. Max had already worked with Tom, but their styles were too complementary for this work. Max decided to go with Aaron Grant over Ximena Ortiz. Grant's overall demeanor and vibe were a stark contrast to Max's. If need be, one could play Devil's Advocate to the other or good cop/bad cop if any interviews came up.

Max met Aaron Grant the following Tuesday at the *Chronicle* office in Allentown. Max was still working out of the Nesquehoning bureau, so Monday was devoted to wrapping up some local stories and assembling some year-in-review pieces related to Carbon County politics.

The two men found an empty conference room outside the newsroom tucked alongside the HR office. Max flipped the light switch on, and with a crackling that sounded like angry fireflies, the room lit as they took seats across from one another at a small round table. Max had filled Aaron in on his early digging into Donahue's background, and the older reporter was glad to partner with his younger colleague. Grant was well aware of the chemical dumping series's work and saw a chance to capitalize on Max's passion, keen sense, and instinct. Aaron knew that with Max's eagerness would come a chance of rookie mistakes.

"I'm not sure how much you know about Mark Donahue, but since you've worked here for a while, I wonder what you might know about some of the questions regarding him getting companies to relocate here."

Grant paused, sizing up his new work associate. On the surface, they had nothing in common. It was obvious to Grant, based on Max's accent and cadence, that he grew up in a big city—most likely Philadelphia. You could fit thirty Dothan, Alabamas in the city limits of Philadelphia. Grant admired Max's longish hair in contrast to his own rapidly receding hairline. He also grinned, measuring his starched white shirt and tie compared to Max's brandless old button-down and khakis. Grant also surmised Max to be Jewish while he was a Southern Baptist through and through, not that it mattered to him. *Opposites work well together,* Grant thought to himself. *Isn't that what they say?*

"I know a little about the mayor," Grant said with just a hint of Southern drawl. "I did a piece a few years back about his wife and her work with local nurses. I got to meet Donahue when I went to their house to do the interview."

"What I was thinking was a little bit of misdirection," Max suggested. "What if we approached Donahue by saying that we're doing a feature on the development successes he's led. In the meantime, we can poke around and see what we can find about his connection to the companies that moved here."

"I can arrange for the interview," Grant said, signaling he agreed with Max's approach. "How about I check into the toy company and typewriter firm, and you can focus on the local contractors who did the construction on the remodel of the building on South 7th."

"Should we tell Jack Devlin what we're up to?" Max asked.

"I'll take care of that. I see him every day. Let's touch base at the end of the week."

After meeting with Grant, Max drove up to Nesquehoning for his regular shift at the bureau. He stopped at McDonald's for a burger, fries, and Coke a meal he indulged in more often than he should, but sometimes expedience trumped the need for healthy food. As he opened the door to the *Chronicle*'s suburban enclave, a burst of cold air accompanied him, causing everyone to turn around and pretend to shiver.

Max sat at his desk and wolfed down his high-calorie, high-carb lunch while looking through the few pieces of mail on his desk. After his last visit to the Carbon County Chamber of Commerce, he figured he was *persona non grata*, but there was an invitation to the chamber's Christmas party in living color. Max chuckled and tossed the glossy piece of mail in the trash. He made a note to RSVP in the negative in the next day or so.

Al Hickey was finishing up a phone call as Max, still munching on the few fries left in the small, greasy paper bag, approached Al's desk. Wanting to follow Devlin's instructions, he gave Al a recap of his meeting with Aaron Grant and the plan to approach the Allentown mayor using a bit of an end-around. Max asked Al, the assignment editor at the bureau that day, to pass on his message to the managing editor. Max knew that each day around 5 p.m. Devlin had a phone conference with the bureau editors to get an idea of what stories were cooking for the next day's morning edition.

"Wait, before you go," Al said, putting up his hand as if he were stopping traffic. "Let me tell you about Joe Taylor. Taylor has earned the nickname 'Bull' for a good reason. He's a pitbull, built like a linebacker, and is well known as Donahue's fixer. He became part of the mayor's team when he first took office in 1970. I've heard rumors that paint him in less than favorable light."

As Max turned to walk back to his desk, Al added four words that would be turn out to be eerily prophetic: "Be careful out there."

Max found out that Sue was given the assignment to cover the Marian Catholic High School basketball game. This was no ordinary game, as Tamaqua's Marian was undefeated in the state and ranked number one. That night's game, a semifinal in the Pennsylvania AA Girls Basketball Conference, was against Delone Catholic, a team with only one loss. Max hadn't seen Sue in a few days and had hoped to thank her for her willingness to help with his spycraft.

Before heading out to a school board meeting in Jim Thorpe, Max called Aaron Grant to see if he had an interview scheduled with the mayor.

"I'm waiting to hear back. I forgot to tell you: there's this guy, Joe Taylor, who has to approve any interview with the mayor. I've dealt with him before, and he's a bit of a prick—pardon my French."

"Okay, keep me posted," Max said. The second time in fifteen minutes, he heard the name Joe Taylor, and it was not followed by "What a great guy."

On the same legal pad Max used to list possible targets for investigation directly above the words "Payoffs" and "City Officials," Max wrote the name Joe Taylor—Bull. *Who is this guy?* Max wondered. Whatever the case, Max knew who he had to call to learn more. The sooner, the better.

Chapter Thirteen

Barrett searched through the Yellow Pages to find the uniform store closest to his condo. He planned to rent, if possible, the uniform of a janitor, which would allow him to work undetected on the elevator in Allentown City Hall. Because the building was the city's political nerve center, it would be impossible to plant an FM transmitter in one of its elevators without causing suspicion. Barrett made a "closed for cleaning" sign he would place outside the elevator while he fiddled around inside to plant the eavesdropping device.

The plot was thicker than just sticking a transmitter behind the billboard in the lift. There were three elevators, and it was Barrett's job to figure out which one the major and his attack dog, Bull, most often used. Barrett would have to sit at key times in the city hall lobby and take notes to learn that. Well, for most people, it would mean take notes—given Barrett's well-studied memory tricks, it would be easy to remember.

Max was working in parallel to attack his reporting mission on two fronts. Task one was to dig into every piece of information—no matter how trivial—related to Mark Donahue's time in Springfield. Max wondered if he left Springfield for more than the reason for relocating to be closer to his wife's family. Max also quietly—as quietly as he could without raising suspicion—poked around to get the scoop on Joe Taylor. Any access he and Aaron Grant would gain to the mayor would undoubtedly have to go through Taylor, a.k.a. Bull. As a reporter, Max felt it would be wise to know how much clout Taylor had.

Unbeknownst to Max, Joe Taylor was busy on the phone learning as much as he could about Max Rosen and Aaron Grant. Grant had been with the *Chronicle* for years, so putting together a dossier on him was simple. Taylor leaned on his contacts at the newspaper who would fill in the blanks on Grant—Where did he live? Was he married with kids? What did he do in his spare time?

Taylor was frustrated with his results in getting the skinny on Max Rosen. He learned that Max was born and raised in Philadelphia, went to college in Allentown, and joined the *Chronicle* less than six months ago. The only color Bull found out was that Max was a huge sports fan. Immediately, Taylor wondered how he could use that fact to his advantage. As a fixer, Taylor had an additional layer of sources he could call on for more info on Max Rosen. As the appointed mayoral gatekeeper, it was his job to keep his boss safe from harm, be it political or personal.

Jack Devlin brought the Sunday Squad together for a status meeting as the days drew closer to Christmas. The calendar showed ten shopping days left before Santa's arrival, and most of the *Chronicle* staff was winding down doing holiday shopping and planning for the newspaper's big Christmas party. Some were even spending their expected holiday bonuses on the currently popular game, Simon, a memory game in which players had to repeat colored lights patterns, assuming they could find one in stock somewhere.

Devlin intended to hear what his team had unearthed in their first week of work. Aaron, speaking for the pair, gave a quick summary of their plan and encouraged Tom or Ximena to pass on anything that could help in their work. Tom was digging further into chemical dumping and its possible trickle-down impact on the entire state's economy. Ximena was focused on the issue of rental discrimination against recent immigrants to the Lehigh Valley.

It was a short meeting with Devlin, who suggested a conference call for the following Tuesday with another update. The managing editor wanted to begin scheduling some feature stories for upcoming Sunday editions. Putting together a calendar allowed Devlin to arrange for the necessary art and graphics for these front-page features and promotional ads. Devlin and the publishers hoped that the work of the Sunday Squad would yield new subscribers and advertisers.

Friday afternoon, Max was back at the Nesquehoning office when Aaron Grant called. Grant was able to lock down an interview with the mayor the following Wednesday. The appointment was to include lunch at Donahue's private dining room with Joe Taylor also on the menu. Taylor, who spoke to Grant to arrange the logistics, asked if Max and Aaron could provide a list of topics or questions they wanted to cover. Grant relayed the request to Max, who thought to himself, *Like hell we will*, but instead said the two would put together some fairly nonspecific angles for their upcoming lunch.

Taylor's request signaled a bright red flag to Max. Other than major celebrities or sports stars with agents wanting to protect their golden geese, it's rare for reporters to be asked to submit their queries in advance. While it wasn't Max or Aaron's aim to catch Mayor Donahue off guard, the notion of giving an interview questions in advance makes for a less-than-spontaneous dialogue.

No more than a minute after Max ended his call with Aaron, the phone rang. The caller was Doug Finkle of the *State-Journal Register*, the newspaper of record in Springfield, Illinois. Max had lobbed a call into Finkle, hoping to get some background on Donahue from his days as a city councilman in the Illinois capital city. Like any seasoned reporter, Finkle's guard was up and wondered why Max was interested in some minor political figure who left town more than two decades ago.

"Thanks for returning my call," Max said, summoning up as much collegial warmth as possible. "Mark Donahue is a popular figure here in Allentown, and we're doing a feature on his success in getting companies to relocate here. I was just wondering if there was anything you might add on background that would show how he developed his business acumen," Max said.

"Business acumen," Finkle responded. "I guess that's one way of putting it. He wasn't exactly run out of town on a rail, but there were some issues with Donahue and a fellow city councilperson, if memory serves. Sylvia McGrath, I seem to recall, was her name. Anyway, after a few days of speculation, the whole matter disappeared. The reporters digging into the story always suspected a payoff. Most of us believed he moved away to save his marriage," Finkle added. "While you're at it, you may want to check into his car dealership. That's about all I am comfortable saying."

There was a long pause as Max was scribbling notes as fast as possible. For a moment, Finkle thought they were disconnected before Max responded, thanking his fellow journalist for his time and assistance.

Max was scheduled to work Saturday, but being so close to Christmas, it would be a slow news day. Saturday night, there were two *Chronicle* holiday parties—one for the reporters and staff at the bureau at six, with an eight o'clock celebration at the Hotel Pennsylvania in Allentown for all *Chronicle* employees.

The party in Nesquehoning was very low key, given the events that led to the retirement of Ray Tomjanovich. Many of the support staff and those in circulation and advertising were unaware of the circumstances under which Ray left. Still, the rumors led all to believe it was a family matter.

At seven fifteen, Max excused himself to drive down to the *Chronicle* party in Allentown, which was certain to be a lively and festive affair. Max was not much for these social events, but he felt he needed to make an appearance given his new, high-profile assignment. Earlier in the day, he asked Sue if she would like to go with him. No sooner were the words out of his mouth than she answered in the affirmative.

"It's a date," she said with a laugh.

Max was surprised at how much he enjoyed the Allentown celebration at the Hotel Pennsylvania. The newspaper had a good year financially as both ad revenue and circulation were on the rise. The night kicked off with a perfunctory speech from the publisher, Tim Daniels, but the three-hour affair was mostly one of good food and an open bar. Max had a Bloody Mary, which he carried around while Sue was giddy after three glasses of sparkling wine.

Sue never left Max's side, and when the night was over, they drove back to Nesquehoning, where Sue had left her car before the bureau event.

"I'm way too drunk to drive home," Sue said in a voice as soft and breathy as she could muster. "Can I stay at your place?"

"I guess so . . ." was Max's shaky response. He was unprepared for this situation. As Sue awaited a more exciting answer, Max's associative memory pulled up a series of sad past events that tugged at his heart. What did Sue expect to happen that night? What did Max want to happen?

Max and Sue got out of his car and quietly made their way up the stairs to his apartment. Sue was getting wobblier, so Max held her arm as he opened the door. That day was a rare one as Max straightened up before leaving for work and even made his bed.

"Why don't you take my bed, and I'll sleep on the couch," Max said with little conviction.

"Are you sure?" Sue responded with more than a hint of sadness in her voice.

"Yeah, I think it's for the best."

"Okay," Sue said as she turned toward the bedroom with tears running down her cheeks.

Sue was up an hour before Max and wanted to avoid the awkwardness leftover from what was generally a wonderful night. She didn't know if Max didn't find her appealing or something was going on with him, causing him anxiety in potentially intimate situations.

Too tired to delve deeper, Sue left a note thanking Max for taking her to the *Chronicle* party, kissed him on the cheek, and walked to the bureau parking lot to find her car.

Sunday, Max planned on spending his day poring over Donahue's background. Sunday afternoon, after he compiled a timeline for the mayor's political ascent, he planned on calling Aaron to discuss a strategy for their Tuesday lunch. He hoped they would finalize the questions they would offer Bull before the big event. Max also would call Barrett to put the second phase of their eavesdropping plan into action. If knowledge was power, Max hoped that Barrett could provide the fuel that would put Max and Aaron's investigation into overdrive.

Monday afternoon, Max was set to meet with Aaron in Quakertown, halfway between the Nesquehoning bureau and the *Chronicle*'s main office. The Dunkin' Donuts where Max met Barrett six weeks before seemed to be a safe place, where customers kept to themselves. While not one that was dealing with national security, their conversation had some sensitive info the two reporters would rather keep to themselves. At least, for now.

Max was seated by the window waiting for his black coffee to cool off. It was at least thirty degrees warmer inside the donut shop than outside, and the window to Max's left was coated with condensation. A vintage Chevy Camaro pulled up with some sort of gospel music pouring out of the car's open windows. The hymn continued for at least thirty seconds before Aaron

Grant turned off the engine. Max noticed Aaron was behind the wheel with his eyes closed, deeply engrossed in the music. "When the time is right," Max muttered under his breath, "I have to ask him about that music."

Grant smiled as he walked in the door. Max waved him over to his table and asked if he wanted coffee or a donut. A fresh batch of cinnamon crullers appeared from the shop's back and the scent of freshly baked—or fried—pastries filled the air.

"Nah, I'm good, but thanks," Aaron said as he sat down across from Max. "So, whatcha got?"

"A few things. First, I sent over a list of topics to Joe Taylor that we might cover tomorrow. The questions I sent are softballs about his many accomplishments. And while the list is sort of bogus, it keeps him from thinking we're going to launch into a verbal assault.

"Second, I have been talking to some folks from Springfield—you know, where Donahue lived before he moved here—and what I learned is more than revealing. A reporter from the local paper hinted there was something fishy about the mayor's auto business. Although he wasn't specific, it was enough to raise suspicion."

"This sounds good," Grant said, rubbing his palms together in expectation.

"I called the Better Business Bureau, and they told me there was a suit against Donahue's car dealership. It had something to do with not paying off a customer's existing loan when they had a trade-in. It became a small class action suit and cost Donahue $65,000."

"I guess that's something," Grant replied with a look of disappointment. "A shady car dealer? That's not news."

"Wait, there's one more thing. There was a rumor that one of the reasons Donahue left Illinois had to do with some woman he saw on the side while he was a city councilman. That gives a bit of credence to something my editor at the bureau told me related to him carrying on with a secretary that led to an under-the-table settlement."

"I don't know, Max," Grant responded. "We have the car dealership thing and some rumors. That's not much to go on, and certainly not enough ammo to catch Donahue off guard at our lunch. Let me tell you what I have, Max," Grant added. "The construction company that was hired to do the remodeling of the toy company that moved here is run by one of Donahue's largest contributors. I found this out through another reporter at the *Chronicle* who covered the groundbreaking.

"Craig Gentile, head of the construction company, is a bigwig in the Lehigh Valley Democratic Party. The word is, he's backing Donahue to run against Shapp in the next gubernatorial primary."

"That's some great stuff," Max said, grinning ear to ear. While he chose to work with Aaron through a process of elimination, he knew Grant was the real deal . . . and more.

In the heart of downtown, Allentown City Hall was built in 1962 for a cost of $3.1 million by Everett Associates, a local architectural firm. The brick-façade building is made up of six floors with the mayor's office on the top floor. The top floor also houses the office of the police chief, Charles Van Dyke. Between the mayor and police chief's office are several conference rooms and a large banquet hall used to entertain high-ranking visitors. That day, it was set up for a white-tablecloth lunch with four chairs.

Max and Aaron sat outside the banquet hall, waiting for their hosts. The meeting was called for one thirty, and the two reporters were a few minutes early. A short, matronly looking assistant to the mayor asked the two guests to take a seat as Donahue and Taylor were just wrapping up some city business.

The chairs turned out to be plush leather wingback chairs far nicer than either man could afford for their homes. Max sat with his briefcase on his lap and stared off into space. It may not have been the best time for introspection, but Max couldn't help but rewind the clock. It had been four months since Max left his parents' house in Philadelphia and moved to Nesquehoning. From a city of close to three million people to a township of 3,300. The change was bigger than a relocation; it was a do-or-die time for Max if he wanted to fulfill his goal of being a star newspaper columnist for a major daily. It was do-or-die time for a man whose life experience and personal growth had been limited to four years living in a college dorm where his emotional state had more ebbs than flows.

Reflecting on that first day of work, when he nervously walked from his car to the office, Max remembered that moment when he knew that to succeed, he would have to leave the past behind with all its doubts and fears. From that warm August afternoon that marked his first day of work up until the current moment when he was sitting by the mayor's office, Max felt proud of how he had grown as a person on the cusp of a major investigative story. What Max realized was that, like so many others, his life was ruled by varied emotions that fight with one another for control. In the past four months, his usual feeling of vulnerability and loneliness had been overtaken by one of strength and confidence. It was not as if moments of sadness and weakness had disappeared; but in the battle between personal strength and weakness, the good guys were winning.

Max returned to earth when the mayor and his *gendarme* approached the banquet room, where the two reporters were seated. Max and Aaron got up to greet their hosts, shaking hands and trading opening pleasantries. The mayor led the others into the room where lunch was to be served. Max was surprised by the degree of formality when he noticed place cards with names were located by each place setting. Max and Aaron were to be seated across from one another.

As Max pulled out his chair to sit, he found a package on his seat, wrapped neatly with a blue bow. Aaron, too, had a gift waiting on his seat, albeit in a smaller package. Aaron and Max traded curious glances across the table, wondering about this unusual gesture.

"Guys, open your gifts," Mayor Donahue said, gushing with warmth. "These were specially selected for you."

Max went first. In the box was a 1978 Phillies yearbook autographed by Mike Schmidt, Greg Luzinski, and relief pitcher Tug McGraw. Aaron then opened his box to find the record album, "How Great Thou Art," a classic gospel recording from Elvis Presley. This rare Elvis LP was out of print and considered a rare collector's album.

The *Chronicle* had a strict policy on reporters receiving gifts of any sort, but the rule stated the gift could not be worth more than twenty-five dollars. The Phillies yearbook had a five-dollar price tag, and the Elvis album, even rare, was not worth close to twenty-five dollars.

"I don't know what to say," Max told the men seated on either side of him. "I went to my first Phillies game when I was six and have been a fan ever since. You sure know how to make a great first impression."

Across the table, Aaron was shaking with emotion. He was trying to reach for the right words, but all that could come out was a weak "Thanks. I love Elvis's gospel music."

The meal was served, and the small talk took over. Mayor Donahue did most of the talking while his sidekick listened intently, quietly eating the small salad placed in front of him. Taylor appeared to be making detailed mental notes as if he were looking for points in the conversation that could provide him clues about the two *Chronicle* reporters' intent. Using Taylor's research, two office interns were sent shopping for the perfect gifts that reflected careful personal research. Bull's brilliantly subtle goal was to let Max and Aaron know how easy it was to find out details about their lives.

After serving the main course, the two waiters disappeared for good. The conversation was about to get serious, and the pair of servers were sent to the kitchen by Taylor with a wave of his hand. Coffee and a tray of Christmas cookies were waiting for the four men back in the mayor's office. The deputy mayor stood, and Max was struck with the imposing nature of the man they called Bull. He was Max's height at six foot two, but easily thirty pounds heavier and all muscle. Max was not intimidated but knew he had to choose his words carefully when they adjourned to Donahue's office.

The mayor's office was decorated in muted holiday cheer with a real miniature tree off to the side. A few ornaments adorned the tree, but a large star sat on top that seemed too large given the smallish evergreen. A half dozen presents were alongside the tree, waiting for the last workday before the holiday to be unwrapped. Max wondered if those gifts were as thoughtfully selected as his yearbook and Aaron's Elvis masterpiece.

Donahue's secretary—the same woman who earlier told Max and Aaron where to wait for lunch—came into Donahue's office and poured coffee into four cups without asking. A cloud of tension filled the room as the mayor and Aaron reached for a cookie at the same time. Breaking the ice, Taylor initiated the post-lunch talk.

"So, I understand the two of you have been doing some homework for the story you're working on," Taylor said as his boss munched on a cookie topped with a likeness of Santa done in red icing. "Why don't you tell me what you're looking for, and maybe I can help you?"

Even though Aaron was the more experienced of the two reporters, he was caught off guard. Long before lunch was over, Max came to realize the whole afternoon had been well orchestrated—the gifts, the seating arrangement, and even the use of the mayor's office for the possibly contentious interview. Max was ready, with his game face on, to get down to business.

"Mayor Donahue, I want to talk a bit about your time in Springfield, if that's okay," Max said to kick things off. "I understand you ran a car dealership and were active in local politics."

Mark Donahue exchanged glances with Joe Taylor, who sat with arms crossed to the right of Max. As with lunch, Max and Aaron were across from each other while the mayor sat at the head of a long rectangular table. Aaron, looking for visual cues, watched Taylor while Max addressed Donahue directly.

"That was a long time ago," the mayor answered. "How is that relevant to a story on my work in bolstering the business climate in Allentown?"

Max stumbled for a reply. "Mr. Mayor, if I might add," Grant interjected, "we had heard through some folks in Springfield that you had some issues with a lawsuit involving your car dealership. With that as background, it leads me to wonder about some of the questions regarding your convincing companies to move their headquarters."

Before the mayor could respond, Taylor took over the conversation. Earning his nickname Bull, the deputy mayor shot his cuffs and sat up ramrod straight in his chair, striking a posture anyone would consider imposing. It was clear who was in charge, and questions or topics not submitted in advance were out of bounds for the interview.

"Gentlemen, there wasn't anything about Mark Donahue's time in Springfield on the list of things you wanted to talk about," Bull said, trying to calm things down. Before resorting to less direct ways of dealing with nosy reporters, Taylor wanted to try the sensible approach. Other options would always be available if the situation warranted.

"We think the topic is appropriate to shed light on whether the mayor brought some of his less-than-ethical tactics to bear in his redevelopment plans," Max replied, tag-teaming with Aaron. "I think it's a fair question if we are to paint an accurate picture of Mayor Donahue."

While Max, Aaron, and Joe Taylor sparred, the mayor tried to look busy, staring at his leather Day-Timer but hanging on every word. He looked up at his second in command and quietly nodded his head.

"You know, this interview is over," Taylor said as he rose from his chair. "The mayor has an important meeting with his staff. I want to let you know how much we enjoyed meeting you both. Any further questions you have can be directed to me."

With that, the man they called Bull strode to the door and ushered Max and Aaron to the outer office. "Thanks again for coming," he said to the two reporters with a shit-eating grin. He turned, went back into the mayor's office, and firmly closed the door.

The meeting in the mayor's office did not go well. In what seemed the blink of an eye, Max found himself sitting behind the wheel, too angry to turn the key in the ignition. *"What was that?"* Max said out loud, the chill of the cold afternoon air turning his breath into steam. Before he could head back to the bureau, he had to make sense of the last twenty-five minutes. He remembered drinking coffee and posing a simple question to the mayor.

As he started unscrambling the afternoon's odd events, Max was attempting to understand the narrative of the story he saw unfold. Perhaps he had to take some blame for the way the meeting went by starting with questions about the mayor's past in Springfield instead of his recent accomplishment in Allentown. Now, it seems, it was time to call in the big guns and get Barrett to eavesdrop on the mayor and his handler. Several pieces were missing from this story, and he was determined to learn the truth one way or the other.

Back in the mayor's office, Mark Donahue sat behind his desk, a bit shaken by the *Chronicle* reporters' interaction. What started off to be a pleasant lunch, he thought, sure turned ugly quickly.

Nonplussed, Joe Taylor raised his hand to stop the mayor from fretting.

"Listen, Mark. I'm here for a reason. I will take care of this, so you have nothing to worry about. All you need to know is that when it comes to gathering dirt, I'm the best of the best."

The mayor smiled and let out a sigh of relief. "I think I know what you have planned. I don't want to know anything about it . . . but you have my blessing."

Chapter Fourteen

Barrett looked out of place as he walked into the lobby of Allentown's city hall at 10 a.m. two days after Max and Aaron's disastrous meeting with the mayor. He was wearing a second-hand janitor's uniform and a heavy woolen outer coat. The winter coat was gray, a top-of-the-line Burberry that the ex-attorney bought when he went on a ski weekend two years ago in Vermont. Barrett never actually got on skis, but he loved the chalet's fireplace and won five hundred dollars hustling guests at backgammon. The coat was a reminder that, while he'd never go skiing again, it was nice separating so-called backgammon experts from their cash.

As Barrett entered the lobby, he spotted a woman sitting on one of the benches in the middle of the main floor. Max had described Sue perfectly, and while Sue and Barrett had never met before in person, they briefly spoke the night before to review plans for the planting of the FM transmitter.

Sue got up as Barrett approached and was all smiles. Max had called her Tuesday night and given her a recap of that day's bizarre events. She listened intently and asked her friend how she could help.

"If you're serious, I want you to call my friend Barrett," Max told her Tuesday night. "He's the point man for this project. I am sure he'd love to have your help, and I think you'll like him—he's a shorter version of me."

After recognizing each other in the lobby, they shook hands, and both noticed that at five-foot-six, Sue was face-to-face with Max's lifelong friend. In his mid-twenties, Barrett knew that he would not have another growth spurt, so being short was his destiny. He always said that being vertically challenged had its advantages, but he'd yet to discover one to that point in time.

The plan was simple: Barrett would put an "Out of Order" sign on the middle elevator and work on placing the surveillance device behind the billboard at the back of the structure. Barrett had the sign, the transmitter, a soldering iron, and a steel wool pad to clean up any excess solder in his satchel. While Barrett performed his duties, Sue would stand guard and tune in the transistor radio Max bought for her the day before.

Everyone agreed on using 92.9 FM for this undercover mission. The trick was finding a spot on the dial far enough away from other local radio stations to avoid interference. The placement of the device and Sue's observation went smoothly. Less than twenty minutes after Barrett arrived, the job was done, and the two spies for the day left city hall, said their goodbyes, and went on their way.

Max arranged with Sue to take the first eavesdropping shift. The mayor and Joe Taylor left for lunch daily at 12:20 p.m. on the dot. Max knew this from his one thirty lunch meeting on Tuesday. He remembered asking Donahue's secretary if it was customary for her boss to eat lunch so late. She indicated that Donahue and Taylor left the office for lunch at that time nearly every day.

Sue had an hour to kill. She walked two blocks over to the *Chronicle* office, flashed her badge, and walked up the stairs to the newsroom. She found an empty desk and called Max to let him know that the Max-Barrett-Sue caper was in progress.

At precisely twelve twenty, Joe Taylor pushed the down button for the middle elevator on the city hall's top floor. Standing to his right was a man in his early thirties of medium build and closely cropped hair; not Mayor Donahue. The doors swung open, and the pair quietly entered the forty-two-square-foot chamber. The door closed, and the two men were alone.

"So, from what I gather, his landlord and downstairs neighbors don't much like him," Taylor said to the man he carefully recruited for a specific task. "I have seen pictures of his place, and there's only one phone, and it's in the kitchen."

Taylor's accomplice stood quietly, hanging on every word. He nodded his head, indicating he heard the instructions loud and clear. Paul Revere, the man who would later be identified by his code name, walked off the elevator toward the exit while Taylor stood by its closing doors. Revere had a limited window to get his job done, and he wasn't one to waste time.

Revere walked past a woman sitting on a bench with an earpiece plugged into a new Zenith transistor radio on his way to the exit. Max's previous intelligence was spot on, and Sue turned on the radio at twelve fifteen and waited for the broadcast on 92.9 FM to start. She heard every word of the discussion between Joe Taylor and the shady-looking individual who walked by her on the way to some nefarious task. Putting together the overheard conversational puzzle pieces, Sue knew Joe Taylor was sending Paul Revere to bug Max's telephone.

Sue didn't want to wait to return to Nesquehoning to warn Max, so she dashed over to the *Chronicle* building and looked for an empty conference room with a telephone. She found one by the newspaper's library, which was used for reporters wanting to do quiet research. The lights were off, so Sue took it to mean it was unoccupied, and since she wouldn't need the room for more than a few minutes, she knew she was safe.

Max was in the office and picked up on the second ring. Given the time, he suspected it was Sue but didn't expect to have any information from their transmitter stakeout so soon.

Sue spoke softly. "Max," she said, "have you ever see the *Mad* magazine cartoon 'Spy vs. Spy'?"

"Okay, I'll bite. Yes, I have."

"Well, that's what we have going on. Joe Taylor is sending someone to your apartment to bug your telephone. I found this out from our bug in the city hall elevator."

It took Max a few seconds to comprehend Sue's statement. He was in disbelief.

"What? I find that hard to believe. How do you know this?"

"Taylor described your apartment to this guy who looked like an ex-military officer and told him where your phone was located. I know it's you because Taylor told this man that your landlord and downstairs neighbors don't like you."

That detail further rattled Max. Finding those sorts of personal details was unnerving. Sure, the landlord wasn't his biggest fan, and the older Pennsylvania Dutch couple below him didn't like him running up the stairs, but how does someone get that information?

"What do you think I should do?" Max asked Sue.

"I know one thing," she said, raising her voice slightly. "Don't make any calls from your house that you don't want to be spied on."

"You know," Max said, gathering his wits. "Your reference to 'Spy vs. Spy' is perfect. That gives me an idea."

Max deliberately stayed at the bureau to give Bull's right-hand man time to place the bug on his home phone. He planned to double-cross Taylor and his cohort. He called his parents from the office and told them there was some work being done on his apartment building, and all the phones would be out of order for a few days. Max then called Barrett and told him about the plan to set a trap for Taylor and his helper. The idea was to let Taylor think he was pulling a fast one, but Max would use his ruse to dispense false information. Max added that they should hold off bugging the federal building until this countermove played out. That ploy, Max assumed, would provide some clear runway to complete the investigation.

It was a perfect plan except for the fact that Joe Taylor was two steps ahead of Max. Max didn't know that Taylor and his helper were more than a fixer and a suspicious errand boy. The two men met in the early sixties when both were stationed in Poland during the Cold War. The naïve reporter didn't realize that he was up against real spies and that Joe Taylor was far more than the mayor's fixer. Until Mark Donahue first ran for mayor, the Springfield, Illinois transplant had never met or even heard of Joe Taylor. For reasons that Donahue never knew, Taylor came with his initial campaign supporters. At a Lehigh Valley Democratic fundraiser, Bill Hinke, the then-head of the party, introduced Donahue to Taylor and said that Joe would be a big asset to his run for office. After that day, Taylor was by Donahue's side whether the mayor wanted him there or not.

Unaware of his more-than-worthy opponent, Max went into action. Sue had just returned to Nesquehoning from her shift in the city hall. Max wheeled his chair across the office's aisle and put his hand on her shoulder, indicating he had something personal to share.

"Since we spoke after you left the city hall, I put together a scheme. I will make a bunch of calls from my home that will throw Taylor off the scent. I'd like to call you first. All you need to do is play along."

Max left the office and drove the few miles to his home. As he pulled into his assigned parking space, Max looked for a van or truck used to monitor his phone calls. Not a single car, van, truck, or even scooter was in sight, leaving Max puzzled about how they would listen to his phone calls in real-time. Nonetheless, he was set to move forward with his first fake phone call.

Remembering the issue with his downstairs neighbors, Max went slowly up the stairs to his apartment. His footsteps were measured as if he were walking a tightrope between two skyscrapers. He opened the door, put his coat on a chair by the door, and made a beeline to the phone.

"Hi Sue, this is Max. Did I catch you at a good time?"

"I have a couple of minutes. What's up?"

"So, you know I'm working on this story about the mayor for the new Sunday feature section, right?"

"Yes, it's all you've talked about."

"Well, I have hit a dead end. I have nothing, and I'm going to have to dump the story. I am going to meet with Aaron later today because he has nothing either."

"I'm sorry. I know how much you've put into it. Do you want help coming up with another feature idea? I have one or two that might work."

"Let me meet with Aaron and get his take. How about a beer after work?"

Paul Revere was parked two blocks away from Max's house. He got a good laugh out of Max's charade and couldn't wait to return to Allentown and tell Joe Taylor. This caper, if you could call it that, was nothing compared to some of the stunts Revere and Taylor pulled off in their service to their country.

On his ride back to Allentown, Paul Revere was surprised that he and Bull were able to fool Max so easily into believing that their elevator stunt was successful. Revere chuckled to himself at the bad acting on Max's call to Sue, pretending he didn't know his phone was bugged. *This kid isn't as sharp as Joe thinks*, Paul Revere thought to himself.

To Max, unaware he was losing the Spy vs. Spy game, things were falling into place. The fact that Joe Taylor had his phone bugged was an indication that he and Aaron were hot on the track of a story that would bring Mark Donahue down. Yes, there were some missing pieces, but Max planned to meet with Aaron on Friday afternoon to fill in the holes which would complete their investigation. While Max was playing cloak and dagger games, Aaron was off checking his sources to learn more about Donahue's involvement in political pay-for-play deals or similar types of illegal activities in Allentown.

"Timing is everything," Taylor told Paul Revere as they met in Revere's spymobile, parked down the street from city hall. It had taken Bull's partner an hour to make the normally forty-minute trip from central Carbon County back to Allentown. It was three days before Christmas, and the roads were jam-packed with working stiffs on vacation doing heavy-duty holiday shopping.

"So, what's next, Bull?" Revere asked. He left his engine running to keep the car's defroster going. The two men were trained to always be aware of their surroundings, no matter how safe things appeared. The streets were practically deserted, but even in a simple counterintelligence action—such as the one they were presently in—you never could be too careful. While Paul Revere didn't think much of Max's skills as a covert tactician, Taylor wasn't as quick to dismiss the young reporter.

"Now, we wait," Taylor explained. "At some point, given the gravity of the story, the newspaper will have to check the facts and offer Donahue the chance to refute the claims of union kickbacks. Until then, it's business as usual."

"By the way," Revere asked his long-time friend and co-conspirator, "are you going home for Christmas?"

"Nope. I'm going to spend it the same way I did in 1964, if you remember that."

"How can I forget?" Revere replied, letting out a huge sigh.

While Taylor and Revere were finishing up their debrief, Max met with Aaron Grant just a few blocks away at the *Chronicle* headquarters. Shortly after his make-believe phone call with Sue, Max drove down to Allentown, mighty pleased with what he thought was some pretty damn good Spy vs. Spy action. *Mad* magazine founders Harvey Kurtzman and William Gaines would be proud.

What Goes Up

Max and Aaron Grant found an empty conference room and spread their notes around the large round table. Grant looked over Max's notes and smiled.

"This is some great stuff," Aaron said, beaming. Max had detailed notes from follow-up conversations with reporters from the Springfield newspaper and an assortment of local Illinois politicians who spoke, on the record, about Donahue's less-than-honorable stunts.

"How about we put together a draft of the story?" Max asked. "First, let's decide whether we want to do this in a series or cover it in one big story?"

"Here's an idea," Aaron responded. "Let's cover the details related to payoffs first, and then present Devlin the option of having us expand about his Springfield issues in that story or make it into two or three parts?"

"Works for me."

Max and Aaron pounded away on typewriters they brought into the conference room from the newspaper's supply closet for the next two hours. They were not IBM Selectrics, but they were more than adequate to get the job done. Every twenty minutes, the pair stopped and played "cut and paste" with their sections. That process involved physically cutting a paragraph or sections and arranging them in a cohesive order. The last part of the action was a misnomer—the assembly medium of choice was Scotch Tape.

By the time Max and Aaron were done, it was well past dinner time. Max suggested they drop off the copy in Devlin's inbox. The managing editor could get to it that evening—if he was around—or first thing in the morning. The two reporters knew the process ahead before the story could be published. It would need to be reviewed by the managing editor, the publisher, the *Chronicle*'s lawyer, and then offered to Donahue for a chance to rebut or clarify anything that would go into print.

Max was glad he and Aaron would get a chance to have a meal together. Max wanted to get to know his new partner better. There also was this question about Grant's love for Elvis's gospel recordings. Max knew Elvis's hits like "Hound Dog," "Jailhouse Rock," and his favorite, "Return to Sender," but when it came to gospel music, Max had zero knowledge.

The two men drove over to the Paddock, a restaurant/bar known only to locals. Grant said he'd never heard of it despite living in the area for several years. Max explained that it was a favorite haunt of his when he was in college because he loved their thin-crust pizza. It was also where Max and a few friends watched the Ali/Ken Norton fight in 1973, so the place held a special spot in his heart.

Max nursed a Ballentine Beer and shared a large pepperoni pizza with Grant. Aaron had a Yuengling and ordered a side of chili. He explained to Max that a man is only as good as his ability to make great chili down in Alabama, so he wanted to see if the Paddock was up to the challenge.

The night was cut short as Grant remembered he had some last-minute holiday shopping to finish, and he was running out of shopping days. He told Max he was married and had a nine-year-old son who was getting into football in a big way. Grant said he wanted to buy Aaron Jr. (Bud, his nickname) his first pair of football cleats to play pee-wee football.

Max drank about two ounces of his beer, so he was safe getting home. There wasn't much to his liking on the car radio two days before Christmas, so he listened to Bob Seger's *Stranger in Town* at full volume in his car's 8-track player. Max was in a good mood, sensing accolades on the horizon for another job well done. "We've Got Tonite" was just finishing when he pulled into his designated spot at his apartment building.

It was blistering cold when Max opened the entry door and gingerly walked up the stairs into his second-floor unit. Even though he was off the day before Christmas, he planned on driving down to Allentown on Christmas Eve day to talk to Jack Devlin in person about the draft of his and Aaron's story. After a long and tiring day, Max fell asleep shortly after his head hit the pillow.

The bank sign on Catawissa Street on the outskirts of Nesquehoning read twenty-four degrees as Max passed by on his way to meet with the managing editor the next day. He picked up right where he left off on Bob Seger's hit album with "Hollywood Nights," "Still the Same," and "Old Time Rock 'n' Roll," guiding him along his route to Allentown. With no traffic, he reached his destination in record time.

Jack Devlin was at his desk wearing what looked to be the grand prize winner in a local Ugly Christmas Sweater competition.

"Max, you and Aaron knocked it out of the park," Devlin said as Max approached his desk. "We want to take our time and give the series all the promotion it deserves."

Even with some recent successes, Max was still terrible at reacting to compliments.

"When do you think you'll run it?" the young reporter asked.

"Hmm. Well, as you know, it has to go through internal review, and then we have to offer the mayor a copy to respond. I was thinking of sending it over there today. Even though his office is officially closed, I have it on good authority that Donahue is around today."

"So, do you think it will make this Sunday?"

"Here's what I'm thinking," Devlin responded, putting his managing editor hat on. "January 7 is the first Sunday next year. We can begin teasing it several days before to get it the attention it deserves."

"That sounds terrific," Max said, slightly underenthused. He was ready for instant gratification and wanted to see it in the following Sunday paper, this weekend. But, realistically, he knew with the holiday and the need for mayoral review, that was not going to happen.

"Have a great holiday," Devlin said to Max as the younger man turned toward the doors that led to the *Chronicle* parking lot.

Max planned to see his parents the next day to spend the holiday with them and his sister. The myth that Jewish people celebrated Christmas by eating Chinese food was not true with the Rosens. Max hated Chinese food and preferred it when his mother made something like a brisket or roast for such occasions. This Christmas Eve, Max planned to cook a frozen lasagna and watch the Sixers play the Knicks at Madison Square Garden. Max was still living off the high of the 76ers 1976–1977 season when the team made it to the NBA Finals, only to lose to the Portland Trailblazers.

After a Sixers win, 109–94, Max cleaned up from dinner and was about to get ready for bed. It was 11 p.m. when the doorbell rang. *It's a little early for Santa*, Max joked to himself. He had no clue who possibly could be at the door at this hour on Christmas Eve.

Max quietly walked down the stairs in case his neighbors below were asleep. With condensation on the window, he couldn't make out who was there, but he could tell it was a man, and a big one at that.

"May I come in," the man standing outside said, stating rather than asking.

There stood Joe Taylor looking more menacing than ever. It was in Max's best interest to comply.

Max led Bull up the stairs and into his apartment. Taylor closed the door behind him.

"Wanted to let you know we got a copy of your story," Taylor said matter-of-factly. "I thought it was best to come to talk to you in person."

Even at the same height, Max was physically and emotionally dwarfed by Taylor's presence.

"Okay," Max said.

At that moment, Taylor reached into the pocket of his tan camelhair coat and pulled out something that he wrapped around his right hand. He then opened his hand, and there in Taylor's palm sat the FM transmitter that Barrett had placed in the middle elevator in Allentown's city hall.

With a smirk of victory on his face, the next words out of Taylor's mouth nearly caused Max to faint: "I believe this belongs to you."

Chapter Fifteen

"Listen. Tell your friend, or whoever it was, that if you're going to pose as a janitor or maintenance man, it's smart not to wear a thousand-dollar coat while doing it," Taylor said with more than a hint of laughter. "Kid, you'd better sit down. Let me get you a glass of water."

Max was getting ready for bed when the surprise knock at the door came. He was in one of the oversized T-shirts he wore to bed but was still in his corduroy pants. He backed up and sat down on the couch, taking the glass of water from Joe Taylor. Taylor chose to stand to maintain his frightening presence.

"Did someone tip you off about the device in the elevator?" Max weakly offered.

"Between the guy in the rich man's coat and the woman with the transistor radio, the guard on duty was suspicious. He called up to me, and I took care of the rest. Without going into details, when it comes to Cold War surveillance, I am lightyears ahead of you and your buddies."

Taylor continued, taking off his coat and draping it over his arm. "I do have to hand it to you. You did fairly good for a couple of rubes. With a little work, you might be good enough to get shot in a real situation."

Taylor couldn't stop laughing at his remark. Max gulped the water as his hands shook.

"So, now what?" Max asked. "Are you going to call the publisher and have me fired . . . or maybe you're going to have me arrested. Which is it?"

"Neither, kid. A lot is going on that you don't know and probably won't ever know. But for now, what you're going to do is kill that story. Or, better yet, tell that Devlin guy you need more time because you found out some new information."

"What sort of information?"

"That's not important. Just make sure that story doesn't run on January 7, as your managing editor said. This thing here," Taylor said, holding up the small FM transmitter, "this is my sword of Damocles hanging over your head. You know that story, right?"

Max nodded.

"Okay, I'll be on my way. I think you know that I'm a serious man who doesn't make idle threats. Just keep up your end, and it will all be fine."

With that, Taylor lumbered down the stairs, possibly rattling the china closet of the downstairs neighbors. Intentional or not, it was a nice touch.

It took Max a good hour to process the last twenty minutes of his life. Could he go from screwup to the hero and back to screwup all in two months? He knew there was more at stake than his job here. Max had no idea what sort of bullshit he could hand Jack Devlin to put the story on hold. He was heading home to see his parents first thing in the morning. Two days away might give him time to come up with a solution.

It was rainy and windy, and thirty degrees, as Max drove to Philadelphia on Christmas morning. Instead of taking the turnpike, he drove on Route 309 south from Nesquehoning and Allentown through Bucks County. Eventually, 309 turned into County Line Road, a straight shot to his parents' home. The only place open at 8 a.m. was a gas station in Richland, where he stopped to get a lukewarm cup of black coffee. The rancid joe did little to brighten Max's outlook on the day, and to be honest, he was going home because he promised his parents he'd show for the second night of Hanukkah. His mom and dad were also anxious to hear everything about his new assignment with the Sunday Squad.

Max pulled into the driveway of his parents' home a little bit before ten. Max's mother parked her bright yellow Volvo in the garage, so the driveway was clear. While Max never gave it more than a passing thought, his father did not drive and was never inclined to learn. His parents were a one-car couple, which became somewhat of a challenge after moving away from Oxford Circle, where public transportation was more widely available. After turning off the engine, Max realized he drove the entire forty-eight miles with the radio off and his 8-track player silent. It was going to be that kind of day.

Walking up the two flights of stairs to the house, Max took a deep breath and tried to focus on putting on a happy face. At that point, he had decided not to tell his parents the details of his current calamity. With sympathy would come advice and possibly admonishment. He was looking for neither and hoping to make a clean getaway on the twenty-seventh.

Max pulled out his key and opened the door. He heard his mother on the phone in the kitchen, talking either to his sister or her sister. When she realized Max was home, his mother hung up the phone and rushed to greet him at the door. He gave her a perfunctory hug and kiss on the cheek.

Instead of saying "Welcome home" or "We're glad to see you," the first words out of her mouth were, as always, to the point: "What's wrong?" she said, holding her son's shoulders at arm's length. "I know something's wrong."

"Nothing. Nothing's wrong," Max responded with little conviction. "It's just that I'm tired and have a lot on my mind."

Max had a lengthy history of not being able to safely extract himself from these encounters. He was hungry, wanted a strong cup of coffee, and wanted to be left alone.

"Can we talk about it later, please?" Max pleaded.

Max's mother didn't reply. Instead, she walked a few steps to their open kitchen and put together a hearty breakfast for her son. As Max dug into a plate of home fried potatoes and scrambled eggs, Harold Rosen came into the kitchen. The senior Rosen kissed his son on the top of his head and sat down across the kitchen table. Harold was not a coffee drinker, instead opting for a glass of V8 juice.

"I didn't hear you come in," Harold Rosen said between sips. Max's mother served her husband the same breakfast, adding a piece of rye toast to the plate. As she placed the dish in front of him, she whispered something into her husband's ear.

"Listen, I'm finished," Max said, clearly not in the mood for any sort of family discussion about his career. "I'm going downstairs to look for the winter coat that I left here."

Max's mother was about to say something, but Harold raised his hand toward his wife, indicating it was best to let their son go to the basement and think things through. Looking for his coat, which was actually in an upstairs closet, was just an excuse to be alone.

The Rosens' five-year-old home was a duplex with a good-sized basement. When Max was in college, and then later in graduate school, it was his domain. A large oak desk faced a picture window looking out at the backyard, and a red and gold sofa—a relic from their previous home—sat against a wall on the right side of the room.

Max remembered everything he ever wrote on the monstrosity of a desk at the bottom of the stairs that sat thirty feet straight ahead. His first paycheck was a hundred dollars for an op-ed he wrote on the future of media that ran in the *Hartford Courant* just one year before. He sent the finished piece to thirty newspapers, never expecting to get a single bite. But, when the *Courant* accepted his work, Max knew he had found his calling. That op-ed was part of a portfolio his mother had put together of everything he had published, including the series on chemical dumping for the *Chronicle* that put him on the map.

Max sat down at the desk and lifted the protective sleeve that sat on the IBM Selectric—the same kind he used at work—and remembered how that electric typewriter changed his life. He reached down and opened the large file cabinet drawer and pulled out a folder overflowing with paper. Each piece of paper was a rejection letter from a newspaper Max had applied for full-time work. There were a hundred sheets in all, but on sheet number one hundred—the last one in the stack—was the *Chronicle*'s response offering him an interview for a full-time job.

The nostalgia hour wrapped up as Max reached for the phone that sat on the far corner of the desk. He had two calls to make, both to people he knew should be home and available Christmas Day, as they were Jewish.

"Hey Barrett," Max said, with anger rising in his voice. "What kind of idiot wears a luxury winter coat over a janitor's uniform to pull off a clandestine operation?"

"Merry Christmas to you too," Barrett replied, none too happy about the reprimand. "You weren't there. It was freakin' cold, and there was no heat in the lobby of City Hall."

"Well, thanks to you, I am in deep shit. I don't want to talk about it over the phone. I am home today and tomorrow. Let me see how today goes, and I'll get back to you."

"Whatever. Happy Hanukah," Barrett replied with deep sarcasm and hung up.

Max's next call was to Norm Weiss, his friend who used his legal prowess to throw the book at Anderson Trucking for its chemical dumping role.

Norm was not home, so Max left a brief message on his friend's answering machine asking him to call back as the matter was urgent and private.

Max sat on the red couch in the basement that graced the previous Rosen house for many years before his parents moved to this new home. This family heirloom of sorts was long enough for Max to stretch out and sleep, which he had done on more than one occasion. Those were memories not worth digging up, so Max went back upstairs just as he heard the front door open, signifying the arrival of his sister, Nancy.

Even if he was unwilling to acknowledge it, the day of family togetherness did him a lot of good. Max and Nancy talked about their all-time favorite Hanukkah gifts—Max's was his first Strat-O-Matic baseball board game while Nancy's was the *Sgt. Pepper's Lonely Hearts Club Band* album right after it came out in 1967. Neither sibling grasped the meaning of the songs or their social implications, but given that The Beatles were the soundtrack of their youth, they just loved the music.

Before a dinner of corned beef, oven-roasted potatoes, fresh string beans, and salad, Max wanted to call Barrett and apologize to him for his earlier outburst.

"Now what did I do?" Barrett answered, half-joking.

"I'm sorry about before. When I tell you the entire story, you'll understand why I was so angry. What are you doing tomorrow?"

"I was thinking about going to Atlantic City to play blackjack, but I think I'm banned from most of the casinos," Barrett replied, boasting about his notoriety.

"How about we meet for lunch before you go? My treat."

"Sure, why don't you grab some Chinese food and bring it over," Barrett said, knowing all too well his lifelong friend hated every type of Asian cuisine.

"Funny guy. I'll surprise you."

Before dinner, the Rosens lit the candles for the second night of Hanukkah. It was Max's job to recite the blessings. His mother's usual comment was she wanted to see if the money they spent on religious school paid off. After many years of hearing the same line, Max chose to ignore the remark.

Max brought holiday gifts for his parents and sister and laid them on the dining room table. He got the new cookbook for his mother, *Julia Child & Company*, which was based on the French Chef's new TV show. He had a pouch of imported pipe tobacco for his father—something that caused his mother to shake her head—and for his sister, he bought a new cassette player.

Everyone in his family chipped in and bought Max a beautiful leather briefcase for Hanukkah. Unlike the one he had, which resembled a small suitcase, this one was made of soft imported leather and had a strap so it could be slung over his shoulder. Max loved it but couldn't help thinking about his new gift's value if he lost his job . . . or worse.

The family gathered around the living room and their new color TV and watched a rerun of *M*A*S*H*, followed by *WKRP in Cincinnati*. Afterward, Nancy said her goodbyes, and the Rosens—who considered 10 p.m. the middle of the night—got ready for bed. Max said goodnight to his parents and thanked them for the gift.

Once his parents left the living room, the warm spirit of the day also left. The headwinds facing Max were overwhelming, and any solution to avoid the wrath of Joe Taylor while fulfilling his commitment to the newspaper seemed out of reach. Max got up from the living room couch and did something most would consider odd that gave him comfort in times of stress—he sat down in the corner between the living room and dining room with his back flush against the wall.

With Taylor holding Max's future in his hands, the young reporter felt scared and vulnerable. Fighting against that object panic was a conflicting feeling of strength and power that inspired him. In what amounted to an episode of fight or flight, Max decided it was time to get beyond the looming, palpable threat and use his brain and courage to beat the odds. He would find a chink in Taylor's armor and be the co-author of a tremendous story of greed and corruption.

For Max, his time putting himself in the corner felt like ten minutes, but it was a full hour. In the cool air of the Rosen house—his parents rarely turned the heat on—Max was soaked with sweat. It was as if his inner engine worked overtime and created a massive amount of excess heat.

After a brief shower, Max crawled into bed with a plan—at least the framework of a plan. He would need to meet with Barrett and Norm Weiss to fill in some of the gaps. If things went his way, Max would head back to Nesquehoning on the twenty-seventh with a course of action. He did not have any other choice.

There were some loose ends to tie up when he got back to Carbon County. Max had to come up with an explanation to Jack Devlin about delaying the story, and then there was the heads-up for his reporting partner Aaron Grant. That could be tricky; Max wanted to tell him the truth, or some version of it. And then there was Sue. Max wasn't sure what to tell her since she was spotted in the city hall lobby. Max put a Sue update at the bottom of his pile of major issues for at least the current moment.

After breakfast with his parents the morning after Christmas, Max said he had plans to visit Barrett before lunch. His parents had known Barrett for as long as their son had and considered the former-attorney-turned-hustler a good man and loyal friend to Max. Max's mom and dad told Max to send Barrett their regards.

Max stopped at Brooklyn Bagels on Bustleton Avenue and picked up a dozen assorted, a small amount of lox, and some cream cheese. He knew Barrett missed Sunday breakfasts with his parents, who had left Philadelphia for Florida's sunny weather. He saw them only a few times each year, finding the wall-to-wall elderly Jewish people of Miami depressing.

There was no traffic to speak of, so it took Max only twenty-five minutes to get to Barrett's condo, which overlooked the Delaware River. With the two-bedroom place came a picturesque view of beautiful Riverton, New Jersey, a borough known for forbidding alcohol sale. Barrett got his unit before the complex was complete and was looking to sell it when the price was right.

Max knew the code to the condo building's front entrance and made his way to the top floor where Barrett lived. Max knocked on the door, and ever the wiseass, Barrett replied, "If that's the Avon Lady, I'm out of toilet water." Max's friend opened the door in hysterics, laughing at his rather lame joke.

"Hey Barrett, remember the time we saw George Kirby perform at the hotel in Puerto Rico? You couldn't get over how funny he was."

"Your point being?"

"You're no George Kirby. Don't quit your day job. Wait, you don't have a day job."

The banter was short-lived. Max and Barrett sat at the kitchen table, and Max watched while his friend devoured a poppyseed bagel with cream cheese and lox. Barrett didn't usually have much of an appetite in the mornings, but he ate this late breakfast as if he hadn't eaten in several days. While his friend munched away, Max filled him in on Taylor's Christmas Eve bombshell. Barrett put his bagel down, wiped his face with a napkin, and interrupted Max.

"Did this guy see me plant the FM transmitter in the elevator?"

"No, he didn't. Come to think of it, even if he got a call from the lobby, how did Taylor know to look for a transmitter in the elevator? There's something here we're missing regarding this guy Bull, the mayor, and this story we're planning on running."

"I have something that might help. I called my parents last night down in Miami—by the way, they send their regards—and told my dad a little bit about our little scheme," Barrett said, hoping Max wouldn't interrupt him. "My dad had a lot of political friends in Philadelphia when he was a lawyer and said the story of the mayor and his more-than-able assistant reminded him of a case from the past."

"I take it you didn't tell him about the eavesdropping, did you?"

"No, I made it seem like I was part of your investigatory work. He liked that. By the way, stop interrupting me. You're going to like this."

"Proceed, Your Highness."

"Two similar cases were going on involving FBI stings in the early seventies. One became famous, called 'Alscam,' and the other had no name but involved Congressman Teitelbaum getting money under the table. Remember him? We went to Hebrew school with his kids."

"Right. There was a daughter your mother used to call 'Nanny' because she had a face like a goat."

"My father helped Teitelbaum get a job after he was arrested for taking a bribe to help rig the bid for a new wing of Albert Einstein Hospital. He lost his congressional seat when he got caught in a low-level FBI sting. He paid a big fine but never did any jail time. Alscam—the one in which FBI agents posed as wealthy Albanian businessmen wanting to get casino licenses—got the headlines. Both were elaborate FBI stings."

"And?" Max said when he realized Barrett was done with his story.

"My dad said it's worth talking to some people who work for the mayor to see what's behind Donahue's alleged wrongdoing. Someone might be trying to set someone else up. Not sure if a third party is setting up the mayor or Taylor."

Max sat, processing everything his friend told him. He added these new threads to the massive array of events—past and present—involving Donahue, Taylor, or the Lehigh County Democratic Party. And then there are possible bribes to the recently relocated toy manufacturer and typewriter companies from local unions. Max realized he needed the assistance of a more experienced reporter to do some sorting of the facts, and he immediately knew Tex was the man for the job.

Barrett motioned Max into the living room where a Franklin Sports table hockey game sat on a table in the middle of the room, the version in which two players pulled levers back and forth to move the players and puck from end to end.

"Before you leave, we have to play one game," Barrett said with an ear-to-ear grin. "It's a relic from our youth. Remember, we used to play in my basement after I beat you in table tennis."

"Do you have the Doors album we used to listen to?"

"Glad you asked." Barrett walked over to his stereo console and flicked it on.

You know the day destroys the night
Night divides the day
Tried to run
Tried to hide
Break on through to the other side . . .

Max smiled. Some things are worth remembering.

The third night of Hanukkah is usually not a big deal in Max's family. But, with Max's recent success, his parents wanted to show their praise. His mother cooked a brisket—avoiding the traditional Jewish-style onion soup mix braise—but more like the way such things are done in Texas. While his mother had never been to Texas, she adopted the low and slow method by using an old cast iron pot and placing it on a gas grill in the backyard. Even in December, the Rosens made good use of the Weber they got as a gift when they had purchased their new home.

A dinner of moist, savory down-home style brisket and potato latkes was a nice send-off for Max. Knowing her son would be leaving early in the morning, Max's mother wrapped the leftovers for him to take back to Nesquehoning after dinner. In addition to placing the food in a brown paper shopping bag, she slipped in a note with a big red heart on it, telling him how proud she was of his work.

Max wanted to get going early on Wednesday morning, the twenty-seventh. He was up and out the door before eight o'clock while his parents were still asleep—or pretending to be asleep to save him the embarrassment of a touch-feely goodbye. Max grabbed a bagel, popped it in the toaster, and then lightly buttered it on one side to eat during his journey.

Max had stopped by his apartment to drop off his clean laundry and leftovers before making his way to the office. There were no other reporters around because, with their seniority, most had enough vacation time to take off from Christmas through New Year's. There was only one colleague Max was interested in seeing.

"Tex, sorry to bother you at home," Max said, speaking from his desk at the bureau. "I need to see you in a fairly important matter. Is there any way you can spare an hour or two for me today?"

"Well, yeah," Tex responded in a somewhat affected drawl. "My in-laws are here, and I'm looking for an excuse to get away. Where should we meet?"

Max thought for a moment. "Can we meet at my apartment around three? I can do later if that's better."

"No, my friend. Three works."

Max had three hours to make a list of all the puzzle pieces he hoped Tex could help him unravel. As a grad student, Max learned a lot about research, so he made a rough Venn Diagram with overlapping circles. Each circle had a name or action in it, such as Mayor Donahue in Springfield in one circle, Joe Taylor finds FM transmitter in another . . . and so on. At that point, Max realized he'd have to tell Tex everything that happened dating back to putting the eavesdropping device in the elevator at the Carbon county courthouse and how it led to Chris Albrecht's arrest and a prison sentence.

At two o'clock, with several sheets of legal paper in his brand-spanking-new briefcase, Max headed home, making a quick stop at Weis Market to grab some beer and snacks for his guest. Before Tex arrived, he wanted to straighten up and set up a card table in the middle of the living room. The card table was a family relic once used at family cookouts. It came with two folding chairs that Max kept in his bedroom closet for rare occasions when he had more than two guests.

Tex arrived at three o'clock on the button. He parked his luxury car a block away to avoid getting his precious wheels dinged. Tex was a man with many passions in life, but none topped his love for his BMW. Even in the dead of winter, the car was immaculately detailed, looking like it just came out of the showroom.

Tex took the steps two at a time and saw Max poke his head out of the apartment. "Hey, man, nice to see you. You saved my life; my in-laws were ready to show slides from their trip last month to New York City. It was the first time they'd ever been there."

Max welcomed in and handed him a cold Yuengling, Tex's favorite beer.

"So, what's all this?" Tex asked, pointing at the stack of paper on the card table. "Are you writing a book about your memoirs? It's a little early, no?"

"Sit down; I have a long story to share," Max replied, waving Tex over to the couch.

Tex listened without any sense of surprise to the details dating back to Max and Barrett planting an FM transmitter in the Carbon County Court-house. Not one detail was left out.

"So, Joe Taylor stood right over there," Max said, pointing to the spot where the mayor's assistant planted himself on Christmas Eve. "And now, you know everything."

"I always wondered how you got the goods on that prick Albrecht," Tex said. "Now it all makes sense." Tex got up from the couch and stood at the card table. "These papers over here. What's this all about? They look like pages from an old geometry textbook."

"I compiled a list of everything and everyone that was part of Aaron's and my investigation, plus a few things I added from my interactions. I put them in a Venn Diagram, which is supposed to show the relationships between all of these people and things and see where they overlap."

"What did you find out?"

"So far, nothing. I think I am taking the right approach, but being new to the area, I am missing a lot of background info. Like, for example, this Bill Hinke guy—he seems to be involved somehow, but I'm not sure how or why."

"Hold on a second," Tex said, holding up his hand like a stop sign. "Craig Gentile. How do you know him?"

"I don't know him. I've never met him."

"Well, he's your man. You know, the missing link. My uncle Matt was a union delegate for Gentile's construction company, and from what Matt tells me, Gentile is a crooked SOB."

"So, what's your suggestion? Can I talk to your uncle?"

"I'm sure he'd be willing to talk, especially if you promise him one of these," Tex said, holding up his empty bottle of Yuengling. "I know one thing he'll tell you," Tex said, walking to the fridge to grab another beer. "Follow the money."

Tex opened his second beer and stood next to Max and put his arm around his young friend's shoulder.

"You may not be out of the woods yet," Tex said, winking. "But there's a clearing up ahead, and you're heading straight for it."

Chapter Sixteen

Max recognized Matt Carpenter without ever seeing his picture. Carpenter stood about five feet, ten inches tall with a hefty beer gut and forearms like tree trunks. On his left bicep was a tattoo of Chesty Puller, the mascot of the US Marine Corps. Uncle Matt, as Max was told to call him, served in the Korean War in late 1952. He was awarded a Marine Distinguished Service Medal for his heroism in the Battle of Old Baldy, a series of battles in West-Central Korea that cost more than three hundred American lives. When Tex told Max about Uncle Matt's time in the service, he advised his young colleague to avoid the topic.

The day after talking to Tex, he arranged to meet up with Uncle Matt, who was sitting at a high-top at the Coal Miner's Bar & Grill in Lansford, a short ride from Max's apartment. He was more than halfway through a draft beer when Max approached. Tex had given his mother's brother a good description of Max, so Matt rose out of his chair and extended his hand to Max. Even though Max had a good five inches on the older man, Max's hand disappeared in the grip of Tex's uncle.

"Tex told me a lot about you," Uncle Matt said, pointing to the stool on the opposite side of the table. "How about a beer?"

"Sure. Do they have Miller Lite?"

The belly laugh that ensued gave Max his answer.

"Make that a Budweiser, then."

"So, kid, Tex tells me you wanted to talk about Craig Gentile. Now there's one guy who has his hand in everyone's pockets. When I was a shop steward at Teamsters Local 773, we used to call that prick 'Craig the Crook.'"

"Local 773, is that involved in the building trades?"

"Sure is. Mostly bricklayers and electricians. I'd say we were involved in every job in Lehigh Valley that was more than a simple home remodel."

"Were you still active before Donahue became mayor of Allentown?"

"You bet. Why?"

"When he got elected and got the typewriter and toy companies to move to the Lehigh Valley, was there any union involvement in the recruiting?"

"Do you mean do I know if there were any under-the-table payoffs? Pretty sure there was."

"How much can you tell me?"

After a long pause, Uncle Matt signaled the bartender and held up two fingers.

Max was two sips into his Budweiser when a second bottle arrived along with a pint of whatever Matt Carpenter was drinking.

"I owe a lot to that union, kid. No way I could have retired on my pension from the service, and I'm not old enough for social security. The union takes care of its own, so I need to be careful of what I say. And, anything I tell you cannot come back to me. You know that, right?"

"I respect that, sir. My dad fought in World War II and is a member of the VFW in Philadelphia, so I know about the loyalty among vets and union guys."

"Okay. Now that we got that straight, I'll give you coupla leads. This Donahue guy, for one. No one ever heard of him before he got here. I know the story that he moved here because of his wife, but that's total horseshit. I have it on good authority that the mayor had a connection that brought him here to save his marriage. It was common knowledge he was playing slap and tickle with his secretary."

"I've heard that from other people as well," Max responded, taking another sip from his original bottle of Budweiser. Uncle Matt was way ahead in the drinking competition.

"One last thing," Matt Carpenter said, in a soft voice, barely above a whisper. "As big a crook as Craig Gentile is, I wouldn't trust that Bill Hinke guy as far as I can throw him. And with my sore shoulder, that wouldn't be very far."

"Hinke. He's the head of the Lehigh County Democratic Party, right? What sort of business is he in?"

"Let me think. Yeah, I remember. Hinke is in real estate. He owns a bunch of property—mostly crap apartments on the outskirts of downtown and some undeveloped land out near the college. He's been pushing to get gambling going on the land owned by the Lenape Nation out near Easton."

"He's a busy man," Max said, wanting to bring his meeting to an end. His head was spinning with an entirely new set of facts that he wanted to piece together and maybe create a new set of Venn Diagrams.

"I can tell you're ready to go, kid. It's no big deal—you got some big fish to fry. It was nice having a drink—well, part of a drink—with ya," Uncle Matt chuckled.

"Uncle Matt, if I can call you that," Max said as he stood up, extending his hand, "thank you for all of this. I promise to keep it on the Q.T."

Max left the dark, smoky bar and sat in his car, engine off, in the Coal Miners Bar & Grill parking lot. It was cold, but Max's brain was working overtime, providing more than enough heat to keep him from feeling the freezing temperature.

The pieces were all there with some visible points of connection. Any time you have a crooked union official, a political party honcho, a big city mayor, and the potential for a large influx of money, there are multiple opportunities for some palms to be greased. What Max needed was a timeline of events and to determine where Joe Taylor fit in this mysterious situation. With his emerging reporter's intuition, Max visualized a few scenarios, but knew it was time to bring Aaron Grant into the picture. Grant's experience and wisdom could be just the thing needed to make sense of this multi-sided puzzle.

Max knew he had to walk a fine line. As he started the engine, he made a mental checklist of next steps. Max had to let Jack Devlin know there was more to the story, and it would be ideal if he could delay publishing the blockbuster story a week or two. Max knew he'd need a very compelling argument for that to happen. Next on the list was to meet with Aaron and reveal the info Uncle Matt shared. Lastly—and this was a big one—Max realized he would benefit from talking to someone on the inside of the city hall, and he already knew the perfect person.

It was almost dinner time as Max drove from Lansford to Nesquehoning. He was in no mood to make anything for dinner. Since he wanted to save his mother's leftovers, Max stopped for a hoagie at Cabrera's Pizzeria & Restaurant, which was halfway between the Coal Miner's joint and home.

Max was not a big hoagie guy—something no native Philadelphian should admit—but that night it sounded good. He was hoping the place had a veal parm hoagie on the menu.

Max, his veal parm hoagie, and a bottle of A-Treat Sarsaparilla soda spent the evening watching the Flyers play the New York Rangers on TV. The Flyers were still living off the high of their 1975 Stanley Cup victory on their way to a second-place finish in the Patrick Division. The team's pugnacious "Broad Street Bullies" identity was fading with such players as Dave "The Hammer" Schultz and Don "Big Bird" Saleski either gone from the team or in the waning stages of their careers.

A 6–5 Flyers victory took Max's mind of the complex situation at hand. He decided to take the entire night off from reviewing and analyzing the information he had collected from Tex and his Uncle Matt. At that point in the process, Max decided he would present the new findings to his reporting partner Aaron Grant. Max decided to call his colleague before the hockey game even though Grant was off on vacation. Aaron was glad to hear from him and invited Max over on the twenty-eighth to talk about new developments that might materially change their story. Grant, who lived in Catasauqua, suggested that Max come over for lunch and sample some of his family's down-home cooking. Not sure what type of cuisine was in store, Max agreed but decided to bring a sandwich along for the ride home, just in case.

The following morning, Max padded around his living room in his new bedroom slippers, a gift from his sister for Hanukkah. Since four, Max had trouble with his feet, a genetic gift from grandparents of Eastern European extraction. The soft lining of the slippers made his often-sore arches and enlarged bunions feel warm and comfortable. He stood staring at the stack of papers sitting on the card table he put up after watching the hockey game. A new day gave Max new insight into the fragments of guidance that sat in a series of circles on yellow sheets from two large legal pads.

The drive from Nesquehoning to Catasauqua took a shade under one hour. Max brought Aaron's wife some flowers and a box of cookies he bought at Connie's Cakes and Cookies, which had just opened after being closed for the holidays. He decided against bringing a bottle of wine for several reasons. The primary one was that Pennsylvania State Stores, the only place you could legally buy alcohol in the state, did not have much of a selection.

Loretta Grant, Aaron's wife, greeted Max at the door. Once inside, Max immediately got that warm feeling that comes with being a guest in a cozy, inviting home. Christmas decorations were still up, and a collection of toys cluttered the living room floor. The kitchen counter was an opened box that housed a new multi-speed blender, a welcome gift for any serious home cook. It was apparent that all in the Grant household had a good holiday.

Aaron came out of his home office to welcome Max and officially introduce him to his wife. His son played in his bedroom, and Aaron promised he would make an appearance come lunchtime. Aaron suggested that, before lunch, they meet in his at-home work sanctuary.

Max carried his mountain of paper in his new briefcase and proceeded to empty them on the couch in Aaron's home office. Aaron pulled out a large coffee table, and Max put the pages in neat piles. Each stack represented a different piece of the puzzle, starting with one that said *Donahue in Springfield*. All told, there were twelve piles to go through.

Aaron surveyed each pile, picking up the top page, slowly thumbing through each sheet. As a seasoned reporter, Aaron Grant knew what he was looking for. Grant would periodically stop, pull a sheet from the pile, and carefully study every word. He would then take those sheets he reviewed and put them in a separate pile off to the side. This process went on for twenty minutes, during which Max sat silently on an overstuffed recliner in the back corner of the office.

"Look here," Grant said, holding up his pile of papers. "There's a common thread here and an answer to one of your big questions."

"What's that?" Max responded inquisitively.

"The center of this whole operation is a relationship between the union and the Lehigh Valley Democratic Party. I'll bet you were still in school when there was a big downturn in construction projects here that was putting a lot of people out of work."

"I wasn't living in the area from '75 to '78 when I was in graduate school and working my first job as a magazine flunky."

"Well, the backstory is that the unions, who are huge contributors to the Democratic Party in these parts, leaned on Bill Hinke to make something happen. My hunch is Hinke looked for a puppet—a frontman, if you will—to come to the Lehigh Valley and start handing out money for favors. I'm not sure how they picked Donahue, but that's not important. He's just a figurehead for some guys playing fast and loose with the law."

"You figured that out from those notes I have here," Max said, pointing to the stacks of paper. "That's pretty amazing. You must have come across this kind of scheme somewhere else."

"I have, but in a different form. This plot is much thicker than any I ever have run across, but when I was working for the *Dothan Eagle*, I got a PhD in crooked politicians."

"You mean that good ol' boy image you see on TV and the movies is for real?"

Aaron laughed. "They tend to exaggerate in the movies, but the book *All the King's Men* is pretty close to the real thing. Have you read it?"

"I read it in high school, I think. The movie, with Broderick Crawford as Willie Stark, was really good. My dad and I watch it every time it comes on."

"Really? I've never seen it. Hang on," Grant continued. "There's more. This Joe Taylor guy. This may sound crazy, but I don't think he works for the mayor, and it's even possible that's not even his real name."

"You discovered that in my notes? How?"

"No, it's just a feeling I have. After the Dothan newspaper, I worked for the *Charlotte Observer* for five years, and something about this investigation reminds me of a corruption case down there. After the dust settled, some of those under suspicion just up and disappeared. At the time, some of us working on the story suspected they were some sort of undercover agents—maybe with the FBI or Treasury. We never were able to confirm that."

Max's rapidly maturing reporting instincts were working overtime. "We need to find someone inside city hall. It needs to be someone close to the mayor and asks some questions. What do you think?"

"I like it. Who do you have in mind?"

Max explained his idea of who he thought was the person to ask for the information they needed. Someone in city hall made out weekly timesheets or distributed paychecks to employees. Not necessarily an employee in a highly sensitive position, just an aide or secretary who kept track of employment records. Max offered two possible names, one of which Aaron rejected because of past dealings with this man.

"He's not someone we can believe," Aaron said. "Plus, he's likely to immediately tell the mayor or Joe Taylor that we were snooping around."

"That leaves one person, right?" Max said. "We both know who she is, but do you know her name or how to contact her?"

"Not directly, but her husband is a typesetter at the paper. I've never met him, but I know a bunch of others in that department, so I can get an introduction."

"Once you get a handle on the guy and get his wife's contact info, do you mind if I speak to her?" Max asked. "Before I forget, don't you think we should ask Devlin for some more time before publishing to flush out this new direction we've uncovered?"

"Yes, to both questions." Aaron looked at his watch. "Holy crap, we're way past lunchtime. I hope Loretta isn't mad; we've been holed up in here for two hours. I'm pretty sure my son Bud already ate, so it will be just us."

Lunch was not what Max expected. Instead of hog jowls or grits with a side of ham hocks, Loretta Grant prepared an array of salads with trays of freshly baked bread and a wide assortment of cheeses. It was a make-your-own-sandwich lunch, and everything looked delicious. Max was not prone to great table manners, so he had to remind himself to wait patiently for his hosts to describe what was on the table. Max also had to remember not to reach across the table for food and to put a napkin on his lap. Despite there always being a lot of great food in the Rosen household when Max was growing up, table etiquette consisted of not chewing with your mouth open.

After lunch, Max left the Grant household, thanking Loretta and Aaron for their hospitality and saying that he hoped to return their kindness with his own home-cooked meal.

"Do you cook?" Loretta Grant asked as she walked Max to the door.

"I know how, but I rarely get the chance to cook for anyone but myself and occasionally my parents. It would be nice to have a chance to show off for you and Aaron."

On the ride back to Nesquehoning, Max replayed his two-hour meeting with Aaron. Max was astonished at his colleague's reporting sense and ability to comb through the stacks of papers, ultimately coming up with an impressive overview and significant findings. He was also pleased, but ashamed, that he didn't have to tell Aaron about the hidden FM transmitter and the confrontation with Joe Taylor.

A few minutes outside of Nesquehoning, snow flurries began to lightly coat the road. It was 4 p.m. in late December, and snow was common in Northeastern Pennsylvania that time of year. The bank clock showed the current temperature was thirty-two degrees, which meant there was only a fifty-fifty chance of the snow sticking to the ground in any meaningful way. Even though his current residence was only seventy miles from where he grew up, the weather was much colder, with an inch or two more of snow each year.

With three days left in the year, Max spent the night contemplating whether he was interested in writing an end-of-the-year recap going over his highlights, such as the Chris Albrecht trial and the chemical dumping series. From a personal perspective, he thought about inviting Sue over for New Year's Eve. He could utilize his lightly tested culinary skills while they watched Dick Clark narrate yet another ball drop in Times Square. Max knew in advance the complications such an evening would bring.

After a quick nap and a light dinner, Max read through the Thursday edition of the *Chronicle* while he listened to American Top 40's countdown of the top songs of 1978. When he turned the radio on, Casey Kasem was up to number ten, "Three Times A Lady," by the Commodores. Max tried his hand at guessing the nine remaining songs, and he failed miserably. He missed the top song, "Shadow Dancing," by Andy Gibb, which he didn't even have in his top five, and chose "Fool (If You Think It's Over)" by Chris Rea as his number one. Max was only eighty-three songs off on that call.

The twenty-ninth of December was another cold one, with the high in Nesquehoning expected to barely crack freezing. Max gathered up his stacks of papers and headed into the office after a quick breakfast. Other than a few people from circulation, the bureau was empty. With the place so deserted, the heat was on sixty-eight, forcing Max to leave his coat on while he worked. His first order of business was to see if Aaron had come through with a contact within the city hall.

Aaron answered on the first ring and sensed it was Max calling.

"Max, I knew it was you. I got a late holiday gift—the secretary in the mayor's office is willing to talk to you. She remembered us from the lunch with the mayor and Joe Taylor and thought we were nice gentlemen."

"Is she working today?"

"Nope, you're in luck. I spoke to her husband at the paper and passed on our message. City Hall is closed till January 2, so she's home with her grandkids."

"What's her name?"

"Marjorie. Marjorie Nelson. She's expecting your call."

"I'll get right on it. After I'm done, I'll call you right back."

Max put the phone down and walked toward the back of the empty office. He took a few deep breaths and returned to his desk. With a lot on the line, he picked up his desk phone and dialed.

"Hello," said the voice on the other end, "Nelson residence." Marjorie Nelson's voice was significantly less harsh than when she led Aaron and Max down the hall outside the mayor's office and instructed them to sit outside the conference room before lunch.

"Hi, Mrs. Nelson. This is Max Rosen from the *Chronicle*. Your husband said you might be expecting my call?"

"Why, yes. Are you having a nice holiday?"

"Yes, ma'am. Thank you for taking the time to talk to me on your time off. The reason I am calling is about Mayor Donahue's office. I take it you are familiar with Joe Taylor, the mayor's assistant."

A long pause. "I'm not sure what you are asking." Marjorie Nelson's voice quickly went from cheery to defensive. "I know Joe Taylor, but I think you're interested in something else."

"Like what?" Max responded.

"You probably don't know this. Well, I am sure only a few people know this. Joe Taylor doesn't work for the mayor. He doesn't get a paycheck from the city, and I have some doubts as to whether that's even his real name. I call him the Mystery Man—but never to his face."

Chapter Seventeen

As soon as Max hung up from his call with Marjorie Nelson, he called Aaron Grant to give him the details. While surprised, Grant's experience prepared him for nearly all imaginable twists and turns in their newspaper investigation.

"I think I'm glad to be right," Grant said with some hesitation. "I also think it's time to hit the pause button on our investigation for a few days. People will be difficult to get ahold of until after the first of the year. We also need to talk to Jack Devlin, and I know he's on vacation with his family in the Poconos. They have a place up there."

Max was sad to hear that Aaron wanted to slow things down until after the first of the year, but he knew that it was the wise course of action from a practical sense. It would also provide a cooling-off period from the ultimatum given by Joe Taylor and provided Max with a sense of relief in the short term. Max also took comfort in knowing that no other news outlet covered this possible corruption case, especially since the *Chronicle* was the only major newspaper within seventy miles, and the Lehigh Valley didn't have a single network-affiliated TV station. While it was always difficult for him to be patient, Max conceded to Aaron's suggestion.

"I will yield to your wisdom and experience," Max said half-heartedly. "I hope you, Loretta, and your son have a great rest of the holiday. Let me wish you an early Happy New Year."

Max hung up the phone only to realize that his adrenaline—which had been on full tilt for months—was beginning to wane. And quickly. In the past, when his internal fuse was not lit, Max became depressed. Knowing that he was currently working toward personal and professional growth, it was important to find something to look forward to for the next few days to avoid feeling down.

Max rose from his desk, hoping to see if, by some chance, there were any assignments listed on the editor's board for him. En route, he passed a desk on the other side of the room that had a vase on it with a single yellow rose. Max knew it had to be where Sue last sat, given she was the only female reporter in the bureau and that she loved roses. Remembering the warm feeling he experienced when Sue kissed him on the cheek, Max realized it had been more than a week since he spoke with her. With an unexpected empty slot in his upcoming social calendar, Max wanted to arrange to spend some time with Sue. He didn't know whether she was at her apartment during the holidays or visiting with her parents in Easton.

With no one else in the office, prying ears would not be privy to Max's calls. He dialed Sue's home number, and he was just about ready to hang up after eight rings. Out of breath, Sue answered as if she just finished a cross-country race.

"Hello," she said while trying to catch her breath.

"Sue, it's Max. How are you?"

There was a long pause. Max was concerned that Sue might have hung up. "I'm fine. I was running to the phone because I am trying to clean up since my parents are coming over for dinner tonight. They know I am a slob," she said with a laugh. "I'm working on an early New Year's resolution to be a neater slob."

"Well, that's a New Year's resolution I'd never be able to keep," Max joked. "As long as I can find whatever I am looking for, then the place is neat enough." Max cleared his throat. "The reason I called was to invite you over to my place for dinner on New Year's Eve. You may not know this, but I have some decent cooking skills. I'd like to make a thank-you dinner for your help with the city hall elevator caper."

"Ooh, that sounds good. I was going to have takeout with my sister and her husband, but this invitation is much more fun."

"Is there anything you don't or can't eat?"

"I don't like Brussels sprouts."

"Don't worry. They are out of season. Why don't you come over at about six thirty? We can have some wine before we eat and watch my buddy Dick Clark do his thing at midnight after we're done with our gourmet meal."

"Your buddy?"

"Yes, I'll tell you the story when you come over."

Max hung up the phone and found himself grinning ear to ear. Besides planning his menu, he decided against putting too much thought into the New Year's Eve dinner. Was it a date? Did she expect to stay over? Max moved those stressful thoughts to the side and focused on impressing Sue with his cooking and having a good time.

After his call, Max headed home. There were no pending assignments, and any catch-up work, such as going through his mail, could be done at his apartment. Even after living in eastern Pennsylvania his entire life, Max never could get used to how early it got dark in December. It was four thirty in the afternoon as he walked to his car, and the streetlights in downtown Nesquehoning were shining brightly. Max had a quick flashback to his freshman year in high school. Due to overcrowding, his school had to add a late shift in which students started their classes at ten thirty in the morning and ended their day at four thirty in the afternoon. Starting high school was difficult enough, but to add the concept of your last class letting out in the dark made life extra stressful.

Max ate the leftovers from the family Hanukkah dinner his mother had packed for him. The brisket and all the side dishes were just as good as when he first ate them. Between watching his mother cook and viewing countless episodes of *The French Chef*, Max inherited some of his mother's talent in the kitchen. For Max, cooking was therapy. He enjoyed lending a hand to his working parents by getting dinner started, especially in the summer. Nirvana, to Max, was peeling potatoes and making the salad for dinner while listening to the Phillies play the Cubs at Wrigley Field in an afternoon game. To show what sort of baseball nerd he was, Max even kept score while puttering in the kitchen.

Excited about his upcoming New Year's Eve non-date, Max went to sleep with something to look forward to. Due to his lack of seniority, Max was scheduled to be in the office on the thirtieth to handle the phones and take on any assignment that might come up.

December 30 was bitterly cold. Even with his bluff about looking for his winter coat in the basement, Max brought his heaviest overcoat back from his recent visit to Philadelphia. He got up early, put a bagel in the toaster, and grabbed it on his way out the door. Not expecting anything earth-shattering, Max went to work in a flannel shirt and corduroy pants.

He lived close enough to the office that he could change into something more businesslike if need be.

As with the day before, the office was empty save for two circulation employees. Instead of sitting at his usual desk, Max moved up to the bureau editor's desk if a call came in. He grabbed the day's paper, and since it was a Saturday during a holiday weekend, the *Chronicle* was half its normal size.

Midway through his bagel and the *Chronicle* sports section, the phone rang. There were three lines on the bureau editor's phone, and the one flashing was a direct line from the newsroom in Allentown. Max figured a nervous editor at headquarters was checking in to ensure someone was in the office. Max picked up in the third ring.

"*Chronicle*, Max Rosen speaking."

"Max, are you the only one in the office?" The voice at the other end was unfamiliar to Max. "It's Charlotte Robb. I'm the editor working with all the bureaus today. We have a skeleton staff down here. I have what looks to be an important story I need someone to follow up on."

"I can do it," Max said.

"Okay. Here are the details as we know them. There's been a kidnapping—the wife of Arnie Mitchell, publisher of *Tickle* magazine. The FBI is holding a press conference in Scranton at 2 p.m., and we need someone there. You up for that?"

"Do you know anything more about the kidnapping?"

"All we know is that Mrs. Mitchell was grabbed outside her home sometime yesterday morning. Normally, they wait forty-eight hours, but because of Mitchell's high profile, the FBI was called in right away."

"I'll find the address for the FBI office in Scranton. Do you need to tell them I'll be attending the press conference?"

"Taken care of. Please check in on the way in case there are any updates. You can call me collect."

Max wrote down Robb's number, grabbed his coat, and headed to the parking lot. In the brief time Max was in the office, his car's windows were thick with frost. Max popped open the trunk and pulled out his trusty yellow scraper courtesy of S&H Hardware.

Traffic was light on the Northeast Extension of the Pennsylvania Turnpike, and at the rate Max was going, he would be an hour early. Max pulled off to fuel up, maybe grab something to eat, and check in with Charlotte Robb. A block off the turnpike in a small town called Avoca, Max found an Esso station next to the Tipsy Turtle Airport Pub. Max braved the cold and pulled up to an open pump while looking across the airport restaurant's parking lot. It was 11:45 a.m., and the pub's lot was packed. What made things curious was that more than half the cars were the police of some sort—Lackawanna County Sheriff, Pittson City Police, and at least five state police vehicles.

Max got back in his car after filling up and drove to the edge of the gas station's lot that bordered the Tipsy Turtle. A phone booth sat on the gas station side of the adjoining lots. A simple robbery, Max thought, wouldn't bring out so many cops—especially state troopers. It had to be something major.

Most of the law enforcement personnel weren't engaged in whatever was going on, so Max walked over to a group of three state troopers leaning on their Ford Torino with a long pigtail antenna. Using a bit of logic, Max selected the three men's oldest and spoke quietly but directly.

"Officer, I'm Max Rosen, a reporter with the *Allentown Chronicle*, and I'm on my way to the FBI office in Scranton to hear about a kidnapping. Is this related?"

The older officer, with the name Wayne on his badge, looked at his fellow troopers.

"What kidnapping? We're here because we got a call about a disturbance at this place. That's all we know."

Max smiled and walked around to the front of the building. With police from all over the state crawling over one another, it was impossible to get a handle on what was taking place. There were no ambulances or aid cars, which would signal that no one was seriously injured or worse. The read was the sort of utter confusion that takes place in the aftermath of a big event.

The phone booth next to Max's car in the adjacent parking lot was still unoccupied. Max reached into his pocket for a dime, stepped into the small enclosure, and closed the door. He slipped the dime into the appropriate slot and dialed "0" for the operator.

"Collect call for Charlotte Robb from Max. Will you accept the charges?"

"Yes, operator," Charlotte responded. "Max, what's going on? Our police scanners have been on fire for the past half hour. Something big is taking place where you are headed."

"You mean, where I'm standing. I'm in a phone booth next to the Tipsy Turtle a few miles south of Scranton. Either a major crime took place here, or there is an impromptu law enforcement gathering with free donuts."

"Max, you must have the luck of the Irish. You are in the right place at the right time. Apparently, from what we hear on the scanners, a kidnap victim was set free at that pub. I'm betting that's what the FBI press conference is all about."

"For starters, I'm not Irish," Max said with a laugh. "As far as a kidnapping goes, I guess I'll get all the details at the local FBI office. I'll check in after the press conference."

Max got back into his car and drove another fifteen miles to Exit 122 for Downtown Scranton. Having never been north of Wilkes-Barre, Max checked his Thomas Guide for the FBI office's location in Scranton. The map showed that Washington Avenue was only a few blocks from the exit, which would put Max right on time for the press conference. He did wonder if, after this new development at the Tipsy Turtle, the press event was even still happening as planned.

The FBI had seven offices in Pennsylvania, with the largest one located on Arch Street in Philadelphia. The one in Scranton was relatively smaller but had the same security level as its largest outpost in the state. Max showed his *Chronicle* ID and Pennsylvania driver's license and was handed a badge and sent to the third-floor conference room.

For a small FBI office, this one had a large, almost-banquet-sized conference room. Chairs were set up in the front with thirty feet of space between the first row and the stage. There were reporters from the Wilkes-Barre and Scranton newspapers, and WBRE-TV, a UHF station that served most of Luzerne County. A man who looked no older than sixteen, and appeared out of place, was sitting on the front row in the last seat from the door. Max casually walked by and read his tag, which identified him as a stringer from the *Philadelphia Inquirer*.

After a prolonged wait of thirty minutes, an FBI spokesman made his way to the stage and laid out all the details of what was initially determined to be a kidnapping but ended up being a simple miscommunication. Michelle Mitchell, the wife of porn publisher Arnie Mitchell, was reported missing, and, because of her husband's profession, everyone assumed there was foul play involved.

The FBI spokesperson inferred that there was a kidnapping, but it was meant to warn Arnie Mitchell for something the authorities would not disclose. His wife was released safe and sound at a restaurant ten miles south of Scranton. Since Arnie Mitchell refused to press charges, the investigation would not proceed any further.

The TV reporter, wanting to impress her peers, asked a few questions about what circumstances led to the kidnapping to which the FBI representative answered, "No comment."

It was 3 p.m., and Max realized he wasted most of the day on what turned out to be a non-story. Looking for a silver lining, he told himself that he did get to see Scranton, the birthplace of Delaware's two-term Senator, Joe Biden. On the other hand, he was totally behind schedule planning the New Year's Eve dinner for Sue.

Before heading out, Max asked the FBI agent who led the press conference where the closest restroom was. It was a long ride back to Nesquehoning, and Max was in no mood to stop along the way. Walking along the corridor to the men's room, Max was taken with the pictures of decorated FBI agents from as far back as the mid-1950s. Some had small plaques under the photos with the agent's name and the reason for the award.

Just as Max reached the restroom, he stopped dead in his tracks. In a crisp black and white photo, dressed in a neat shirt and striped tie, there was someone painfully familiar—Joe Taylor. Underneath the photo, there was a small plaque that read "'Joe Taylor'—for bravery beyond the call of duty." Unlike the other FBI heroes' pictures, the name Joe Taylor was in quotes, indicating that it was not his real name.

Max stood, staring at the picture for three solid minutes. He put his briefcase on the ground, rubbed his eyes, and refocused them on the photo.

And in a voice that was just loud enough to gain everyone's attention, Max let loose: "Holy shit. That's him!"

The entire office came to a standstill with Max's outburst. Without looking around, he ducked into the men's room, hoping everyone would get back to their own business by the time he came out. Max waited ten minutes before leaving the bathroom, but no sooner had he stepped two feet out of the men's room when a tall, reed-thin, extremely fit man approached him.

"Are you all right?" the FBI employee, who was an agent assigned to desk work, asked Max. "You gave us all quite the scare."

"I'm fine. I was just overwhelmed by some of the feats of the men and women honored on the wall here."

Max was not very convincing in his response, but the FBI agent who approached him was only ensuring their visitor was not injured in some way. Satisfied that Max's rant was nothing serious, the agent smiled and said, "Well, let me know if you need anything."

Not wishing to press his luck, Max left the FBI office as quickly as he could without drawing attention. Even though his mind was spinning out of control with what he just discovered, Max focused on getting to his car and starting on the ride back to Carbon County.

Max needed a distraction after starting his car, so he tuned into the area's sports talk station, WEJL. Luzerne County was hardcore Penn State territory, so the talk centered on the Nittany Lions changes against Alabama in the Sugar Bowl. The game was set for New Year's Day, with the winner likely crowned the national champion. The team lacked many future NFL stars save for Matt Millen, the latest string of great Penn State linebackers.

Max stayed with the Scranton sports talk station until he was out of range, at which point he switched to WEEX, Allentown's station devoted to sports talk. It was no surprise the same topic was discussed, given that Penn State's Millen was a local kid from the Lehigh Valley. The succession of mind-numbing calls praising the team and its coach Joe Paterno allowed Max to focus on his driving. He drove straight to the bureau to talk with Charlotte Robb and get her opinion on what to write about the kidnapping, if anything.

The office was locked with the lights off, which was expected as it was five o'clock on the thirtieth of December. The heat was off, so Max left his coat on and raised the temperature to a bearable sixty-eight degrees, figuring he might be there for a while.

Charlotte Robb answered her phone on the first ring. "Max, I was expecting to hear from you an hour ago. What's going on?"

At that moment, Max realized that after seeing Joe Taylor's picture at the FBI office, he forgot about the kidnapping and his assignment.

"I am so sorry," Max responded, trying to sound apologetic. "As it turned out, the FBI wouldn't come out and say it was a kidnapping. The truth is, given Arnie Mitchell's business, the FBI realized it was what you could call a 'business issue' between the porno publisher and some disgruntled enemy. I think it's a non-story."

"While there probably is something there, unless we knew who was involved in the 'abduction,' there isn't much to report. It would make for some juicy news, but my instinct is to leave it alone."

"I'll tell you what, Charlotte. I think it's worth keeping an eye on in the future, but now isn't the time to speculate."

"Right, Max. Listen, have a Happy New Year. Talk to you in '79."

Max was relieved that he didn't have to write a story on what turned out to be something the FBI preferred to sweep under the rug. He did have the feeling the agency's decision to punt was a temporary one to allow it to dig deeper into the business of Arnie Mitchell, a notorious figure in the Lehigh Valley.

It was close to 6 p.m. and Max had some serious shopping to do for his big dinner party the following evening. He was concerned that some of the supermarkets would have shortened hours on the thirty-first, so he left the bureau and headed off to Falk's, a higher-end food store that likely would have everything Max needed. Before he left the office, he called, and Falk's was open until nine with limited hours on New Year's Eve day.

Falk's had just opened a new branch in Palmerton, a town between Nesquehoning and Allentown. Max had been there shortly after it opened, and he bookmarked it in his mind as a place to shop in case he ever needed fresh produce and choicer cuts of meat. While hardly what anyone at the time would call a gourmet supermarket, it was far better than the smaller, run-down places that were common in older parts of Carbon County.

Max pulled into Falk's parking lot and was surprised to see very few parking spots left. He was not the only one who had a dinner party planned for New Year's Eve. He grabbed a cart and pulled out the shopping list he'd been working on since Sue accepted his invitation. Max planned to keep things simple, as this was the first time he cooked for anyone other than his family. Tackling something too exotic, such as homemade ravioli stuffed with three kinds of cheese in a light ragù, would make it seem like he was trying too hard to impress.

After loading three bags of groceries in the car, Max remembered he had one more stop to make. It was a stop he thought long and hard about. The last time Max had Sue at his house was after the company holiday party, and a drunk Sue was disappointed that her host did not make any attempt to join her in bed. It was a scene that the socially and sexually inexperienced Max replayed countless times in his mind. What should he have done? What would he do if he ever had such a chance again?

That chance now appeared on the horizon as a logical outcome of an intimate New Year's Eve dinner, and Max wanted to be prepared. On his way back to Nesquehoning, Max pulled into the parking lot of a Rite Aid, the largest pharmacy chain in the area. Hands shaking, Max walked into the pharmacy, whose bright florescent lights caused him to squint. Embarrassed to ask a clerk or the pharmacist for help, Max wandered the aisles until he found the male contraceptives section. His knowledge of condoms was limited to what he learned in his tenth grade sex ed class. At an all-boys high school such as the one he attended, sex ed classes were filled more with laughter than actual instruction. So, when it came to condoms, Max was on his own.

Since Trojan was the only brand he'd heard of, Max grabbed a box off the shelf. Before heading to the checkout stand, Max was thinking ahead, should he have an overnight guest. One aisle over from the condoms, he found a Colgate toothbrush, which would be a thoughtful gesture for the morning after a possibly memorable evening. For a second, Max paused, worrying that his planning might lead Sue to think that he expected to have sex with her. Rather than stand in the middle of a brightly lit drug store and debate the pros and cons of his purchases, Max told himself to stop overthinking things. He closed his eyes, thought about Sue kissing him on the cheek, and being overwhelmed by her exotic scent. Max paid for his purchases and drove home.

It was too late to call Aaron Grant and tell him about the revelation regarding Joe Taylor. Max realized that on January 2, when business at the newspaper resumed, Taylor would still be some sort of FBI agent. Given that, and that it was a holiday, there was no point in rushing the announcement. A face-to-face meeting with Grant would allow them to plan how to best utilize Max's discovery.

Before going to bed, Max worked on the timing of the dishes he would serve Sue for their big night. His menu consisted of an appetizer plate of olives and cheeses which they could nibble on while having a glass of wine. Next would come individual salads—Max's specialty—and a light soup. Of late, Max had read a lot of recipes for interesting soups, and although he'd yet to prepare one, he was confident he could handle it. Their main course would be veal piccata, which he had prepared for his family on many occasions. With the veal, he'd serve roasted potatoes and string beans. Not being big on desserts, Max bought a pint of Breyer's mint chocolate chip ice cream to top off the meal.

The trick Max knew from overdosing on TV cooking shows was to prepare as much as he could in advance. Doing that would allow him to focus on his guest and knock out the remaining courses in real-time. The thought of having a woman over and serving her a memorable meal would be a big step forward in his growth socially. If the evening ended the way Max hoped it would, it would also represent a milestone for him in other departments.

It was 10 p.m., and Max had one last call to make.

"Hi, Max, is everything all right?" his mother asked. "You're calling kind of late."

"Everything is fine. I have something I want to talk to you about. I have a friend coming over for dinner tomorrow night, so I'd like us to wish each other Happy New Year's now. And I'd appreciate it if you didn't call me New Year's Day too early."

There was stone silence on the other end of the phone.

"Who's the friend?" Max's mother asked.

"No one you know. Just someone from work."

"I gather that it's a woman. Is she your girlfriend?"

"Not really. We've worked together since she joined the bureau, and we enjoy each other's company."

"Having a woman over for dinner on New Year's Eve is a big statement. I hope you know what you're doing?"

"If I did, it would be a first," Max said sarcastically.

"That's not necessary," his mother replied with a hurt tone in her voice. "How about you call us before she comes so you can talk to your father and me?"

"Okay, but just for a few minutes."

"Talk to you tomorrow. I'm sure you're excited to have someone other than your family to cook for."

"Good night," Max said, ending the call.

Max shook off the guilt he felt after talking to his mother. *It could have gone a lot worse*, he thought to himself.

It was unusual for Max to set his alarm on a day off, but he was up bright and early at seven thirty on December 31. His first job was to clean his apartment. It was small, so it only took Max ninety minutes to vacuum the rug, clean the bathrooms and kitchen, and put away a lot of clutter. Listening to music always helped, so WFMZ's countdown of the past year's top hits helped move things along.

Before lunch, Max started his prep work and made the salad and appetizer plates. He made a fresh stock for the minestrone early in the afternoon. Max peeled the potatoes and soaked them in water with lemon and baking soda to keep them fresh. He decided to do the potatoes about the same time he cooked the veal, an hour before his guest arrived. The last thing was the fresh string beans—which cost a fortune since they were out of season. He washed them and put them in a steamer basket in the fridge. He would steam them while he and Sue enjoyed their wine and appetizers.

Max knew nothing about wine. He remembered his college classmates drinking Mateus, a rosé wine, when they were trying to impress someone. He had kept one on hand in case he ever entertained, so he dug it out from his so-called pantry and put it in the refrigerator. He laughed, thinking about the other option he recalled from college—Boone's Farm.

The time flew by, and before he knew it, it was 3:30 p.m. Max took a break and, as agreed upon, called his parents. With his father on the phone, his mother didn't ask too many questions, but Max could feel a distinct chill in her voice. In the past, such a guilt trip would make Max extremely sad and close to tears, but he refused to buy into her trap on this day.

Max showered and put on his lone button-down polo shirt purchased on a trip to the outlet stores in nearby Reading. He found a clean pair of khakis and put on a dash of Paco Rabanne cologne for good measure. Max stood in the bathroom after putting himself together and stared at himself in the mirror for a good thirty seconds. If his life was governed by the competing forces of vulnerability and strength, the latter was finally in charge. Max smiled and almost cried, thinking about the progress he had made in his personal life.

At 6:30 p.m. on the button, Sue rang Max's doorbell. When he opened the door, his friend stood there smiling in a long flowing dress with sequins across the bodice. She had a button-down cardigan sweater, dotted with sequins, covering her arms. She had chosen a simple yet elegant pearl necklace, perfect for New Year's Eve. Her makeup was understated, but the familiar scent of her perfume nearly knocked Max to his knees.

"Are you going to let me in?" Sue joked. "It's cold out here."

Sue handed Max a pretty bouquet of snapdragons in a frosted green vase.

"These are for you," she said, handing Max her gift as they walked up the stairs. "I took it for granted you didn't have a vase, so I put the flowers in one of mine."

When they entered the apartment, Sue nearly gasped. Max turned his card table into a makeshift dining room table with a plain blue tablecloth draped across the top. Not owning anything other than a set of everyday Melmac dishes, Max dressed them up with some floral napkins he had bought the night before at Falks.

"Let's sit on the sofa and have a glass of wine," Max said as casually as he could. Inside, he was nervous and excited, pushing any self-doubts aside so he could enjoy the evening.

Max and Sue drank their wine, ate their appetizer plates, and talked. Sue was curious about where Max picked up his culinary talents. He gladly went into great detail about his love for cooking shows, the heritage of Eastern European cooking he inherited, and even told her the story of how he acquired an entire collection of *Gourmet* magazines.

Sue looked straight at Max as he spoke, finding his story charming, revealing a part of his personality she had never seen before. *This is a special man,* Sue thought. As Max finished his long *geschichte*, Sue reached out and placed her hand on top of his.

Max's face was flushed with Sue's gentle touch, but he had to break the mood by putting the finishing touches on her meal.

"I'm so sorry, but I need to go to the kitchen and finish a few things. To be continued?"

Sue smiled back at Max, giving him an answer without speaking.

An hour after her arrival, Sue and Max sat down to the multicourse meal that was several days in the making. They ate slowly, with Sue astonished at the effort Max had made. As if in perfect order, salads were placed on the table, followed by soup, veal, potatoes, and steamed string beans.

"Sorry, but the string beans are a bit overdone," Max said apologetically.

"You're serious?"

"It's just that I wanted everything to be perfect."

"Believe me, it is. I have never had a man cook for me before, let alone someone who could work at a gourmet restaurant."

Max blushed. "Cooking relaxes me. I never cook for myself; I'm a frozen lasagna guy on most nights."

Sue passed on dessert. Being a good guest, she helped clear the table. With a stack of dishes from a fancy dinner, Max was fortunate that one of his place's nice perks was a built-in dishwasher.

"Can you please help me load the dishwasher?" Max asked. "I was never allowed to do it growing up."

"Sure, I have a degree in dishwasher loading."

Space was tight in Max's small kitchen, and when Sue's lithe body brushed against Max's hip, the warm feeling of lust and passion filled him from head to toe. He took a deep breath and suggested they watch a movie on TV until Dick Clark emceed the Times Square festivities.

"Before that, you said Dick Clark was a buddy. Is that a joke?"

"Actually, no." Max proceeded to tell Sue about his appearance on a popular game show hosted by Dick Clark. Before the show started, the world's oldest teenager introduced himself to the contestants and found out Max was from Philadelphia. As that was the location of Dick Clark's big career break with *American Bandstand*, the two had something in common. Max assured Sue he and Dick Clark hadn't seen each other since.

TV programming was light on New Year's Eve, but *60 Minutes* interviewed Joe Paterno, the legendary coach of Penn State football. In the Lehigh Valley, love for JoePa was required. Each year, Paterno would make a recruiting trip to the Allentown area where top players would wait in line for a chance to play for the Nittany Lions.

After *60 Minutes*, Sue moved closer to Max on the couch and held his hand. In a repeat of one of Max's great memories, she kissed him on the cheek. He returned her kiss, but instead of on her cheek, he pressed his lips against hers. Max's heart was pounding as Sue kissed him back, drawing him closer.

It was only one hour until midnight, but Max knew he could not wait. He got up from the couch and was about to ask her to join him someplace more comfortable when time stood still. There was a loud knock at the door, followed by two rings of the doorbell.

Max looked at Sue and she returned his look, equally bewildered. Max knew it wasn't an emergency as someone would have called rather than show up at his door on New Year's Eve. Max shrugged his shoulders and walked down the steps to see who was at the door.

As if hit by lightning, Max stood frozen at his front door, recognizing the man standing out in the cold.

"Max, let me in," the man said. It was none other than Joe Taylor, your friendly neighborhood FBI agent.

Max opened the door, and Joe Taylor—or whatever his name was—took off his gloves and put them in his heavy overcoat. "I need to talk to you."

The two men walked up the stairs, with Joe Taylor two steps behind. Max entered his apartment and smiled at Sue, who seemed puzzled by what was going on.

"So, you must be Sue," Taylor said. "Sorry to interrupt, but this is important."

"What is it?" Max asked impatiently.

"I hear you've been asking around about me," Taylor said sternly. "We had a deal, so that's a no-no. You remember this?" Joe Taylor said, pulling Max's clandestine FM transmitter out of his coat pocket.

"I sure do. I also know something else."

"And what's that?" Taylor responded angrily.
"You're an FBI agent, that's what."

Chapter Eighteen

Given his work and experience with the FBI, it took something major to catch Joe Taylor off guard, but Max's revelation put Taylor immediately on the defensive.

"Where did you get that idea?" Taylor said, raising his voice.

"At the FBI office in Scranton. I think it's nice how the agency honors the men and women who risk their lives for our country, don't you?"

"What I did or did not do for this country is not the subject at hand," Taylor said, regaining his composure. "So, I'd say we have a situation on our hands."

"We do, and if you don't mind, I'd like to get on with my evening. Why don't we agree to meet on the second and discuss our options? I need to include my reporting partner, Aaron Grant. He knows the entire story, including the hidden FM transmitter and the fact that you are an FBI agent."

"You told him?"

"I sure did. We trust each other and are doing the investigation into the mayor together. He's a good man with a lot of journalistic experience."

"As you wish. We can meet at 10 a.m. on Tuesday. I'd like to do this somewhere out of the way. We've come too far to let anything derail the work we've done."

"Who's this 'we' you are talking about?"

"Depending on our conversation Tuesday, I may tell you who 'we' is."

With that, Taylor buttoned his coat and walked toward the door of Max's apartment. He turned around one last time. "Happy New Year, Max. Happy New Year, Sue. See you later."

Max stood with his back to Sue as Taylor stomped down the stairs and out the door. The Joe Taylor New Year's Eve Drama took the wind out of the intimate moment Max and Sue were about to share. Sue hadn't said a word the entire time Joe Taylor confronted Max, and she had no idea how to rekindle the magic they felt during and right after dinner. She waited for Max to say something and took his silence as an inability to process the clashing events of the evening. Sue assumed she knew what was going on but wanted to give Max room to figure things out.

"Max, come sit with me," Sue said softly. "There's plenty of time for you to come up with a plan for Taylor and the mayor."

It was ten minutes before midnight when Max joined Sue on the couch after turning on the TV. With an earpiece in his left ear and the noise of a massive crowd in midtown Manhattan, Dick Clark turned to face the giant ball in Times Square as the seconds ticked away, ending 1978.

When the countdown ended, and confetti rained down across the TV screen image, Max leaned over and kissed Sue. It was a warm, pleasant kiss, but without the passion from the previous hour. The mood had passed and would need to be reignited on another night.

Max got up and turned off the television. There was plenty of wine left from dinner, so he grabbed two clean glasses and poured. He brought them over and handed one to Sue. She seemed unphased by the mayor's assistant's strange visit but didn't show any interest in discussing it further.

Sue raised her glass and turned, facing Max, sitting a comfortable distance away on the couch. "Here's to a successful 1979," she said, clinking glasses. "I am looking forward to an exciting year."

Expecting something a bit more personal, Max paused for a second and simply responded, "Hear, hear," to her toast.

Time flew by for the next two hours as Max and Sue drank their wine and talked about life. Each recounted their college days with Max explaining his failures in the romantic department and his underachievement academically. He also talked about the fact that he was not involved with his college's newspaper and came to the world of news reporting relatively late.

Sue said her lifelong dream was to be a journalist, keeping a diary from age ten on. She worked on her high school's newspaper and excelled in her college courses related to her future career. In her senior year, she became editor of the Shippensburg State *News-Chronicle*, the school's daily paper. Her move to a position at the *Chronicle* was the next logical step in her career path.

Max and Sue talked for hours until neither one could keep their eyes open. It was 4 a.m., and the mood for anything other than sleep was not in store for the two New Year's Eve celebrants. The evening began with wine, flowers, and a thoughtfully prepared meal and ended with Max and Sue falling asleep on the couch. Max slept at one end while Sue was at the other, their legs resting on one another.

Some four hours later, Max opened his eyes and found Sue standing in his kitchen, boiling water to make instant coffee. She only had one cup in front of her, figuring she would let Max sleep while she loaded up on caffeine before leaving.

"Why are you up so early?" Max asked Sue, who was stirring her coffee, facing away from the living room. She was looking in the fridge for milk to take away the bitterness of the instant brew.

"I have to get going. My parents are having a New Year's brunch, and I promised to help set up the tables."

"I understand. Do you want to get some breakfast before you leave?"

"No. I'm still full from dinner last night," Sue said, turning to face Max. She had a radiant smile on her face, which made her host feel better about her early departure.

Sue gulped down her coffee and went into the coat closet for her sweater. Max sat up on the couch, filled with disappointment and confusion, while he watched her prepare to leave. He rubbed his eyes, in part to get the cobwebs out, but more to hold back the tears he felt welling up inside.

"I had an amazing time, Max. I think we're going to have a great 1979." Sue bent over and kissed Max on the cheek as she buttoned her sweater. She found her purse on the faux dining room table, put it under her shoulder, and headed down the stairs.

Max's New Year's Eve dinner, with a dash of intimacy as a nightcap, was officially over. He started replaying every minute of the night before and concluded that the Joe Taylor Show was the cause for the sudden romantic course correction. Simultaneously, though, Max was puzzled that Sue didn't ask for any details about Joe Taylor's visit. It wasn't as if Joe was scheduled to appear like a delivery from the local pizza parlor. Max was about to fall victim to one of his major foibles—trying to explain the inexplicable.

With a cup of coffee in hand, the reality of life was setting in for Max with a litany of challenges to tackle in the next several days. He debated calling Aaron on a day most family men spent with their spouses and children. He knew it was important to share his discovery about Joe Taylor's identity because Max had agreed to a meeting between the two of them and the FBI agent on January 2. Next on the list was to get Jack Devlin to delay their blockbuster for Sunday the fourteenth. Max hoped that either Tom or Ximena's stories were ready for publication, which would allow Max to delay his and Aaron's story to allow the Joe Taylor situation to come to a resolution.

It took Max until mid-afternoon to work up the courage to call Aaron Grant. In addition to informing his reporting partner about Joe Taylor's identity, it was time to come clean about the hidden FM transmitter plot. Going back to the one he and Barrett planted in the Carbon County Courthouse was not important; however, the device Barrett, with Sue's help, put in the elevator in city hall needed explanation.

Loretta Grant answered the phone. "Good afternoon, Grant residence."

"Happy New Year, Loretta. It's Max. I hope you, Aaron, and Bud had a great celebration. May I speak to your husband?"

"Sure, he's right here," Loretta called to Aaron in the living room and told him Max was on the phone.

"Max, Happy New Year. What's up?"

"I am sorry to bother you today, but we must talk. Can you get away for a few hours? It isn't something we can discuss on the phone."

"Sure, sure," Aaron answered, a bit perplexed. "Where do you want to meet?"

"There's a place called the Golden Gate Diner on Union in Allentown. I checked, and they are open today. Can we say in ninety minutes?"

"Yeah, sure. See you then."

What a way to start the year, Max thought as he got ready to leave. Meeting Aaron for a tell-all chat was not what Max figured he would be doing on the first day of 1979. Up until the late New Year's Eve events, Max fantasized about spending the day with Sue after their night together. Instead, his focus was on finding an easy way to confess to Aaron his plan to bug the mayor's elevator. Max wasn't sure to lead with the difficult news or the discovery of Joe Taylor's identity.

Max was fifteen minutes early and found a booth near the back of the diner. He was surprised at the number of people at the twenty-four-hour restaurant. There were three bowl games in progress, including the Sugar Bowl in which Penn State was playing Alabama for the NCAA Football crown. In contrast, New Year's Day in Philadelphia was a big one with the Mummers Parade—the city's answer to Mardi Gras. Locals lined the streets to watch men in glittering costumes strum their instruments and waltz down Second Street to the delight of half-sober onlookers.

Aaron showed up right on time. Max waved at him to come to the back booth. Max was so wrapped up in his dilemma, he didn't realize it was twenty degrees outside. Aaron took off his heavy overcoat, scarf, and gloves before sitting down.

Before Aaron even got comfortable in the booth, Max could no longer contain himself.

Following a series of deep breaths, Max spoke. "I have a few things to tell you. One you won't like; the other you will. Where should I start?"

"That's up to you."

"I was blown away by Devlin selecting me to be on this new Sunday Squad, and I wanted to do well. Anyway, I read about how, in the Cold War, the Russians and Americans spied on each other using FM transmitters."

"Yes, I know all about the bug in the Great Seal," Aaron replied, expecting the worst.

"After talking about some of the strange things regarding Mayor Donahue's background and ability to bring companies to the Lehigh Valley, I wanted to get an edge."

"So, you bugged his office, is that what you want to tell me?"

"No, with the help of a friend, we bugged his elevator."

Aaron nodded, not that he liked what he heard, but as a sign of acknowledgment. "So why are you telling me this now?"

"That's the other part of the news," Max said, saddened by Aaron's response. "I had an assignment on December 30 that involved a kidnapping. I was told to go to the FBI office in Scranton for a briefing that afternoon. To make a long, boring story short, I saw Joe Taylor's picture on the wall of heroes at the FBI office."

"What happened with the kidnapping?" Aaron asked, matter-of-factly.

"That's a story for another day. On New Year's Eve, I had a friend over for dinner, and Joe Taylor stopped by right before midnight to ask why we've been asking around about him. That's when I confronted him with my discovery."

"How did he take it?"

"Not great. But, see, here's the thing: he found out about the FM transmitter in the elevator. I'm not sure how, but he has it and is using it to threaten me away from writing our story. But now that I have something on him, we're in a stalemate."

Aaron Grant continued to shake his head as if he was hearing someone spin a fanciful yarn that was essentially bullshit. For a moment, Grant wondered if Max was making this all up. Having worked with Max, though, he knew what he was being told was not only plausible but most likely true.

"As difficult as it is for me to believe, I understand everything you're telling me. So, how did you leave things with Joe Taylor or whatever his name is?"

"I agreed that we'd meet him tomorrow morning. We, meaning you and me. I told Taylor that I already told you about his covert identity."

"Max, this is a lot to process. Have you set a time and place for this meet?"

"No, what do you suggest?"

"I don't think you'll like this, but right after you called, Jack Devlin called and said he wanted to have a Sunday Squad meeting at 10:30 a.m. tomorrow. How about we arrange to meet the mysterious Joe Taylor at 8:30 a.m. here. This place is out of the way for all of us. How are you supposed to let him know when and where to meet?"

"He's supposed to call me tonight."

Aaron Grant sat, staring at his reporting partner, wishing he had been paired up with Tom or Ximena, or anyone else for that matter.

"Let's talk before he calls. I need some time to think about this. You need to go home and make sure you don't miss his call."

It was a shade past 4 p.m., and the sun was beginning to set as Max got in his car. The temperature was beginning to drop as Max headed back to Nesquehoning. He was relieved that he unburdened himself of his misdeed to Aaron and hoped that his partner and now friend had the experience and practical wisdom to find a way out of this mess. Even more than Aaron not having a viable solution, the biggest concern was Jack Delvin's meeting scheduled for the next day. What if Max couldn't convince the managing editor to hold the front-page Sunday story?

Max had no sooner walked in the door to his apartment when the phone rang. He rushed over and grabbed the receiver off the cradle affixed to the wall in the kitchen. Out of breath, Max answered.

"Hi, this is Max."

"Max, it's Joe Taylor. I want to arrange our meeting tomorrow."

Before Taylor could say anything further, Max interrupted.

"I spoke to Aaron Grant, and we came up with 8:30 a.m. at the Golden Gate Diner. Do you know where that is?"

"I do. That works. Bring a copy of the draft of the story you and your pal wrote for the paper when you come. You know I've seen it, but there are some things I want to straighten out."

"Okay."

After his call with Joe Taylor, Max called Aaron to lock down the time and place. They spoke briefly, and Max reminded Aaron to bring the draft of the story they submitted to Devlin before the managing editor left on vacation.

With chaos in both the personal and professional parts of his life, Max slept poorly. Again, he thought how things could have been if New Year's Eve had ended differently. Max had no time to dwell on the what-ifs of his life; there were a series of hurdles he needed to clear to preserve his job and steer clear of any legal action.

Running on pure adrenaline, Max was up and out the door at seven in the morning. Traffic was light even with folks getting back to work. It took him only forty-five minutes to get to the east side of Allentown. He parked outside the diner, where he stared off into space and took stock of his situation. Max remembered a close friend in college telling him to the best way to assess your position in any crossroads is to think of the best and worst that could happen. In this case, Max was hard-pressed to think of the best case; far too many things would have to fall in place for him to emerge unscathed. As far as worst-case, it was too dangerous to go down that path as it would have a paralyzing effect.

Max spotted Aaron pull up in front of the diner. As Aaron got out of the car, Max got out of his and called his colleague's name. Aaron turned around and waved but had a stern look on his face. This was not how the more senior reporter wanted to spend the morning on his first day back at work for the new year.

The two men entered the diner and grabbed the same booth they shared the day before. Seated across from each other, the two men ordered coffee but nothing to eat. No words were exchanged, and at 8:40 a.m., Joe Taylor walked in. Taylor was skilled at hiding in plain sight as he walked over to the booth without looking at anyone.

"Gentlemen. Aaron, nice to see you again. I've heard a lot about you over the past few years. Your reputation precedes you," Taylor said, taking off his coat and sliding in the booth next to Max.

Aaron nodded but said nothing in response.

"So, here we are. You two know about me, and I have some incriminating evidence against you. Well, at least against Max."

Max was in over his head, fighting for the right response. Luckily, Aaron was armed and ready.

"Joe, or whatever you name is, I know you are more than familiar with the concept of Mutually Assured Destruction," Aaron said forcefully, staring directly at Joe. "I think you would agree that's what we have on our hands here."

"I get your point," Taylor said, realizing he was up against someone with more guts and guile than Max. "How do you propose we proceed?"

"Neither of us has anything to gain by giving away each other's secrets," Aaron said in response.

"Oh? Then what do you propose?"

"Depending on where the FBI is in its investigation, we agree to hold our story until your case is wrapped up. We also want your help in fleshing out some of the details we may have missed in our work."

"In principle, that's fine, but I can't legally tell you where we are in our work," Taylor said. "We're close, but just how close I cannot share."

"Do you think you'll be done by January 14?" Max asked.

"Most likely, but not definitely," Taylor said, turning to face Max, seated to his right.

Max and Aaron exchanged glances. The two men had recently spent enough time together for them to get a read on each other's mindset.

"You have a deal," Aaron said, reaching out to shake Joe Taylor's hand.

"From now on, you can reach me at this private number," Taylor said, handing Aaron his card. "Let me review this draft of your story and see where I can add some color."

The men rose from the booth one at a time, led by Joe Taylor. Max left a five-dollar bill on the table to cover the two coffees. Aaron put his hand on Max's shoulder, indicating they should let Joe leave first.

Max looked at his watch and reminded Aaron they had a meeting with Jack Devlin and the other Sunday Squad members. It was 9:45 a.m., which gave them plenty of time to get to the *Chronicle* building a few miles away.

Before pulling away from the diner, Max felt some hope he'd be able to get out of his self-inflicted dilemma, not only without getting caught for his illegal transmitter. He even dared flirt with the possibility of an award-winning story at the end of this saga. There was reason to be hopeful, but Max knew many things could still go wrong and throw their deal with Joe Taylor off course.

Jack Devlin, Tom, and Ximena were in the *Chronicle*'s conference room when Max and Aaron walked in. It was ten thirty on the button, but Devlin was eager to get started.

"For starters, welcome back. I have some wonderful news. I spoke with Tim Daniels last week while I was on vacation, and we agreed to push your story on the mayor up to this weekend. Starting tomorrow, we have a full-scale promotion in place announcing the launch of the Sunday Squad. Kicking it off on the seventh with a blockbuster will boost circulation and put us in contention for some big awards."

Ximena and Tom stood and applauded Max and Aaron. In any other circumstance, Max would be proud of the recognition from his peers. In this case, not so much. He reached for something to say in return for the kind gesture from his peers but came up empty. Instead, his eyes locked on Aaron Grant, who was seated across the table. Calmly, Grant returned Max's stare with a half-smile. Max knew what he was thinking.

Holy shit. We're in trouble.

Chapter Nineteen

For the remaining forty-five minutes of the meeting, Max was there only in physical form. After the managing editor's gleeful declaration that Max and Aaron's investigative work would run in five days, he had no memory of what happened in the conference room. On his way out, Max did remember Tom Monahan saying that he was happy for Max getting star treatment for his work.

As Max left the *Chronicle* and walked into the parking lot, Aaron yelled at Max to get his attention.

"Max. Max! Wait a minute!"

After hearing Aaron, Max stopped dead in his tracks. He turned around and met his reporting partner halfway between their parked cars. While Max felt like he had the wind knocked out of him, Aaron appeared energized.

"I think we need to talk," Aaron said in a major understatement. "I see we have two options, and I'd like to talk them over. Call me here at the paper when you get back to Nesquehoning."

Max nodded and got into his car.

After starting his car and turning on the heat and defroster, Max had an unexplained urge to make a detour on his way back to the bureau. He made a right turn out of the parking lot, went three blocks, and made a left on Chew Street. He drove past the West End Cemetery and the Allentown Fair Grounds before he reached his destination.

Max parked in the lot of Keneseth Israel, the synagogue where he taught during his four years in college. He got out of his car, walked to the corner where Chew Street ended, and stood, surveying his alma mater that occupied the next several blocks. To the left stood the fraternity he had joined, but he was only a social member. Ahead on the right was the school's Commons building, which housed the cafeteria, bookstore, and the student radio station, which held Max's best college memories. Beyond the Commons was the dorm Max lived in for the last three years of school.

After fifteen minutes of standing silently, Max returned to his car and got on the road back toward the bureau. As he drove, Max tried to comprehend why he felt compelled to visit the school he graduated from nearly four years earlier. The best he could come up with, at that moment, was to try to understand the path that took him from four tumultuous years as an undergraduate student to where he was in his personal and professional life on January 2 of the new year.

After Max reached the parking lot of the *Chronicle*'s Nesquehoning bureau, it was evident that the forty-five-minute ride did little to provide any answers to Max's existential dilemma. It was 12:30 p.m. when Max walked into the office, filled with reporters and circulation department personnel. Tex, Al, and even Ervin came over and wished their star reporter a happy new year. Tex gave his friend and colleague the once-over since he was the only one in the office who knew about Max's pressure.

"I'm in the office," Max said softly, after reaching Aaron on the phone. "We can talk, but I have to be careful about what I say at this end."

"I get it. As I see it, we have two options. What if we came up with a better story than the investigation into the mayor? That kidnapping you talked about that happened last week—what if we were able to break that open?"

"In four days? I'm not sure about that."

"The other choice is to go to Jack Devlin and come clean."

"I like the first choice better," Max said with a major sigh. "Give me until the end of the day to see what I can find. I thought of an idea that I can tell you about after calling a friend who is a lawyer in Philadelphia."

After getting off the phone, Max looked through his new briefcase to find the number of Norm Weiss, his friend and lawyer in Philadelphia who had been a great help during the chemical dumping story. Norm was instrumental in getting Dan Bigelow a settlement against Andersen Trucking. Since working on that case, Norm Weiss's firm made the headlines regularly for its work in an emerging class of whistleblower cases. With that work, Max hoped, Norm may have made some contacts at various law enforcement agencies.

The purpose of Max's call was twofold: Norm may have some background on the kidnapping case involving Arnie Mitchell's wife, and he possibly may know more about the timing of the FBI investigation into Mayor Donahue and his varied associates. Norm was the kind of man whose character was such that he gained trust from everyone he worked with. It was not too far out of the realm of possibility he might have a contact at the FBI office in Philadelphia.

The switchboard operator at Fogel-Rothchild-Hess, Weiss's firm, told Max that Norm was out at a trial but would be calling in for messages. Max left word that it was important that he reached Norm before the end of business and gave both his work and home phone numbers.

Before making his next call, Max walked back to the series of file cabinets jammed against the wall between the assignment editor's desk at the back office where Ray Tomjanovich once sat. In each file cabinet was a series of small manila envelopes stuffed with newspaper clippings. This section of the bureau represented the bureau's archives and was handled with great care by the reporters. Anytime a folder was removed, it was returned to its designated spot, which was in alphabetical order by the year—the files dated back to 1969, before which stories were on microfiche.

Max removed the folders for Arnie Mitchell and a separate one for *Tickle* magazine. He took them back to his desk just as his phone rang.

"Hey, Max, I'm returning your call." It was Norm Weiss, who sounded like he was in the middle of a busy intersection. "I'm at a payphone near City Hall, and I got your message. What's up?"

"Without a long explanation, I was wondering if you could find out some information on two matters. One is related to a kidnapping last week in Allentown. It is the wife of that porno publisher Arnie Mitchell. To make a long story short, the FBI claimed it was not a kidnapping, but I suspect there's more to the story."

"Uh-uh," Norm responded. "What else?"

"This is the big one. I know the FBI is investigating the mayor of Allentown on corruption charges. I would imagine they would need indictments in advance; is there a way you could find out when those are likely to be handed down?"

"Hmm," Norm said, "those are some tall orders. I'll tell you what—I feel I owe you because that chemical dumping case put my firm on the map, and we've taken off. Give me some time, and I'll poke around."

"Anything you can do would be great," Max said, hoping for a small miracle. "My clock is ticking."

After the call ended, Max opened the envelopes he had taken from the file cabinet and learned more than he cared to know about Arnie Mitchell and his magazine. After reading about how Mitchell built his empire—by eliminating the competition one way or the other—Max concluded this was not a story he could put together in time to offer it as a substitute for the mayoral investigation.

In need of a friendly voice, Max dialed Sue's home number to see how her family's New Year's Day Brunch went. Instead of reaching Sue, Max got her answering machine with a message that was short and sweet: "I'm not here. Please leave a message."

"Sue, it's Max. I was just checking in to see how your family brunch went and wish you a happy New Year. Call me back today when you get a chance."

Max looked up to see Ervin had gotten off the phone after a long conversation. Max left his desk and walked up to speak with Ervin, who was on as editor that day.

"Ervin, have you seen Sue around? I wanted to talk to her."

"I got a call from Allentown that she's on some sort of special assignment for the rest of the week. I took her off the calendar for any assignments."

"Special assignment?" Max asked with a puzzled look.

"I have no idea what that's about. Are you ready for an assignment? The Tamaqua Borough Council has an emergency meeting tonight. Something happened to the high school's water main, and they must figure out where to get the money to repair it. The borough's 1979 budget hasn't been approved yet."

"Sure. I wanted to head out that way to talk to someone for another story."

Max stopped to say hello to Tex, grabbed his coat and briefcase, and headed for the parking lot. It was three thirty, and the emergency meeting was scheduled for six. That gave him plenty of time to meet with one man who could provide some help with his race against the clock and the FBI.

Matt Carpenter was sitting at the same table at the Coal Miner's Bar and Grill as he was when Max first met him. Uncle Matt was finishing a pint and watching the Cotton Bowl on TV when Max walked over. Uncle Matt rose and extended his meaty hand.

"Let me finish my beer," Uncle Matt said, never taking his eyes off the game. "I have Nebraska plus four points, and I think my money's safe. Grab a seat. Do you want something?"

"I'm fine, sir. I do need your help, and it's important."

Matt placed his sixteen-ounce glass on a paper coaster, which seemed odd given the table had seen better days. "How can I help you, man?"

"I know you have your ear to the ground on matters related to the union and local politics. I wonder what sort of people you know in law enforcement?"

"Why?" Matt said with a laugh. "You need a parking ticket fixed?"

Max stopped and gathered his thoughts. He needed to tell Uncle Matt what was going on briefly without revealing many gory details. Max had no choice but to trust Tex's uncle.

"I don't need to tell you about the underhanded dealings of the union and its relationship with local politicians. Things are coming to a head based on an FBI investigation, but I don't know when. I must find out when indictments are going to be served. My career depends on it."

Matt picked up his beer and finished it with one gulp. He signaled to the bartender he wanted a refill by holding up one finger.

"Buckley told me you would be coming by," Matt said. "I had a chance to make some calls before you got here."

"Buckley? Who is Buckley, sir?"

Matt let out a roar that shook the table. "Son, that's Tex's real name. Do you think my sister named him Tex?" When he finally stopped laughing, he continued. "So, here's what I know. And, by the way, you did not hear this from me. One of the union guys told me that he was asked to testify against Gentile and Hinke. They told him to be ready over the weekend."

"Do you know if that's Saturday or Sunday?"

"My guess honestly would be Saturday, probably later afternoon, but that's just a guess. Sunday, around these parts, is considered a day off even for the FBI."

182

Max slapped a ten-dollar bill on the table and said, "Uncle Matt, I owe you one. Let me pay for your beer."

Tamaqua City Hall was a ten-minute ride from the bar, giving Max enough time to grab something to eat. An undercooked flame-broiled burger and fries from Burger King served as dinner, after which Max walked across the street from the burger joint to the borough hall. He was right on time, and the meeting was brief. The borough manager, Pete Marshall, suggested the borough take a short-term loan against its cash reserve to fix the high school problem. The motion passed unanimously, and the meeting was over.

It was a long way to go for such a minor story, but Max knew the trip was worth it. The clock was still ticking, but hope emerged that he and Aaron might get lucky, and the FBI would announce the end of its multi-year probe in enough time to make the deadline for the Sunday paper. The timing would be tricky no matter how things evolved as he and Aaron would need time to add to their existing story before the paper went to press at 10 p.m. Saturday.

Max was back at his desk at 8:15 p.m., giving him more than enough time to write up the Tamaqua borough council story. As he reached for some paper to feed into his Selectric, Max noticed a message taped to his phone. It read: "Call Norm Weiss tonight. He has what you asked for."

Max powered through his five-hundred-word story on the water main issue at the Tamaqua High School. Technically, Tamaqua was in Schuylkill County, which was somewhat outside the *Chronicle*'s coverage area. But since people in cities such as Jim Thorpe, Lehighton, and Palmerton had relatives or did business in Tamaqua, the borough was included, for the most part, in the paper's Carbon County edition.

After dropping off the story on Ervin's desk, Max told the night editor that he was headed home, and if there were any questions about his work, he could call him there. Max lived ten minutes from the bureau, so he could hurry back if anything major was required.

Feeling a little queasy after his greasy dinner, Max took a ginger ale from the fridge after taking off his coat. He took a few sips and then picked up the phone to return Norm's call. He knew Norm had kids, so he wanted to reach him before it was time for goodnight stories and last-minute glasses of water.

"Norm, I got your message in the office but waited until I got home to call you."

"That's fine. I have some great news. A friend of a friend who I worked with on my last case involving a whistleblower at the Navy Yard here in the city knows someone reliable in the FBI office in Philadelphia."

"And?" Max pushed, hurriedly.

"There will be an FBI conference at the Lehigh Valley office late afternoon Saturday. Right now, it's about 90 percent certain, but will be locked down no later than tomorrow afternoon."

"Do you know what could prevent it from going down?"

"No, I don't. These things have a timetable of their own. At first, I thought they picked Saturday afternoon to avoid media attention, but I think it's more that they have to bring in some other agencies that need some time to prepare."

Max took a deep breath. "Is there any way I can know it's 100 percent certain?"

"Sorry, Max, there isn't."

"I am deeply indebted for what you did for me, and I will never forget it."

"I am glad to help. You see, I know you, and your intentions are honorable here. You just got a little zealous and maybe took a few shortcuts."

Max didn't respond. He was not about to tell Norm about the transmitter, his run-ins with Joe Taylor, or his pressing deadline. There was no sense in burdening his friend with more than he needed to know.

"Again, thank you. Talk to you soon."

At this point, there was little Max could do but wait. His temptation was to try to bluff Joe Taylor and tell him he knew the FBI would announce the results of its investigation on Saturday. In his past dealings with the undercover agent, however, he had more than met his match. The risk of Max being wrong this late in the game would spell disaster for the young reporter's personal life and professional career. Max's best option was to meet with Aaron and tell him what he learned from Matt Carpenter and Norm Weiss.

Despite being stressed, Max was so exhausted that he slept well. He went through his usual morning routine and was in the office at 10a.m. He picked up the January 3 edition of the *Chronicle* and found his story on the Tamaqua Borough Council meeting buried on page four of the local Carbon County edition. The story was so short that the editor in Allentown had omitted Max's byline, which was customary for such reporting. It recalled the time he covered a car crash in Lansford, and one of the editors in Allentown spelled Max's last name incorrectly.

Max looked at his watch and at eleven he called Aaron Grant in the office. Grant was on the phone, so the call went straight to voice mail. Max asked Aaron to call him back as soon as possible.

With nothing next to Max's name on the assignment board, he could spend the day doing some more background work on the Arnie Mitchell kidnapping case. Max still had the file folders on his desk that he had taken out of the bureau's archives the day before. He emptied the folders and laid out the stories in chronological order.

Arnie Mitchell came to Allentown from New York, where he worked for Bob Guccione at *Penthouse*. Mitchell oversaw hiring photographers for the model shoots but was unhappy with the popular adult magazine's mainstream direction. Wanting to start a competitive, more risqué porno magazine, he chose Allentown as his headquarters because of its proximity to two of the nation's four largest cities.

Max was about to read a profile piece on Mitchell done by *Philadelphia Magazine* in 1976 when his phone rang.

"Max, it's Aaron. What's up?"

For the next five minutes, talking at warp speed, Max updated his partner about his conversations with Matt Carpenter and Norm Weiss.

"So, what's our next move?" Max said with more than a touch of fear in his voice.

"I know I said we had only two paths—tell Jack Devlin or find another story," Grant said firmly. "I think we have another. Is there a way to do a three-way call with our phone system?"

"I'm sure there is. What do you have in mind?"

"We get on the phone with Joe Taylor. If we ask the right questions, we should get the right answers."

"I am not sure I follow exactly, but I trust you. I will find out how we can do the call. Should we say 3 p.m.?"

"Sure. Just call me as soon as you can confirm we can pull this off technically."

Max asked the only person in the office who would know the *Chronicle* phone system's inner workings. Tex was seated twenty feet away on the other side of the office, reading the latest issue of *Rolling Stone*.

"Sorry to bother you," Max said when he was within earshot of Tex. "Do you know how to do a three-way call?"

"You betcha." Tex put down his magazine. Cheech and Chong, the stoner comedy act, was on the cover, but Tex was focused on the album reviews. "It's simple. I'll write down the steps."

Max called Aaron and said the three-way call was a go. Max would first call Aaron and then Joe Taylor on his private number. At that point, Aaron would take over.

The hands on the ancient wall clock in the bureau appeared to Max to be moving backward as he waited for the three o'clock showdown. He was too nervous to eat but nibbled on a bag of Bachman pretzel sticks he brought back from his last trip to see his family.

At 2:58, Max dialed Aaron. Aaron confirmed the connection was clear. He told Max to take deep breaths and dial Joe Taylor.

"Yeah, who is this?" Joe Taylor answered angrily on his private line, indicating he was busy.

"Joe, it's Aaron Grant and Max Rosen. Do you have a minute?"

"I do. Your minute starts now."

"We understand the investigation is over, and the FBI is holding a press conference on Saturday to announce the results. Can you confirm that?"

"Where the hell did you hear that?" Taylor said with a furious visceral reaction. After those words, there was a long pause. "Look, guys, I am tired of this back and forth game. Let's have an honest conversation."

"That's all we want," Aaron responded.

"Your information is correct. I must applaud you for your legwork and the accuracy of your information. You are better reporters than I originally thought."

"It was mostly Max's work," Aaron said.

"The people I spoke to," Max said, joining the conversation, "are good, honest people who have no intention of interfering with the wheels of justice. They are only interested that the truth comes out."

"Yeah, yeah, I get it," Joe Taylor answered with a much softer tone in his voice. "Let me tell you what's going on. In exchange, I ask a favor. Agreed?"

"Depends on the favor," Max said in a lighthearted way.

"Yes, we will announce the termination of our investigation into Mayor Donahue, the union guy, and the head of the local Democratic Party. It will be around three on Saturday afternoon. We will announce the indictments were handed down and give a general recap of the years-long work."

"That must be some favor you're asking for that," Max said.

"That kidnapping you looked into last week—the one with Arnie Mitchell's wife. Well, there's a lot more to the story, as you probably figured out. I want you, Max, to dig into it like you did the mayoral corruption case."

"It sounds like this is personal to you," Aaron said, sensing more to Joe's request.

"This guy Mitchell—he's a real piece of shit. We believe he uses underage girls in his photos, but no one has ever proven it. It's just a hunch, but we suspect the faux kidnapping was from someone or a group looking out for revenge for his slimeball antics."

"I've been going through a lot of background—you know, how he left New York and *Penthouse* because it wasn't bold enough for him," Max said with a determined tone. "I am happy to look into it as far as it goes."

"I want you to promise me you'll bury that guy," Taylor added. "When we meet, I can give you a couple of off-the-record leads."

"When did you want to meet?" Aaron asked.

"How about Friday afternoon? I'd like to go over the draft of your story and help fill in some of the blanks. You should tell your editor—that Devlin guy, right? —that you will have a final version Saturday."

"Where should we meet?" Aaron and Max asked in near unison.

"That same diner works. See you gentlemen then."

As he placed the phone on its cradle, Max's heart raced. It was all over. Looming before him was a probable award-winning story of corruption, with another big piece waiting in the wings. It was the best Max had felt since the moment Joe Taylor knocked on his door on New Year's Eve. Life had been looking gloomy, but now, everything was falling into place.

Aaron Grant called Max to strategize on how to approach Jack Devlin with the news. Since Aaron worked in Allentown's main office, he suggested that he approach Devlin face-to-face. Grant felt that the managing editor wouldn't mind the last-minute changes given the FBI announcement's timing.

Max spent the rest of the day and Thursday poring over every piece of reporting that had been done about Arnie Mitchell since he moved to the Lehigh Valley. Thursday, Max drove down to the Allentown Public Library and sat in front of a microfiche machine reading stories in national magazines and other newspapers about the porno king. By the time he drove back to Nesquehoning on Thursday night, he had three large folders filled with copies of stories related to the smut publisher, his background, family, and other businesses he owned.

Knowing his partner was out of the office, Aaron left a message on Max's home answering machine, stating that everything was good with Devlin. The newspaper had been running promos on its new Sunday series, promising for some blockbuster reporting. Max and Aaron were happy they wouldn't be disappointing the newspaper and its readers.

The meeting with Joe Taylor on Friday afternoon was a brief twenty minutes. Over cups of coffee at the same diner where the three men had their Mexican Standoff days before, the mood was light but with serious undertones. Joe finally went through the draft of the story and made notes in the margins, adding color where necessary and crossing out things that he knew to be erroneous. Before they left their booth, Joe handed Max a blue folder with the FBI logo taken off.

"Here's everything you need to put that son of bitch behind bars," Taylor said, handing the papers over the Max. "You need to let your buddy here help you. I think you have promise, but he's a wily veteran."

Max nodded his head. "Thanks for everything. Will we see you Saturday?"

"Wouldn't miss it for the world. I'll be in the back trying to be inconspicuous with some of the others who worked on this case with me."

A cold drizzle had begun shortly after sunset. The temperature never got above twenty-five on January 4, and there was concern that freezing rain was on the way. The weather was not on Aaron and Max's mind as they drove over to the *Chronicle* office. For the next three hours, they revised their story and added detail to make the words jump off the page. It was close to 9 p.m. when they were done, so Max and Aaron put their final version in Jack Devlin's inbox. Aaron followed that by calling Devlin at home with the word that they were finished and post-editing; the story was good to go.

Max got back to Nesquehoning after ten, but he was far too amped to go to sleep. He hadn't eaten anything since lunch, so he popped a frozen lasagna into the toaster oven and grabbed the phone. Max was on top of the world and wanted to share his excitement. He wanted to share it with Sue.

Max again reached Sue's answering machine with her oddly short message. "Hi Sue, it's Max. Again. I have some great news to share. Call me."

As he hung up, Max realized he hadn't spoken to Sue since January 1, the morning after their romantic dinner was rudely interrupted. As he put his makeshift dinner on the table, Max realized he had heartfelt feelings for Sue. As he ate, he replayed New Year's Eve, and while they never consummated their special time together, he hoped it wouldn't be long before they rekindled the flame of that night.

Max slept in Saturday morning and took his time reading the paper and having breakfast. He devoured the last bagel he had brought back from his last trip to Philadelphia, along with some veggie cream cheese that he lathered on the poppyseed bagel. Max envisioned the Sunday paper's front page with his and Aaron's story dominating the entire section above the fold. While Max didn't necessarily care about the attention and possible awards, he did think about the ninety-nine newspapers that rejected him and how lucky he was that he wound up working for the *Chronicle*.

The FBI office in Allentown was on Hamilton and took up half a block. The building was a mix of old and new with most of the original architecture in place while, per new safety standards, the windows and roof had been upgraded. There was no public parking lot, so Max got a spot down the block in front of the Allentown School District building, closed for the weekend.

Joe Taylor left their names at the front desk, and after showing his ID, Max was led to a large conference room at the end of the hallway on the main floor. He was only fifteen minutes early, but he spotted Aaron seated halfway from the front as he entered the room. Max joined him without saying a word.

Promptly at three, the regional director, Len Breslin, who orchestrated the operation, came up to the stage and spent close to thirty minutes going through the case involving Mayor Donahue and a host of conspirators. Not all names were revealed, but the man in charge described their roles in some detail. Breslin was quick to thank the agents involved in the work, mentioning that some were involved for several years working undercover. Max and Aaron traded glances and smiled.

Once the press conference was over, Max and Aaron got up from their seats and looked for Joe Taylor to offer their thanks. It had been a rocky relationship, but in the end, the undercover FBI agent came through. Max spotted Joe Taylor speaking to a female agent at the back of the room on the far side from where he stood. As Max and Aaron walked over, Joe Taylor saw them and waved the two men to come over.

Max was walking in front of Aaron as they reached the corner where Joe Taylor was standing. He turned his back toward Max and Aaron and gently took the arm of the female agent standing to his left. As she turned to face the two reporters, Max felt a bomb go off in his chest.

"Hi, Max," the female agent said, reaching out to touch Max's arm.

"Sue?" Max whispered as he felt his world cave in.

Chapter Twenty

Max stood motionless. He stared at Sue and tried to take it all in. Everything suddenly made sense.

Sue was working for the FBI, meaning she told Joe about Barrett planting the transmitter in the city hall elevator. She was the one who knew Max would be in Allentown the day of the transmitter planting. Thanks to Sue, the FBI knew every one of Max's moves, which kept them one step ahead. That included the logistics behind the whole fake bugging of Max's home phone.

And then there was New Year's Eve. Sue told Joe Taylor where Max would be that night. Taylor's sudden arrival at Max's home came as no surprise to Max's dinner guest; it was now obvious why she never asked Max why Joe Taylor had shown up.

The New Year's Eve charade hurt the worst. Max took a deep breath, allowing him to keep his composure and hold on to his dignity for a few more minutes. With Max impersonating a statue, Sue broke the ice.

"Max, I need to tell you that this was more than an act. I did not plan on developing feelings for you, and I'm not sorry about that."

Overhearing this heartbreaking conversation, Joe Taylor signaled Aaron Grant and suggested they give Max and Sue some privacy.

"Max, I'll be in the lobby. Come talk to me before you leave," Grant said.

Before Joe Taylor left the meeting room, he reached out his hand to Max.

"Here, this is for you," Taylor said, handing Max the FM transmitter that was planted in City Hall. "I deactivated it, but I thought you might want it as a souvenir. In case we never meet again, I wish you luck in your career—you have great potential."

Max and Sue were now alone in the back of the room, where the details of Max and Aaron's big story had come to fruition. He tried to make sense of colliding emotional forces that gripped his soul. Was Sue's masquerade some sort of cosmic punishment for using spycraft to get the story about Chris Albrecht's trial? The sponge that was Max's memory flashed through every moment he and Sue spent together and realized it was a joke, and he was the punchline.

"Max, please say something," Sue said, softly pleading.

"I don't know what to say," Max responded. He felt the uncontrollable urge to weep, but deep inside, he remained calm. "I guess I have a lot to think about." Max looked toward the door, knowing the clock on his emotional dam was ticking and was about to burst.

Sue reached into her purse and pulled out a small, neatly wrapped package. Before Max could move away, she reached for his arm and gently held him in place.

"This is for you. Please don't open it until you get home. I will never forget you and the time we had together. Someday, I hope you forgive me, but my job can be a tough one on me and the people around me."

Max walked out the door and stopped for a moment to talk to Aaron.

"Are you all right?" Aaron asked Max with deep concern.

"I don't know. Please just let me go."

Max left the FBI building and walked the few blocks to his car. He had placed the decommissioned transmitter and Sue's gift in his new briefcase. Once in his car, Max placed his new bag on the passenger's seat. Knowing he couldn't wait until he got home, Max reached inside and took out Sue's gift.

Inside the gift wrap was a new bottle of Chanel No. 5 with a note:

Dear Max,

I know how much you liked my fragrance. Please give this to the woman you meet who can love you the way you need and deserve to be loved.

"Sue"

With that, the dam burst, and Max wept like never before.

Max let the flood of sadness run its course. After what seemed like an eternity, he started the car but had no idea where to go. He wanted to be alone, but he needed to talk to someone. Max had been with the newspaper for over four months. While he was friendly with many of his colleagues, there wasn't anyone with whom he could share such a personal crisis.

For a brief moment, Max thought about going to Philadelphia to stay with his parents, but that refuge would come with a series of questions. The words "I hope you know what you're doing" from his mother still lingered in his memory. Max was not up for any reminder of his foolishness. He knew Barrett, who was emotionally shut off to such matters, also wouldn't be much help. That left Max with his only choice—go back to his apartment in Nesquehoning and sort things out.

Max knew it would not be wise to turn on the car radio. Any one of several sad or sentimental songs would lead to a stream of tears. He drove in silence the entire forty-five minutes, oblivious to everything around him except for the traffic. Max hadn't eaten since breakfast but had no interest in stopping along the way; he was too busy eating his heart out.

The memory that served him so well throughout school and in his current career was now a curse. Max could relive every moment with Sue over the past few months, including their afternoon pretending to look at apartments in Allentown. Thinking of the night of the company Christmas party, when he drove a drunk Sue back to his apartment, just added to his painful recollections.

Max arrived home in Carbon County just as many people were making their plans for a fun Saturday night. Despite the cold weather, his neighbors were no doubt deciding where to go out for dinner or what movie to see. *Kramer vs. Kramer* had just made its way up to theaters in Lehighton and Jim Thorpe, and both movie houses would be packed that night. For Max, his plan for Saturday night was simple—go to bed and hope that January 6 was just a bad dream when he woke up.

In the middle of the night, hunger got the best of Max. He woke up at 2 a.m. and made himself a cheese sandwich and opened a can of Campbell's vegetable soup. Max dined in a complete daze and returned to his bedroom sanctuary as soon as he put his dinner plates in the sink.

At eight o'clock on Sunday morning, Max opened his eyes and instantly remembered that his and Aaron's big story would be splashed across the *Chronicle*'s front page. He rushed down, grabbed the paper from on top of the mat outside his door, and gingerly walked up the stairs. He went to the couch and took the paper out of the plastic bag that protected it from the elements. The headline screamed across the top of the Sunday edition of the *Chronicle*.

Mayor Mark Donahue, Union, and Political Leaders Busted in FBI Sting

Despite the trauma of the last twenty-four hours, Max took pride in the work he and Aaron had done. The story ran across the entire front page above the fold. The details were shared in powerful prose, which was predominantly Max's handiwork. The reporting went into an elaborate description of the facts: Mayor Mark Donahue was recruited from Springfield, Illinois, where he had a bad reputation as a crooked politician and less-than-honorable businessman. Brokered by his father-in-law, Jim, who was well connected in the Lehigh Valley, there was a secret meeting between the local union and the Democratic Party.

The county had experienced severe economic depression, so the union and local politicians cooked up a scheme to elect a puppet mayor who would act as a front to bring new businesses to Allentown and the surrounding area. The union wanted to focus on manufacturing jobs and insisted they be located in run-down areas where buildings could be purchased at auction. Union contractors would get a huge shot in the arm with remodeling work.

Everything fell into place when Mark Donahue agreed to be part of the scam. Donahue was looking for a reason to leave Illinois, given his business and personal indiscretions. While it wasn't in the story, Max would later find out that it was Matt Carpenter, a union shop steward, who tipped off the FBI years ago that something fishy was going on. At that point, the FBI began an investigation and finessed one of its top undercover agents into the inner circle.

Max's well of despair was lifted. Even though he knew it would take time to get past his quasi-relationship with Sue, he needed to focus on what he and Aaron had achieved. He couldn't overlook the fact that he had another story, the Arnie Mitchell kidnapping, waiting to be tackled.

With the Philadelphia Eagles season over, Max watched the Houston Oilers get shellacked by a stellar Pittsburgh Steelers team 34–5 in the AFC Conference Championship game. It was a big day for Steelers wide receivers Lynn Swann and John Stallworth, with each catching a touchdown pass from quarterback Terry Bradshaw. Max skipped the second game of Championship Sunday as an Eagles fan who hated the team's division rivals. This was because the Dallas Cowboys took on the Los Angeles Rams, with the winner going on to the Super Bowl.

Even though he hated being disturbed while watching football, Max didn't mind answering the phone when congratulations poured in from friends, family, and work colleagues. Max's parents called bright and early to tell him the investigative feature also ran in the *Philadelphia Inquirer*. Max thought about telling them about his breakup—or whatever one could call it—with Sue. He planned on going home Thursday, so his tale of woe could wait. The best call came from Norm Weiss, who was happy for Max and glad to help with his work's late stages. When Max told him about his upcoming visit to Philadelphia, Norm made his friend promise to call so they could get together.

As the day wore on, it morphed into a typical downer Sunday for Max. The excitement of his work faded, and his feelings of sadness over Sue began to take hold. Max knew the amount of personal courage it had taken to get close to Sue, and then having it backfire made him wary about future relationships. His feelings were exacerbated when he realized that he didn't have the kind of close friends he could talk to about his state of unhappiness after all these years. An hour before dinnertime, Max was overcome with exhaustion, so he curled up on the sofa and took a nap.

The downstairs neighbors' door slammed, waking Max up from his deep, late-afternoon slumber. He looked at the kitchen clock, and it read eight o'clock, so he grabbed some leftovers from the fridge and ate them over the sink. It was a far cry from the setting he so carefully put together for New Year's Eve, less than a week before. Still tired, even after a solid nap, Max felt it was time to bring the day to an end, so he turned in for the night.

After a restless night, Max finally gave up and got out of bed. He was awake for an hour, spending that time replaying various events of the past month and wondering what was next. Walking to the kitchen for a glass of water, he noticed a call on his answering machine. For a moment, he hoped it was Sue wanting to provide him with answers to the countless questions that raced through his mind. The call was from eleven o'clock the night before from Jack Devlin, asking Max to come down to the main office as early as possible on Monday.

Max was anxious to get the day going, so he showered and was out the door by seven and on his way down to the *Chronicle*'s main office. Once he arrived there, Max went across the street to the deli for a cup of coffee and a toasted bagel. He didn't figure Devlin was going to provide breakfast for their meeting.

"There he is," Jack Devlin said to everyone within earshot as Max walked in from the parking lot. "The man of the hour." The twenty reporters in the newsroom rose to their feet and applauded the arrival of the hero of the moment. Recognition in the newspaper business was not commonplace, and Max could feel himself turning red from the attention.

"Let's go into my office," Devlin said to Max, putting his arm around the young reporter. "It's difficult to believe you've only been with the paper for three months. It's also hard to fathom how you bounced back after such a rough start," Devlin added with a bit of a chuckle. "We have some big plans for you."

"Really?" Max responded, his voice suddenly going up three octaves.

"I feel bad for the Nesquehoning bureau because, as of today, we're transferring you to the main office. I spoke to the publisher, and we wanted you to be closer to where the action is and make it easier for you and Aaron Grant to work together."

"Wow, that is amazing," Max answered, somewhat in shock. "You may not know this, but I was apartment hunting in Allentown just a month ago. I went to college here, and there's a section of town near the school and the fairgrounds I like a lot."

"Perfect. You up for the new challenge?" Jack Devlin paused a minute and laughed. "Wait, of course, you are. Who am I kidding?"

"I need a break for a few days, so I planned on going to visit my parents in Philadelphia. Can we discuss the details when I get back?"

"Sure. Take as much time as you need—you earned it. I'm sure your family is quite proud of you."

Max drove back to Nesquehoning after he met with the managing editor. Going back to the office made him uncomfortable. Max determined that the best course of action at this time was to stop at his apartment, call into the bureau, and then head down the turnpike to Philadelphia. Max would tell whichever editor was on duty at the bureau that he needed some time off after a hectic week.

Al Hickey answered the phone. Max hadn't spoken to Al since before the holidays, so the call was filled with praise for Aaron and Max's work. "I taught you everything you know," Al joked. "You're a good kid. Take the time and relax."

After gathering up some clothes—including a lot of dirty laundry—Max took off for the sixty-mile ride. The radio was off and had been off since Saturday when Sue's bombshell dropped. While slightly reluctant to turn it on, the long ride needed some sort of musical or talk accompaniment. Sports talk seemed like a great choice, and given that WCAU in Philadelphia had a long signal reach, Max was able to focus on angry fans talking about how bad the Phillies would be in 1979 and the disappointing past season of the Eagles. As one of many millions of long-suffering area sports fans, the gibberish was music to Max's ears.

Max was planning to surprise his parents. But as he pulled into their driveway, he could see into the garage, and his mother's car was gone. At three in the afternoon, his mom and dad were most likely grocery shopping. Max understood the Rosen family fridge was never empty. And then there was the spare chill chest in the basement that would also be loaded, primarily with fruits and vegetables.

After nearly two days of maintaining his emotions, Max broke into tears as soon as he walked in the door. He wasn't sure what sparked this outburst of emotion, but he suspected there were some bad memories in that two-story duplex that remained close to the surface. He hadn't given a lot of thought to what he'd tell his parents about Sue, but there weren't a lot of people he could trust with such deeply personal information, and Max knew he needed to tell someone. It didn't seem like a good dinnertime topic, so Max decided to play it by ear to find the proper time for this heavy download.

While waiting for his folks to come home, Max called Barrett and told his friend and co-conspirator he'd like to see him on Tuesday. It was too cold outside for tennis hustling, so Barrett was free all day. They decided to meet for coffee halfway between their places, which happened to be in the neighborhood where they grew up.

After hanging up, Max heard his mother's car pull into the driveway. He went out to help with the groceries, and after seeing him come down the steps, Max's mother got out of the car, raced over, and hugged him.

"What a wonderful surprise. Are you hungry? If I knew you were coming, I would have made something special."

"I am a little hungry," Max answered, leaving his mother's embrace and walking over to his father. Max put his arms around the senior Rosen and kissed his neck. It was something Max saw his dad do to his father as a show of love, and Max always followed suit.

After groceries were unloaded, Max sat at the kitchen table while his mother magically whipped up a grilled cheese and tomato sandwich and a cup of homemade pea soup. Even with years of practice, Max figured he'd never possess his mother's effortless kitchen skills.

While Max was eating, the feeling he had when he came into the house returned. He put down his sandwich and began crying. Startled, his parents frantically asked what was wrong.

"You've had such a wonderful week, Max. What could be the matter?" his mother said, handing her son a tissue.

With that, as if he were a balloon punctured by a large pin, the words quickly streamed out, and Max told his parents most of the details of the past few weeks. He did leave out the parts about Joe Taylor and the planting of the FM transmitter, but the rest of the saga remained intact.

"You're talking about the girl from New Year's Eve, right?" his father asked.

"Yes, that's her."

"Wow, an FBI agent. That's something," Harold Rosen added.

Max's mother knew her son well and decided not to say anything—at least for the moment.

"Well, at least you're home to think things over. You can see your friends, eat well, and relax. We're always here to talk over anything you want," she said.

"Thank you. I feel better just telling you."

Lunch was getting cold, so Max resumed his meal after sharing his heartache with the two people he knew he could count on. True that sometimes confiding in his parents came with unwanted and impractical advice, but on that day, Max's hurt could only be healed by the ones who loved him most.

With his parents in the living room watching the early news, Max went down to the basement to look around. He was looking for something specific, and after finding the large folder stuffed with nearly a hundred sheets of paper, he sat on the couch and looked at them, one after the other.

The papers were rejection letters from ninety-nine of the one hundred newspapers he applied to in mid-1978. He marveled at each letter's off-white stationery with the embossed name of the paper at the top. They were all worded similarly, thanking Max for his application and wishing him good luck. The reasons for turning him down for a position ranged from lack of experience to no jobs being available at that moment.

After combing through the letters, Max played the what-if game. What if he was offered a job in Charlotte, North Carolina, or Hartford, Connecticut, or even Tulsa, Oklahoma—three newspapers that were at the top of his list when he sent out resumes and clips? What would it be like to live somewhere he had never been, such as Tulsa? Before moving to Nesquehoning, Max had never lived away from home except for college dorm life, which was an experience unto itself. Would he be scared living so far away from family, or would it be a new, exciting adventure?

It was approaching five thirty in the afternoon, thirty minutes past when the Rosens ate dinner when both of Max's parents worked. These days, with both parents retired, things were a bit more casual—dinnertime was 6 p.m. The sound of meat sizzling in a pan drew Max's attention. He went upstairs and asked if he could help by making the salad.

"I'm sure your dad won't mind you pinch-hitting for him," Max's mother said, smiling from ear to ear. She loved having her son in the kitchen while she cooked.

"Did you buy romaine lettuce? You know I hate iceberg—it has no nutritional value."

"Yes, we bought romaine," Max's father yelled from the living room. "We figured you might come home next week, so we wanted to be prepared."

Dinner for the Rosens always included salad and an array of vegetables. That night, Max's mother made spaghetti and meatballs with fresh string beans. It was the dead of winter, but Max knew his father could find fresh vegetables no matter where they came from.

During their meal, Max told his parents that he went through his rejection letters in the basement and brought up the topic of working for a newspaper far from his hometown. His parents avoided eye contact with each other but looked directly at Max to see how serious he was. After twenty-five years, their instincts never failed.

"What brought that on?" his mother asked.

"Like where?" his father asked.

"I don't know. Maybe it's time for me to broaden my career horizons."

"We'll support you no matter what you decide," Max's mother said, not meaning a word of it.

"It's just talking. I'm sorry I brought it up if it bothers you."

Max's sister Nancy came over after dinner. She had a busy day with patients and could not get away in time for supper. "Max, Mother called and told me you came home. Is everything all right?"

"I'm fine. I just needed a break."

"One of my patients asked me if we were related. He read your story in the *Inquirer* and figured that we might be kin since we had the same last name. That's exactly what he said: 'kin'."

"Yes, we be of kin." Max laughed.

Nancy sat on the living room sofa, and Max joined her. Their parents wanted to give their kids time to talk alone and went to their bedroom and watched TV. As per usual, the volume was loud enough for their show to be heard down the block. Max smiled at his sister and chuckled.

"I guess some things never change," he said, pointing down the hall toward their parents' room.

Max and Nancy talked for two hours before they both were exhausted from their respective days. Nancy listened patiently as he told her every detail about his time with Sue. His sister was not one for advice and told him that there are plenty of fish in the sea.

It was after ten when Max climbed into bed, emotionally wiped out. The day began with the managing editor of the *Chronicle* telling his young star reporter that he was being transferred to the main office. It ended in the safety and comfort of his parents' home, something he knew he'd miss if he moved far away.

Tuesday looked to be a low-key day for Max. He woke up at eight to the sound of coffee brewing. *Coffee brewing? In the Rosen house?* Harold Rosen bought his wife a Mr. Coffee brewing machine for Hanukkah. It sat in the box until New Year's Day when Max's mother tried her hand at something other than instant. She bought a can of Maxwell House ground coffee for her new toy and got it perfect for her first time. Max put on his robe and went to the kitchen to enjoy a cup of real coffee.

After breakfast, Max called Barrett, and Barrett asked Max to come over to his house instead of meeting halfway. Max decided to stop for bagels on the way.

Barrett had a beautiful view of the Delaware River from his condo. They sat inside and watched as boats made their way up and down from other ports along the east coast. Max abruptly interrupted the river watching party.

"Did you ever think about moving away and living somewhere else?" Max asked his friend.

"No. Why, do you?"

"Of late, I am. It's possible that my recent work could open doors for me at some newspapers. I've lived in this area for a quarter of a century—it may be time to move on."

"Really? Where would you move to?"

"It's more like where would I not move."

"Such as?"

"North Dakota, Montana, and maybe some places in the Deep South."

"Interesting," Barrett said, curious about Max's question and answer.

Max was about to continue the conversation when the phone rang. Barrett got up from his chair by the window and answered.

"Barrett, this is Harold Rosen. Is Max still there?"

"Yes, he is. I'll put him on."

"Dad, what's up? Is everything okay?"

"No. Your friend, Norm Weiss, was shot. He's in the hospital."

"Which one?"

"Roxborough Memorial Hospital. It's near his house."

"Do you know what happened?"

"No, son, I don't."

"Okay, I am on my way."

Max turned to Barrett, who was listening to one end of the conversation, but it was enough to get the gist of what was going on.

"I have to go," Max said, putting on his coat and fishing for his car keys. "I'll call you later."

Roxborough was on the complete other end of the city, and there was no easy way for Max to get there quickly. He made his way to Roosevelt Boulevard and drove until he reached the Schuylkill Expressway. Traffic was light as many schools weren't back in session, and workers were extending their New Year's weekend well into the following week. To avoid any major road disasters, Max tuned in to KYW, the all news and traffic station, which gave hourly traffic reports. All told, it took Max forty-five minutes to get to the hospital.

A block away from the hospital, on Jamestown Avenue, Max found an open parking meter. He dug out three quarters, which gave him three hours. He glanced at his watch, and it was two in the afternoon. Down the block was a place famous for its cheesesteaks, but seeing his friend was far more important than eating.

Norm Weiss was moved from the emergency room to a private room in the hospital. At the front desk, Max was told he was in room 437. The elevators were right by the reception area, so Max rushed over and pushed the button to go up. Two Philadelphia police officers got off as the doors opened, making Max wonder if they came from Norm's room. He would find out soon enough.

Norm's room was close to the elevator. Outside number 437 stood two police officers, one on either side of the door. Max walked over to the door but was stopped by the larger of the two cops who asked what he wanted.

"I am a friend of Norm Weiss. Someone from his family called and asked me to come down."

"Wait here," the officer said, opening the door and closing it behind him.

After a pause, he returned. "Okay, you can go in."

Norm's wife, Jill, and his parents were seated next to his bed. Norm was wide awake and saw Max come into the room.

"Max, I'm so glad you came so fast. Jill called and spoke to your dad. I see he reached you."

"He did, and I came as fast as I could."

Norm looked around the room. He was propped up in bed with an IV running and some serious bandages across his right shoulder. Norm didn't look to be in serious pain, but hospital painkillers are great at doing their job.

"Jill, Mom and Dad, can you give Max and me a minute, please?" Norm said softly.

"We'll be right outside," Norm's dad, Paul, said, kissing his son on the cheek.

"Thanks."

Once his family left the room, Norm asked Max to grab a chair and sit close.

"I was shot this morning on my way to work. I parked my car in the lot near the office, and as soon as I made it to the sidewalk, two guys were waiting for me."

"Holy shit," a startled Max blurted out. "And then what?"

"One guy took out his gun while the other one looked me in the eye and said, 'Consider this a warning.' After that, things are a bit hazy, but they told me I was shot in my shoulder right below my collarbone. The next thing I remember, I work up here in the ER."

"What are you thinking?" Max asked.

"I don't think it had anything to do with the stuff with the FBI sting of the mayor in Allentown. That's white-collar stuff."

"Don't tell me," Max said, interrupting. "You asked a source about the fake kidnapping of the porn guy's wife."

"Yes, I did."

"Oh man, I can't believe I dragged you into this mess."

"Don't be sorry. Every good lawyer worth his degree should be shot at least once in his or her life."

"That's good. You haven't lost your sense of humor."

"So, here's my request," Norm whispered, quickly running out of steam. "I want you to double down on your investigation into that scumbag. Please don't let me get shot for nothing."

"Seriously?"

"I am deadly serious. Well, I hope not deadly."

"I will get right on it, Norm. Please get well. The Sixers might make the playoffs, and there's a game that has our name on it."

"You bet. Please tell my family to come back in."

Max had plenty of time left on his parking meter, so he went over to Dalessandro's, a place always in the news for its cheesesteaks. Unlike most of his Philadelphia brethren, Max was not a big cheesesteak person; in fact, the ones his mother made at home were better than any at such famous places as Pat's and Geno's. Having skipped lunch though, the greasy, meaty, iconic sandwich called his name. He ordered one to go and ate it one-handed on his way back to his parents' home.

On the ride home, up a crowded I-95, Max switched between sports talk and the news. The radio provided background noise, and he thought about the promise he made to Norm and his conversation with his parents, and then later Barrett. As he drove, he looked at the other cars—heat blasting inside, nose to tail, riding on the pothole marked highway. What would life be like in a place like San Diego? It had to be warmer than the Northeast part of the country, and traffic had to be better. And then there was the beach.

Caught daydreaming, an angry driver behind Max honked viciously when he failed to move with the traffic. He waved as if he were sorry and concentrated on the road ahead. Max knew once he got home—probably just in time for dinner—that he would have to tell his parents he was heading back to Nesquehoning in the morning. He was anxious to dive into the Mitchell kidnapping case and provide some vengeance for his buddy Norm.

Max pulled into the driveway at four forty-five, just as the sun was going down, and the air became decidedly cooler. On his way down I-95 to his parents' home—about five miles as the crow flies—he stopped and bought his mother flowers. He wanted to show his appreciation for her concern and her restraint in providing her flavor of advice.

Having parents who grew up in the Depression, the Rosens were big on leftovers. Everything generally tasted better the second day, so dinner was a replica of the previous night with a fresh salad and the addition of his mother's homemade vegetable soup.

As Max helped clear the dishes, he told his mom and dad that he would be leaving in the morning to go back to work. While he didn't provide specifics—many of which would cause concern—Max told them he was working on another big story dealing with another notorious Lehigh Valley character. His parents were wise not to ask any questions.

Adrenaline pumping from a crazy day, Max barely slept. Small snippets of time he spent with Sue played in his memory like precisely edited filmstrips. Most of all, he thought about how he and Aaron would bring Arnie Mitchell and his slimy cohorts to justice. When he closed his eyes, all Max could see was an exhausted Norm Weiss in his hospital bed urging his reporter friend to nail that porno kingpin piece of shit. Max knew Aaron, a real family man, would love to be along for the ride.

After a cup of coffee from his mother's new Mr. Coffee, Max took a neatly wrapped bagel with vegetable schmear and was ready to head back. He kissed his mother goodbye and hugged his dad, giving him the traditional Rosen kiss on the neck. As he left with a basket of clean clothes, Max promised to return in the next few weeks.

Opting to go the long way back to Nesquehoning, Max got on Route 309 toward Allentown. Until he got out of range, Max listened to WIFI-92 with Byron and Tanaka's morning team. Their odd humor appealed to Max, especially their funny take on the day's news. The duo's spiel made the ride go quickly. Once outside of Allentown, Max looped over to Route 476, which took him right to his destination. After ninety minutes of non-stop driving, Max was glad to be home.

It took two trips for Max to bring in everything he brought back from his trip to Philadelphia. In addition to his laundry, his mother wrapped a brisket she made for him. There were grocery bags of staples such as Bachman pretzels that he couldn't find in Carbon County.

After his last load, Max locked his car and quietly walked up the stairs. It was still before 10 a.m. and he didn't want to irritate the neighbors. He walked into his apartment, turned on the heat, and noticed he had two messages on his answering machine. The first was from a college acquaintance who read his story in the *Chronicle* and wanted to know if the paper had any openings.

The second call stopped Max dead in his tracks.

"Max, this is David Lawrence from the *Seattle Herald*. We have been following the work you have done and were blown away by the mayoral investigation piece. We'd like to talk to you about interviewing for a job we have open. Give me a call."

Max sat and stared at his answering machine. After the events of the past few days, only one thought came to mind:

Be careful what you wish for.

The End

Max Rosen's life at the *Chronicle* continues
with the novella *Tickle Takedown*.

Look for an all-new Max Rosen adventure, *Nosejob*, coming in 2021.

About the Author

Allen Weiner is a writer and technology analyst known for his expertise in areas ranging from sports, publishing technology, and digital media, to cooking, travel, art, music, and the future of food. As an analyst, Allen has been featured in the *New York Times*, the *Wall Street Journal*, *USA Today*, the *Washington Post*, and on CNN, Good Morning America, Bloomberg News, and the BBC.

Allen's career as a multimedia journalist includes his work as a reporter and columnist at daily newspapers, trade and consumer magazines, and digital publications such as *The Daily Dot* and Sportscasting.com. He was also a digital media executive who led the team that launched the first newspaper on the web: SFGate.

What Goes Up is Allen's first novel. A native of Philadelphia, Allen lives with his wife in Ponte Vedra, Florida, and is a diehard Philadelphia sports fan.

Max Rosen is a twenty-five-year-[old] with a powerful digital mind livi[ng in the] analog world of the late 1970s. Hi[s] dream of becoming a lawyer did n[ot] pan out, but his writing talent and great intellect led him to a job as an entry-level newspaper reporter in Northeastern Pennsylvania. On his own for the first time, Max stumbles badly out of the gate in his new job and must use his wits, guile, and some less-than-legal tactics to get his career back on track, before his rofessional—and personal—life implodes.

Allen Weiner is a writer and technology analyst living in Ponte Vedra, Florida.